Death on Dickens Island

Also by Allison Brook

The Haunted Library Mysteries

Booked on Murder

Overdue or Die

Dewey Decimated

Death on the Shelf

Checked Out for Murder

Buried in the Stacks

Read and Gone

Death Overdue

Death on Dickens Island

A BOOKS ON THE BEACH MYSTERY

Allison Brook

NEW YORK

Books should be disposed of and recycled according to local requirements. All paper materials used are FSC compliant.

This is a work of fiction. All of the names, characters, organizations, places and events portrayed in this novel are either products of the author's imagination or are used fictitiously. Any resemblance to real or actual events, locales, or persons, living or dead, is entirely coincidental.

Published in the United States by Crooked Lane Books, an imprint of The Quick Brown Fox & Company LLC.

Crooked Lane Books and its logo are trademarks of The Quick Brown Fox & Company LLC.

Library of Congress Catalog-in-Publication data available upon request.

ISBN (hardcover): 979-8-89242-048-8
ISBN (paperback): 979-8-89242-253-6
ISBN (ebook): 979-8-89242-049-5

Cover design by Mary Woodin

Printed in the United States.

www.crookedlanebooks.com

Crooked Lane Books
34 West 27th St., 10th Floor
New York, NY 10001

First Edition: October 2025

The authorized representative in the EU for product safety and compliance is eucomply OÜPärnu mnt 139b-14, 11317 Tallinn, Estonia, hello@eucompliancepartner.com, +33757690241

10 9 8 7 6 5 4 3 2 1

This book is dedicated to the many readers who love my Haunted Library series. I hope you get to love Delia, Connor, and the other characters in this series too.

Chapter One

"They're at it again!"

I looked up from my calculations of the store's profits for the past month and turned to see my father in the office doorway. Graham Dickens, standing six foot four in his stocking feet, was still handsome and in great shape for a man in his sixties. But these days, since my mother's move to my Manhattan apartment for an open-ended stay, his once powerful swimmer's shoulders hunched forward in perpetual worry. Dad's wrinkled brow told me he was more agitated than usual.

Of course I knew who *they* were: Aunt Reenie, Dickens Island's town manager, and Uncle Brad, the head of the town council.

"Don't let their melodrama rattle you." I waved my hand, wishing it were a magic wand that would banish his concern. "Whatever it is, they'll work it out."

Dad pursed his lips. "If only that were true. Whatever they're fighting about is impacting their relationship. Brad just called to ask if he could stay at my house for a few days."

"Oh." Despite their frequent and sometimes public spats, my aunt and uncle were still as madly in love as when they were teenagers. "That doesn't sound good."

"It's disastrous, for them and for all of us who live on Dickens Island." Dad drew a deep breath. "Delia, you have to talk to both of them immediately. Nip this quarrel in the bud. Remind your aunt and uncle their behavior affects everyone around them."

"Me?" Panic rose in my chest. "Why me?"

"Because you have your mother's ability to remain calm and rational in explosive situations. Since she's not here, you're the next best thing."

"Thanks," I said.

Dad stepped closer and put an arm around my shoulders. "Honey, I didn't mean it the way it came out. Your mother's mediating skills are worthy of the United Nations, but since she's not here, we rely on you to resolve family issues." He cast me a look of pure desperation. "Please, Delia. Talk to Reenie. Talk to Brad. They're letting their emotions run amok. It's putting their marriage in jeopardy."

I grimaced. Not for the first time, I questioned my decision to move back to Dickens Island. I didn't share my father's strong commitment toward the island named after our ancestor that he expected my brother and me to take on. It was one of the reasons why I had continued to live in Manhattan after my divorce.

"We're talking about two sixty-something people," I said. "Grandparents, for goodness' sake! They're old enough to resolve their own problems."

Dad's dogged expression returned. "I'd agree if Reenie wasn't our town manager and my brother the council president, but the entire island shouldn't suffer because of their shenanigans. And that's exactly what will happen if they don't get their act together."

Damn it, he was right. Against my better judgment, I nodded. "Okay, I'll talk to them, but I can't promise any results."

"Thank you, sweetheart." Dad bussed my cheek. "Sometime today?"

"Sure. Why not?"

That settled, Dad glanced down at the papers spread out on my desk. "When do you think you'll have the final numbers?"

"Soon. So far, last month's figures show a definite net increase. The new products we've added to our inventory have taken off, and my suggestions regarding how to trim expenses seem to be making a difference."

My father grinned. "That's because you're back in the family business."

"Only temporarily," I reminded him.

"You won't find another boss that lets you set your hours like I do, leaving you plenty of time to write the occasional article for *The Chronicle*."

Having achieved his goal, my father returned to the front of the Dickens General Store, which he'd been managing all of my thirty-eight years and then some.

I sighed deeply. What had I agreed to? My aunt and uncle were volatile people who loved each other with a passion yet held diametrically opposed opinions about practically everything. Which didn't ordinarily matter, I supposed. A couple could agree to disagree and avoid red-hot topics. But we lived on an island barely nine square miles in size. Shaped like an egg lying on its side, Dickens Island stood smack in the middle of the Long Island Sound between Long Island and Connecticut.

Reenie, my mother's younger sister, was Dickens Island's main realtor and had recently been elected town manager. Brad, my father's younger brother, was a lawyer with an office in Mineola and had been a member of the island's town council for years, most of them as council president. It was unusual but not unheard of for a married couple to hold the two most important town positions since the island's population was five hundred at most during the winter months. In addition, both officers were Dickenses, which still carried a great deal of prestige. But prestigious or not, my aunt's and uncle's strongly held views were clashing, and I was the family member who had been designated to deal with them both.

I finished up my paperwork, pleased with the results. Yes, the Dickens General Store, which belonged to my immediate family—my parents, my brother Wayne, and me—was finally seeing an uptick in sales after slowly losing money over the past three years. I had spent hours analyzing inventory, cutting orders that no longer sold, and selecting more appealing merchandise. Finally, this month the store was back in the black.

I closed the office door and walked over to the women's clothing section where my father stood chatting with Toby Withers. She was holding up a white blouse with blue embroidery on the front.

"What do you think, Delia? Medium or large?"

I eyed her large frame, recalling that Toby had tried most diets with little success. "Actually, I'd go with the extra-large for comfort, since that manufacturer tends to run small. And if you're like me, you probably put everything in the dryer, which will shrink it a bit. If I remember, that blouse is one hundred percent cotton."

"Good point," she said as she replaced the blouse with an extra-large. "My dryer tends to run hot."

"Did you notice the pull-on black pants that are on sale?" I pointed to the rack. "They'll go nicely with the blouse. With anything, actually. I find you can't have enough pairs of black pants."

"Hmm."

My father winked at me as Toby ambled over to check out the pants. "You're a natural saleswoman," he whispered as we walked to the front of the store.

"I'm leaving for the day," I told him. "I'll stop by the town manager's office and see if Aunt Reenie's free to chat."

"Good idea. Brad said he'll be over to the house around six, after he's packed up some clothes and a few necessities." Dad's worried look was back. "I wonder how much stuff he plans to bring over this time."

"Try not to worry unnecessarily. It will probably just be for a day or two."

"Last time he stayed close to three weeks," he said wryly.

"Wasn't that eight years ago?"

"Six."

I had no answer, so I blew him a kiss and turned to head for the back door that led to the parking area.

"Delia!" Dad called out, stopping me in my tracks.

"I just had an idea. Why don't you and Connor come for dinner tonight? Say a quarter to seven? Ask Connor to bring along one of his video games. We can play a game or two while you chat with Brad."

"That should be fine," I said. I'd been planning a dinner of leftover meatballs and pasta and a salad, but it could stay in the fridge another night. "Thanks, Dad. What are you making?"

He grinned. "A surprise. Don't worry, it will be one of your favorites."

"I'm not worried." And I wasn't. My father had always been the cook in our family. "See you later."

I stepped outside and scrunched up my shoulders against the March wind as I walked to my car. Enjoying my father's great culinary expertise was one of the few perks I'd gained by moving back to the island, since he often invited Connor and me to join him for dinner. No doubt he was lonely since my mother had taken off four months ago—"for some personal time," as she'd put it. Now she was living in my Manhattan apartment—we had no idea for how long. My son wouldn't mind having dinner there tonight. He and my dad had a close relationship. No big surprise since, until I'd returned, Connor had been living with my parents in the house where I grew up.

Our relationship was strained, which certainly wasn't Connor's fault. Devastated by the change in my husband and our subsequent divorce, I'd left my three-year-old in my parents' care while I lived and worked in Manhattan. It hadn't started out that way. I hadn't meant to leave Connor with them for so long, but day care in the city was expensive and not amenable to the long work hours I often put in. My parents were happy to watch Connor, and soon I was leaving him with them two or three days at a time. Eventually, it became a permanent arrangement.

I spent weekends with Connor at my parents' house, but the setup wasn't comfortable. I felt like something between a guest and a child who had never left home. I soon became aware of the conflict between their parenting style and my own. I was much more lenient about things like diet and bedtime, while they often had the final say according to their rules. After a while, I found myself returning to the island for holidays and to celebrate Connor's birthday and special occasions.

Connor adored my parents, but it did nothing to erase his belief that I'd abandoned him. When he was still quite young, he occasionally asked me questions about his father, whom he'd last seen when he was a toddler and, as far as Connor knew, had dropped off the face of the earth. I'd given him vague answers, hoping he never remembered the last afternoon he'd spent with Mitch. Eventually, Connor stopped mentioning him. Now fifteen, a high school sophomore, and a head taller than me, Connor was distant and reserved. He answered me in monosyllables—that is, when he even bothered to acknowledge my questions or even my presence in his life.

In the four months since I'd moved back, I'd made two attempts to tackle the problem head on. Each time, I'd gotten as far as telling him I loved him very much but that I'd had overwhelming personal problems when he was little. Both times he walked out of the room before I could explain that I'd left him with my parents because I had been certain he was better off living with them. So far nothing had changed his attitude toward me. I needed to fix things between us, but that wouldn't happen overnight and right now my focus was on what I was going to say to Aunt Reenie.

I exited the parking lot and drove along Duxbury Street, our main thoroughfare. I passed shops and businesses, quickly coming to the end of the three short blocks that made up our downtown, and turned right onto Sumac Street. I drove by the Dickens Library on the left and the community church on the right, continued another block, then pulled into the parking lot of the building that housed our police department, post office, and my aunt's office where, no doubt, Dickens Island's town manager was currently holding court.

Chapter Two

I found my aunt behind her desk, chuckling over something one of the three people facing her had said. It was her town manager laugh, which meant she was in total control of the situation and her visitors were in perfect agreement with whatever was under discussion. She stopped laughing the moment she saw me.

"Hi there, Delia. Are you looking for me?" Was that a note of apprehension in her voice? Or was it irritation? Both, I decided.

"I am, Aunt Reenie. I'd like to talk to you when you have a free moment."

She twisted her lips in one direction then the other. At sixty-one, Ravena Dickens was a striking woman. Pretty face, great figure, and her lustrous dark hair streaked with highlights that fell past her shoulders always looked as though she'd just left the salon. But she lacked the natural elegance of her older sister, my taller, slimmer mother, who dressed in flowing garments and wore her salt-and-pepper hair in a simple bob.

"Our meeting's just about over, so I suppose we can talk."

Her three visitors, two men and a woman, took the hint and got to their feet. I smiled at Gregg Fanning, our handsome police chief, and Danielle Rizzoli, the junior-senior high school principal. They said their quick goodbyes and left. Chet Thomas, my aunt's very handsome thirty-something aide, stood but made no move to leave.

"Chet, why don't you make those calls we talked about. You have the numbers?"

"Of course. I'm on it, Reenie."

She smiled at him. "Great. I'll check back with you to find out how they respond to our suggestions as soon as Delia and I are done."

Chet nodded and departed, closing the door behind him. My aunt came around her desk. Arms crossed, she leaned against the edge so we were inches apart. "Okay. Let's have it. I suppose Graham sent you."

There was no point in denying it. "He did. Dad's upset because you and Uncle Brad are fighting."

"And he's worried this means dissention between the council and my office. Well, we can't all bury our heads in the sand and maintain the status quo just because that's how it has always been. Some of us have the foresight to realize that if the island is going to thrive, we have to keep up with the times. Create more housing. Agree to a ferry line between Dickens Island and Connecticut. We need new sources of revenue, more tourist attractions. Otherwise . . ." She shook her head.

I studied Aunt Reenie. She wasn't on her soapbox trying to convince the town council to see things her way. She was worried about our future.

"Want to tell me about it?" I asked.

She thought it over. "Why not?" She dropped into her chair. I sat down too.

"Last week I got a call from a Jim Thornton in Connecticut's Department of Transportation, wanting to know if we'd be interested in starting up a ferry service between Dickens Island and Connecticut. They were thinking the route would go from Branford on their side across to that spit of land just east of the Burton Bird Sanctuary on our shoreline. I thought it was a brilliant idea and the perfect location, since it won't interfere with Marley's Beach or the Bridgeport, Connecticut–Port Jefferson, Long Island Ferry Line.

"I told Jim that while I liked the idea, I needed to discuss it with the town council." Aunt Reenie grimaced. "I can't tell you how many residents have asked me why we don't have a ferry service to Connecticut, and I never have a good answer to offer. Sure, we have water taxis, but they're very expensive and don't fill the need.

"That night over dinner, I mentioned the Connecticut plan to your uncle. His face turned beet-red, and I feared he was about to have a coronary.

"Your uncle said, 'How can you even consider it? There's a reason why we've never put a ferry terminal there!'

"'Really?' I've never heard of any reason,' I told him.

"'It would disturb the birds.'

"'Disturb the birds?' I asked."

Aunt Reenie pursed her lips. "That's what Brad's worried about. The birds."

Her aunt continued to describe the conversation with her uncle. "'Do you think ferries are silent as they come and go?' he said. 'Then there's the pollution from vehicles as they drive on and off the ferry.'

"I told him we could regulate the number of daily trips, and there wouldn't be much pollution since it would be a small ferry with room for ten or twelve vehicles each crossing."

Aunt Reenie rolled her eyes. "I finally got Brad to admit to the real reason he objects to a ferry connecting us to Connecticut. He doesn't want his precious island overrun with more tourists during the summer months because 'they spoil the island for us natives in every way possible. They ruin the fishing; they take over our restaurants; and they cause traffic jams and accidents on the roads.'"

"But most shops and businesses here on the island depend on tourism for their income. I never realized summer tourism was a problem," I said.

"That's because it isn't a problem. In fact, we could use more attractions to draw more visitors. Then maybe we'll keep some of the young people who leave as soon as they're old enough to live on their own."

Like her own two children, I thought.

Aunt Reenie gnawed on her upper lip as she debated whether or not to let me in on a council matter. Finally, she exhaled loudly. "Keep this under wraps, Delia: The town council and my office have arranged to buy the VanPatten Farm as soon as Tim and Velma officially put it on the market. It's a large, very desirable piece of property with a few acres abutting the shore just east of the proposed ferry.

"Tim put out feelers and told us two conglomerates are eager to buy the land, but only if the zoning is changed—which only we can do and why the VanPattens will end up selling to us. One company wants to build a complex of townhouses. The other has plans for a hotel-casino complex."

Not such a big secret after all—at least the selling part. I'd overheard Velma VanPatten talking about it in the general store the other day.

"I bet plenty of New York and Connecticut people would love to have a summer home only a short drive away," I said. "And a hotel-casino complex would be good for the island's economy."

"I'm all for development and growth, and I can see either plan working as long as it maintains the harmony of our island. I've no problem seeing the property rezoned for either—residential for the townhouses or commercial for a hotel-casino. We'll require that whomever we go with hires an urban planning group to determine the appropriate size of the project so it works with our current infrastructure, or will work with minimal additions and expansions. Lots of red tape but doable."

Reenie shook her head, as though she couldn't fathom what she was about to tell me. "At our closed council meeting last night, your uncle came out dead set against both proposals. He wants to keep the property a farm—a working farm, though both the farmhouse and the barns are in terrible condition. I don't know how Tim and Velma manage to live there. It's been a farm in name only these last five years. They raise no crops, have no livestock—just some chickens and a few barn cats, I suppose."

"What do the other members of the council think?"

"Sadie Alvarez and George Simon are all for creating more housing since our last community of new homes was built over twelve years ago. As usual, Pete Osbourne says he has to give the plan some thought since the island economy can benefit from either the housing or the hospitality."

"And Missy?" I asked, referring to the most recent addition to the board.

My aunt made a face like she'd bitten into something awful. "Missy Faraday spoke up in favor of your Uncle Brad's idea. No big surprise since that's what she's been doing the entire time she's been on the council."

"Oh?"

"I'm convinced she doesn't have an original idea in her head. Missy smiles and nods and bats those big baby blues at Brad, then votes in favor of whatever he says."

I laughed. "You're not saying Missy has a thing for Uncle Brad."

"Maybe she does." Aunt Reenie's eyebrows shot up. "Soon as she got on the council, she made it her business to rush up to Brad at the end of each meeting to ask him to explain something we'd been discussing. Because of our work schedules, Brad and I usually drive to council meetings in separate cars, and for a while your uncle was always arriving home a good twenty, thirty minutes later than me."

I thought about Missy Faraday. She was a slender woman with large blue eyes and an expression of constant surprise that made her look years younger than her age, which was about forty-five by my reckoning. Missy worked in the bakery a few doors down from the general store. She always greeted me with a cheery hello when I came in for my occasional breakfast muffin.

Pleasant and upbeat, but not the sharpest knife in the drawer, I wondered how she'd ended up on the council. Actually, I *knew* how she'd ended up on the council—by default. Dad told me her father had been a councilman when he died. Since no one stepped up to take his place, Missy had offered to do so until September, when a new council member would be voted in.

"She stopped her act soon as I made it clear that I was annoyed every time she sidled up to Brad to ask him a question. And I rearranged my daytime schedule so Brad and I could drive to evening meetings together. Still, I couldn't help wondering . . ."

"You can't imagine Uncle Brad is interested in Missy Faraday," I said. "She's . . ." I looked skyward, searching for the right words.

"Sexy and on the loose, from what I've heard. After a bad break up with a longtime boyfriend."

Was Missy Faraday the real reason my aunt had thrown my uncle out of the house?

"Aunt Reenie, you and Uncle Brad are always on opposite sides of island politics and policies. What got you so angry this time?"

"You mean angrier than the other times I argued and cajoled him until we reached a compromise? Or I bit my tongue and went along with his 'keep things as they are' philosophy? These recent opportunities to grow our island and bring us into the twenty-first century with a viable economy made me realize something. I don't want a fight on my hands every time a new expansion idea is proposed. I'm tired of arguing; tired of coming across as the shrill wife who's only a Dickens by marriage and not by birth."

I opened my mouth to argue that what she said wasn't true.

"Yes, my dear niece. There are plenty of old-timers who see it that way. And so I told your uncle to pack up some things and leave while I decided if I wanted to continue our relationship. Well, I've thought, and I've decided I've had enough bickering to last me a lifetime.

"This separation is for good. I'm seeing my lawyer tomorrow to draw up whatever papers are necessary to start divorce proceedings. I want Bradley Harrison Dickens permanently out of my life!"

Chapter Three

I walked slowly to my car, stunned by Aunt Reenie's pronouncement. She was going to file for divorce. *No, that can't be true! She doesn't really mean it,* I told myself. She's angry. Upset. Frustrated. Uncle Brad wanted to keep the island the way it was, but that was impossible. He had to see it needed to thrive and grow and keep up with the times.

I shuddered. Maybe Aunt Reenie would leave the island like my mother had. After all, Dickens Island was Uncle Brad's home. She'd moved here when they married. Both their children, my cousins Katie and Eric, had left the island when they started college and never came back. Eric and his family now lived in Oregon. Katie, who was divorced like me, lived in Connecticut with her two daughters. If she divorced Uncle Brad, Aunt Reenie would have no reason to stay here.

A tremor ran through my body. Maybe I never should have come back here. Though I managed the general store's books and had a hand in proposing new orders and canceling others, along with writing the occasional article for *The Chronicle*, the weekly newspaper owned by my brother, Wayne, who was also the editor-in-chief, I had no full-time job on the island. Nothing nearly as important as the marketing position I'd left behind in Manhattan. I'd only come back because my mother had texted me to say she was leaving Dickens Island and she felt Connor needed his mother.

Since then, I'd wondered more than once if Mom had made it sound so urgent because she'd decided Connor and I should be living together. Her move into my apartment seemed practical at the time. Now I regarded it as an ending of my old life.

I drove along Sedley Boulevard, which cut across the widest part of the island, and turned right on Devonshire. My home was even older than the nearby homes that hugged Rogers Landing, the first year-round community of houses built along the curve of the northeast shore of the island at the turn of the twentieth century. An impressive Victorian, it stood alone on a high ridge that overlooked the northernmost tip of the island. The eleven Rogers Landing homes faced Connecticut. Mine looked out on the open sea.

My grandmother, whom I always called Helena, had left it to me when she died last year at the age of eighty-eight. Helena Catherine Whitcomb Dickens, my father's mother, had been a remarkable woman. At one time she'd been the only elementary school teacher on the island, and she'd taken on managing the general store when her husband died and my father and uncle were young boys. Helena continued to teach and to raise her young sons and soon volunteered for municipal jobs as well. Before long, she was the first woman to hold the position of town manager. Growing up, I admired my grandmother, and I loved her even more.

Because her schedule was so hectic, Helena usually had dinner at our house before putting in a few hours at the store or attending an evening council meeting. Oddly enough, despite our busy schedules, the five of us—my parents, Wayne, Helena, and I—managed to eat together most nights. Our discussions were spirited and covered every topic. Helena always regaled us with stories about the history of the island, and she never hesitated to tell us about problems her office and the council were grappling with, though Dad reproached her for being indiscreet.

"Don't be silly, Graham. Delia and Wayne need to know about the issues and problems we deal with every day to keep our island running. After all, they're the next generation."

At which point, my brother and I would roll our eyes at each other.

Once, when I was fifteen and daydreaming about a guy I had a crush on, I wasn't paying attention to Helena going on about the deterioration of our roads. She admonished me.

"Delia, you need to know everything about the island's infrastructure and how to keep it in good working condition, since you'll be calling the shots one day."

Startled, I said, "No, I won't! I'm out of here after high school."

She fixed her eyes on me. "Perhaps you'll be gone for a while, but you'll return to Dickens Island," she said, and went back to griping about the potholes in the roads.

I didn't take her seriously and instead of coming back to the island, I got married right after graduating college and ended up living in Massachusetts because of my husband's job. But here I was, back on the island, living in the house she left me.

The house was truly a wonderful example of Victorian architecture and had been in Helena's family since it was built almost one hundred years ago. It had two stories and an attic under the traditional steep roof. The walkway from the road led to five exterior steps and a wrap-around porch that swung around the entire left side and extended to the back of the house. Inside, on the left past the center hall, were the kitchen, the dining room, and a small bathroom. To the right was the large room with the rounded turret that had been the living room for generations. But I had turned it into the family room and made the room with the built-in bookcase just across the narrow hall that Helena called the library my living room. A stairway at the end of the central hall led to the four bedrooms upstairs.

Helena had kept up repairs and maintenance as best she could. While all of the appliances were only a few years old, the three bathrooms needed to be updated, and I longed to remove all the busy wallpaper and paint the walls. I also wanted to change the dull gray exterior to a cheerful yellow and refresh the white trim. Though I'd managed to save up some money during the years I worked in the city, the few inquiries I'd made regarding the cost of sprucing up the house made me realize that everything was much more expensive than I'd first thought. I would have to tackle my renovations one project at a time.

I pulled into the driveway instead of the detached garage, which was still jam-packed with Connor's things that he'd brought over from my parents' house. I'd asked him often enough to throw out what he didn't need and to bring what he was keeping up to his bedroom, but four months had passed and, except for transferring his clothes, electronic devices, and a few other items, he still hadn't done it.

As I climbed the front steps, I noticed lights were on in most of the rooms. Connor was home. It was only when I stepped onto the porch that I spotted the bundle of rags beside the door. Not rags, it turned out, but a dog with long, straggly gray and white hair that lay curled in a sleeping circle. As I came closer, he opened his eyes to study me. He didn't seem surprised by my arrival, which I found kind of strange.

"Hello. And who are you?" I said.

The dog blinked and got to his feet. From what I could tell, he wasn't wearing a collar.

"Did you follow Connor home?"

The dog cocked his head as if he were deciding whether or not to answer me.

"Well," I said after a minute, "I'm going inside and you should go home, wherever that is. Your owners must be wondering where you are."

Rock music assailed my ears as soon as I stepped into the hall. I suppressed my annoyance. I had asked Connor not to play his music loud. Then I remembered that, as far as he knew, he was alone. I covered my ears as I went upstairs and knocked on his door. Of course he couldn't hear me. I opened the door. The quilt on the bed was wrinkled, as though he'd been lying on it. Clothes were strewn about the floor and over the back of the desk chair. Thumping music streamed from Connor's laptop on his desk, but my son was nowhere to be seen.

I turned off the sound, went back downstairs, and found my son in the kitchen. Connor was tall and rail-skinny, with dark-brown eyes and flyaway hair he kept raking with his fingers to keep out of his eyes. In a few years, he'd fill out and be a gorgeous heartbreaker like his father. Now he stood by the refrigerator drinking orange juice from the carton, something I'd told him several times not to do. He stopped when he saw me, closed the carton, and put it back in the fridge.

"Hi, Mom."

"Hello, Connor. When did you get home?"

"About fifteen minutes ago."

"Where did you go after school?"

He shrugged. "Nowhere. Trevor and I just hung out."

I shuddered inwardly. Trevor Sykes was trouble, even in the small high school on the island. We storekeepers knew to watch him carefully when he came inside to browse. Not the kind of kid I wanted my son to hang with, but that was a discussion for another day.

"How was school?" I asked.

Another shrug. "Okay."

Connor started to leave the kitchen when I called after him. "Your grandfather invited us to dinner tonight."

"Good."

"Be ready to leave at six thirty. And he'd like you to bring a game with you. To play after dinner."

"Yeah. Sure."

This time, he'd gotten as far as the hall when I asked, "Did that dog I saw outside follow you home?"

Connor spun around. "Yeah, he did. He's still outside?"

"He was lying on the porch when I came in. Who does he belong to?"

"No idea. He followed me home from Trevor's house. I figured he was a stray, so I gave him something to eat."

"You did? What did you give him?"

Connor grinned. "A few meatballs. He gobbled them up in record time. He sure was hungry."

Tomorrow night's dinner. "You let him come inside the house?"

"Don't worry. He was really good. He followed me into the kitchen and sniffed the food. Then he ate the meatballs in two seconds flat, like he was starving. I was trying to decide if I should give him another meatball when he walked over to the door and waited for me to let him out."

"That's weird," I said.

"Really, Mom? What's so weird about a well-behaved dog?"

I waited for him to go upstairs and slam his door shut, then followed him upstairs and went to my bedroom. There were so many things I wanted to talk to my son about, but I hadn't the faintest idea how to go about it. My last few attempts had failed. The only thing I'd seen Connor show interest in was a stray dog, and a dog was the last thing I needed. Hopefully when we next went outside, the creature would have moved on.

Chapter Four

There was no sign of the dog when Connor and I left the house an hour later. I hoped he had a home to go to or, if he had no home, had found a place to spend the night. Since the wind had picked up and the temperature had fallen, I was glad to drive to my parents' house, which, if you went by car, was almost a half mile away.

Connor and I remained silent during the short ride. He probably had nothing to say to me. I had plenty I wanted to say to him, but since they were mostly rules and regulations, it wasn't the right topic of conversation as we were about to have dinner.

My parents' house felt warm and inviting as we stepped inside. I sniffed the delicious aroma and grinned. Lasagna! I loved lasagna. My father, a white chef's apron over his clothes, came out of the kitchen to greet us. He hugged me, then Connor.

"I'm glad to see you brought over one of your better games," Dad said to Connor.

"It's the one you got me for Christmas." My son grinned at his grandfather, his face animated. "It's awesome. You really have to think about moves and make decisions. I got my highest score ever the last time I played it myself."

"I can still beat the pants off of you," Dad teased him.

Connor laughed. "Yeah, Gramps. We'll see about that."

"Anything I can do to help?" I asked.

"You can set the table in the dining room. We're five for dinner tonight."

Five? I followed my father into the kitchen while Connor dropped onto the living room couch and clicked the remote to turn on the TV. He was perfectly at home here. And why shouldn't he be since he'd lived here most of his life?

"Who else is coming for dinner?" I asked. "And where's Uncle Brad?"

"He'll be here soon. He went to pick up his guest."

"What guest? How can he have a guest when he's a guest himself?"

My father pursed his lips. "He didn't say. Brad wasn't here fifteen minutes when he got a call on his cell. He shooed me out of the guest room so he could speak in private. Next thing I know, he's telling me he has to meet someone and asking if he can invite the person to dinner. What could I do but say yes?"

"I suppose that means I won't be having a little chat with him tonight." I suddenly remembered what Aunt Reenie had told me. "Which is just as well. This last squabble is more serious than their usual flare ups. I think they need more than familial help. They need a marriage counselor."

"Delia, what on earth did Reenie say?" my father asked.

But now wasn't the time to go into it. Voices in the living room meant that Uncle Brad had arrived with his guest. My mouth fell open when I saw who it was.

"Of course I know Missy," I said a minute later when Uncle Brad, his hand on Missy's shoulder, steered her into the kitchen to introduce her to Dad and me.

"Delia, how nice to see you!" she chirped. "I had no idea I was intruding on a family dinner."

"You're not intruding," Brad insisted. "After you told me what happened, I thought you could do with a change of scenery."

"What happened?" my father asked.

Missy drew in a deep breath. "I left work at five thirty and was about to cross Duxbury Street to get my car. I'd parked it in the lot behind the shops on the other side of the street. It's larger than the lot behind the bakery, and not so full of potholes. Anyway, no cars were in sight when I stepped off the curb, when this black sedan came barreling down the street like it was determined to knock me down."

She paused dramatically. "I jumped out of its way. When I got to my car, I just sat there panting until I could catch my breath. As soon as I got home, I called Brad."

"Why did you call Uncle Brad?" I said at the same time Connor asked, "Did you see the driver's face?"

Missy looked at my son. "It happened so fast, I didn't see who was driving." Then she turned to me.

"I called Brad so he could advise me about what to do." She smiled at my uncle. "You always know the best solutions for the issues we deal with at council meetings."

"Thank you, Missy," Uncle Brad said, bowing his head, "though that's far from an accurate statement."

"Why didn't you call the police?" Connor asked.

Exactly, I thought.

"I was afraid they wouldn't believe me. I mean, there was no way I could prove that what happened really happened."

Too true, I thought.

My father shook his head. "Missy, do you really think someone tried to hit you intentionally?"

"I do," she said.

"Unfortunately, Missy didn't get the license plate number, and there's no CCTV on the street," Uncle Brad said.

Something Aunt Reenie had proposed but got nowhere with, I remembered.

"There was no one around to see what happened either," Missy added.

Uncle Brad patted her shoulder. "After her ordeal, I thought Missy could do with some company, so I invited her to join us for dinner."

"How very kind of you," I said with a touch of sarcasm. Given his circumstances, he had no business inviting anyone to his brother's house where he was staying because his wife had thrown him out. Certainly not Missy, of all people.

I couldn't help wondering if Missy's upsetting incident was something she'd made up as an excuse to call Uncle Brad. And how fortuitous that he happened to be available to play the benevolent hero. Maybe Aunt Reenie was right. Maybe there was something brewing between these two.

My father put down the oven mitt he'd been holding. "Okay, we get the picture. Missy, I'm sorry you've had a bad experience, but you're welcome to join us for dinner, which I'm happy to serve once you're all seated at the dining room table. Delia, if you'll be so kind as to set the table. Connor, please get the salad and the soda from the fridge. Brad, if you bring over this wine bottle I just opened, I'll manage the rest."

Chapter Five

We sat down at the dining table, and for a while we were too busy eating to make conversation. Dad's lasagna was delicious, and we all opted for a second serving. His baby greens salad was crisp and had the most wonderful tangy dressing. Connor must have liked it because he finished off what I'd put in his salad bowl, something he rarely did at home.

"Gee, this meal is really delicious, Mr. Dickens," Missy told my father as she batted her blue eyes at him.

"I'm glad you're enjoying it. I hope you've left room for dessert."

"What's for dessert, Gramps?" Connor asked.

"Pecan pie." My father grinned. "I happened to find one in the freezer."

"Awesome," Connor said. "With chocolate ice cream?"

"Of course! What's pecan pie without chocolate ice cream?"

Connor leaned over to give his grandfather a high five.

Missy helped me clear the dishes while my father put on a pot of coffee for Uncle Brad and me. Then he brought the pie and ice cream to the table.

"You're so lucky you have a great family," Missy said as we carried dessert plates, mugs, and cutlery to the dining room table. "I missed that growing up."

"Oh?" I said. I knew nothing about her life, except that her father had recently died, she'd taken his place on the town council temporarily, and she worked in the bakery.

"Don't get me wrong," Missy said quickly. "My parents were wonderful people and I loved them dearly, only they weren't much fun. Probably because they were older and I was an only child. "

"I'm sorry for your loss. I understand your father passed six months ago."

"Thank you. Yes, that was a terrible blow. Especially when I needed him to explain—" Missy's hand shook as she set down the dishes, making them rattle.

"Explain what?" I couldn't help asking

Uncle Brad eyes were fixed on Missy as if he was sending her a silent message. Missy gave a little laugh. "How I would manage to live on my own for the first time in my life. It came as a shock, though it shouldn't have. After all, I'm a grown woman."

That's not what you were about to say, I thought.

My father put down the knife he'd been using to slice the pie. "Now who would like a piece of this delicious pie?"

"Me!" Connor said. "With lots of ice cream."

"Coming right up!"

I caught Uncle Brad's nod to Missy, like she'd just said the right thing. *O-kay. There's definitely something Missy's not telling us; something Uncle Brad doesn't want us to know.*

"Connor, anything exciting happening in that school you go to?" my father asked to change the subject.

"Same old. Oh, yeah, my Spanish teacher is planning to take a group of kids to Spain next summer."

"Really?" I said. This was the first I was hearing about it. "Are you interested in going?"

"Maybe," Connor said. "Yeah, I think I'd like to."

"We'll have to talk about it," my father said. "Sorry," he said quickly when he caught my expression. "I mean, you and your mom will discuss it."

"Indeed we will," I said, a bit stronger that necessary.

"Anyway, the trip's more than a year away," Connor said, probably to diffuse the tension. "What do you know about Captain Kidd?" he asked, changing the subject. "Did he ever come to Dickens Island?"

"There's no documentation that he ever set foot on our island, though there's a good chance that he did," Uncle Brad said. "He spent time in the Long Island Sound area and owned and lived on property in Manhattan."

Uncle Brad rubbed his hands together as he warmed to his subject. "William Kidd started out as a privateer hunting down pirates, and then he became a pirate himself. He buried some of his treasure on Gardiner's Island in 1699 before he was hung two years later."

"I wonder if he buried any treasure here on Dickens Island," Connor said.

"There are rumors that he buried treasure all along the coast of the Sound," Uncle Brad said, "but except for what was found on Gardiner's Island—which he reported himself in hopes of gaining a pardon, though it didn't work out—no one knows for sure."

Connor helped me clear the table, then I loaded the dishwasher while Dad put away the leftovers. I wiped down the plastic placemats we'd used and put them away. When I was done, I went into the living room where Connor and my father had started the game that Connor had brought over to play.

"Delia, why don't you take home the rest of the lasagna," Dad said. "There's enough for another dinner for you and Connor."

"Yes!" Connor thrust his fist in the air.

"Or you can eat it tomorrow night. Freeze half of it for a second meal," I said.

My father waved away my suggestion. "You take it, along with the rest of the pie. I'll only gain weight if I eat any more of it."

And I won't? "Okay. Thanks."

Dad returned to their game. Uncle Brad and Missy stood in the hall, their heads bent together as they conversed intensely in low tones. Were they trying to figure out who had almost run Missy over earlier today? Or were they talking about whatever it was Uncle Brad didn't want her to tell us that she'd found out about around the time her father died?

Finally, Uncle Brad patted her shoulder. Missy nodded. They came into the living room.

"I'm going to drive Missy home," Uncle Brad said. "She's exhausted after the day she's had."

Missy went over to my father. "Graham, thanks so much for dinner. It was delicious."

"You're most welcome," my father said. "I'm glad you could join us."

"Goodbye, Connor."

"Bye," Connor said, not looking up from the TV screen as his thumbs moved like lightning on the controls in his hand.

Missy surprised me by hugging me. "Good night, Delia. Enjoy your family."

Before I could respond, she dashed over to Uncle Brad, who was waiting for her at the front door.

"Night, everyone," he called out. "Graham, thanks for a delicious dinner. I'll see you in a while."

They left, and the house was suddenly quiet. Oddly enough, I felt bereft and lonely, as though everyone had something to do and somewhere to go except me.

"You two enjoy your game. I'm going home," I said.

My father shot me a meaningful look. "Don't you want to wait until Brad gets back so you can talk to him?"

I shook my head. "We'll talk tomorrow. Dad, can you drive Connor home around ten? Or if you're tired, call me and I'll pick him up." I caught my son's annoyed expression. "Connor, I'd like you to get to sleep at a decent hour. You have school tomorrow."

"No one has to drive me home. I'll walk—take the shortcut home." Connor's thumbs worked, his eyes never leaving the TV screen.

"In the dark?" I asked. The path that ran from the back of my parents' home to mine cut the half mile drive down to a short walk through a forest of trees.

"Yeah. It's no big deal."

"All right," I said reluctantly.

"See you at the store tomorrow?" my father asked.

"Yes. I want to go through a few more catalogues and websites for more appealing summer items. Don't worry. I'll check with you first before I place any orders."

My father's face took on the worried expression I hadn't seen all evening. "Delia, let's not get carried away. We have to consider the cost of bringing in too many new items that might not go over with Dickens residents. Then we'll be stuck with too much inventory. The people who buy our merchandise require basic items, not trendy designer clothes and accessories."

"Dad, have you forgotten you asked me to revamp the store and bring it up to date? The new orders I've introduced so far are doing well. The back room's filled with merchandise and bolts of cheap fabrics that nobody's bought in years."

"Mom, please," my son complained. "Gramps and I are in the middle of a game."

"Sorry," I muttered. I bent down to kiss my father's cheek. "We'll talk another time."

Dad patted my back. "Good idea. Don't forget the leftovers."

"I won't. Thanks again for dinner."

In the kitchen, I removed the containers of lasagna and pie from the fridge and placed them in one of the many plastic tote bags my parents kept folded in the bottom of the pantry.

I drove home, parked the car in the driveway, and carried the leftovers up the outside steps. The dog was back, curled up in the same spot he'd been in when I'd come home from work hours ago.

"Hi, there," I greeted him.

Some of the rags moved as he wagged his tail.

"You don't want to sleep out here in the cold," I said.

Before I realized what I was doing, I unlocked the front door and held it open. The dog rose slowly and entered the house. But he went no farther than a few feet into the hall, where he plopped down and looked up at me.

"Be right back," I said. I put the leftovers I'd brought home in the fridge, then went upstairs to see what I could find to make the dog a temporary bed. I found a worn quilt in the linen closet. I brought it downstairs, folded it into quarters, and placed it just outside the kitchen. The dog sniffed it all around before settling down and curling up in the middle of the quilt, once again looking like a pile of rags.

I chuckled. "You feel right at home, don't you? In the kitchen, I filled a bowl with water and left it a few feet from the dog. On second thought, I put one of the remaining meatballs on a small plate and set it down beside the bowl. The dog stood and ate it in one fell swoop.

"You sure were hungry," I said, as he curled back into a ball and closed his eyes.

What a strange evening it had been, I thought, as I boiled water for lemon tea. A stray dog had made himself at home in our house. Uncle Brad had brought Missy to dinner. Then Missy told a story about a driver wanting to run her down and later alluded to something she'd discovered around her father's death that Uncle Brad warned her not to tell me.

I couldn't quite get the sense of the nature of their relationship. Was something going on between them like Aunt Reenie suspected? They shared a sense of familiarity. Uncle Brad seemed protective of Missy, and Missy leaned on him for emotional and practical support. But was it also romantic? Sexual?

I still had to talk to him, but what could I say? I carried my mug of tea into the family room. It wasn't my place to tell him Aunt Reenie was planning to divorce him. There was the possibility she'd calm down and decide she wasn't about to do any such thing. I shook my head. Why did Dad ask me to get involved in my aunt and uncle's squabbles? What made him think I could influence how they behaved?

My father presented his own set of problems where I was concerned. When I'd told him I was coming back to live on the island, he had said he wanted me to take an active part in running the general store. Not work there from nine to five, five days a week. He and his salespeople would cover that as usual. But he wanted my input to introduce more updated and upbeat merchandise and to spruce up the place a bit. To lure in more shoppers. People still came in for food and for basics like socks and Band-Aids, but sales had fallen off because people were either buying more expensive items like clothing and household items on Long Island or ordering them online.

I said I'd be happy to and set to work with enthusiasm, only to be told an item was too far-out for Dickens Island, or too expensive, or too weird. It was only after hours of arguing that I managed to introduce some new items. Those sold well and were the reason our numbers had improved. My father and his brother were alike—they fought change and tried to maintain the status quo.

I must have dozed off, because the next thing I knew, Conner was saying, "Sorry I'm a little late, Mom. Gramps and I were in the middle of this really lit game, and it took a while for it to end."

I sat up, rubbed my eyes, and saw it was a quarter to eleven. "Who won?"

"Who do you think? Me."

I grinned. Conner sounded so happy.

"You let that dog sleep in the house?" he asked.

"I found him outside and fed him one more meatball." I yawned. "Tomorrow I'll try to find out who he belongs to. Meanwhile, he can stay with us tonight."

"I don't think so. He scooted out the door when I came in just now."

"Really? I guess he decided to go home after all." *If only Uncle Brad would do the same.*

Chapter Six

A siren woke me minutes before my alarm went off. I stopped in the bathroom, then went to Connor's room to wake him up. I dreaded another morning hassle. Connor was a deep sleeper and definitely not a morning person. He had missed the school bus the past few days, and I'd had to drive him to school.

To my surprise, he was already dressed and downstairs in the kitchen eating a bowl of cereal without any milk.

"Hi, Mom."

"I'm glad you're up."

He shrugged as he stood to get the orange juice. He was about to drink from the container when he caught my eye. "I'll get a glass."

"Would you please pour me some too?" I said.

I made toast and a small carafe of coffee. Connor and I didn't talk as we ate our breakfast, but the silence between us was cordial. I was about to ask if he had any tests coming up, when he said, "I'm going to Trevor's house after school."

"Okay. I'll probably be at the store most of the day. Call me if you want me to pick you up at Trevor's."

"I'll be fine, Mom. See ya."

I looked up at the clock. "But it's only five after eight. The bus won't be by for another ten minutes."

The front door closed behind Connor. I wondered if this was the way all teenagers behaved—mysterious and uncommunicative—or was it the result of my not being with Connor during his childhood? I shook my head. At least the hostility he'd been sending my way lately was absent this morning. Maybe our relationship was improving simply because we were living in the same house and he saw how much I loved him.

I showered and got dressed and decided to stop by my brother's house. Wayne was three years younger than me and a successful novelist. He and his partner, Lauren, split their time between the island and Manhattan, when they weren't traveling. A few years ago, he'd started up *The Chronicle*, our local weekly newspaper. He'd hired people to handle ads and type them up while he, Lauren, and a few others reported on local news and wrote articles of local interest. Recently, Wayne asked me to write an article about the history of the general store. I'd sent it to him a few days ago, and he wanted me to stop by to talk about it.

Their house was at the other end of the island, a modern wood-and-glass structure that stood on a bluff over a sandy beach facing Connecticut. Gertie, their Golden Lab, came out to greet me. She licked my hand, then sniffed my jeans. I wondered if she'd caught the scent of the raggedy dog that had visited us yesterday.

"Hey, Sis!" My brother came outside and wrapped me in a hug. Wayne was six foot four like our dad and as good-looking as any movie star.

I laughed, shaking my head at his sweatshirt and Bermuda shorts. "Aren't you cold?"

"Nah. Come inside and let's talk."

My brother led me to the eating area of their large kitchen, which had floor-to-ceiling windows that faced the Sound. His laptop was open. Next to it was a mug half filled with coffee. Without asking, he poured a mug for me. I took out the milk from their huge fridge and sat down at the table.

"Your article reads well," he said without any introduction. "I'm just tweaking it in one or two places. No need for you to read it again. It goes in the next edition."

"Okay. So why did you want me to come over?"

Wayne stretched out his long legs. "I've been thinking. The paper is doing okay. Glen keeps up on the school sports and Brianna and Rory do a good job bringing in local events. But we need something more solid. A few articles of substance."

"Why are you looking at me?" I asked.

"Because, Sis, you have a natural writing style and more free time than the others."

I glared at him. Though Wayne was my kid brother, he had a way of getting me to do things I hadn't planned to do. "I'm busy modernizing the general store, and I have Connor to take care of."

"You know Dad's not going to let you make any major changes all at once, and Connor's in high school, not kindergarten. You need to make use of that brilliant mind of yours."

"So what do you have in mind?"

Wayne jumped to his feet. "A series of articles about the history of Dickens Island. What the island was like before our ancestor bought it from that English fellow who had settled here in the mid-1800s. The Dickens family. How the island has changed over the years. Write what you want! No need to go in chronological order."

My brother rubbed his hands together, and I knew he was only getting started.

"Okay," I said to stop him.

He grinned. "Okay, as in you'll do it? That's fantastic, Delia." Wayne wrapped me in another bear hug.

"Okay, as in I'll think about it."

"Oh." He pouted the way he used to as a kid when things didn't go his way.

"And I'll get back to you ASAP, got it?"

He nodded and sat down.

"It is a good idea," I said. When he opened his mouth, I held up my finger. "End of discussion. I have a few things to tell you. Family stuff."

I filled Wayne in on our aunt and uncle's shenanigans, how our father expected me to set things right, and last night when Uncle Brad brought Missy to dinner after she claimed someone nearly ran her down.

"Lots of conflict and mystery." His eyes shone, and I knew what that meant. "Don't you dare use any of what I just told you in one of your plots."

"Of course not," he said glibly, and I knew he was lying.

I dropped my head and allowed myself to admit what was bothering me. "I miss Mom. I wish she'd come home and do what she's always done—remind Dad it's not his job to worry about the health and welfare of every Dickens resident." I exhaled. "Or play referee when Aunt Reenie and Uncle Brad have one of their squabbles."

"That's precisely why she left," Wayne said.

"Oh." I looked at him in surprise.

"Mom needed a break from overseeing the overseer. You shouldn't be so quick to fill her shoes."

"Believe me, I don't want to. I'll talk to Uncle Brad, tell him to stop shooting down all of Aunt Reenie's ideas. Not that I expect him to suddenly agree to new housing or a ferry line to Connecticut."

"Both are coming, whether he likes it or not," my brother said darkly. "The island's economy is stagnant. It needs growth."

I shivered. Wayne had always had an uncanny understanding of what was good for Dickens Island's economy. I had no doubt that he knew what he was talking about.

"Where's Lauren today?" I asked, to talk about something else.

Wayne glanced at his watch. "Probably on the Long Island Railroad with her client, on their way to the D and D Building. She won't be home till eight or nine tonight."

I nodded. Lauren was a talented interior decorator and in high demand.

We chatted a bit more, then I got up to leave. Wayne and Gertie walked me out to my car. My brother hugged me and held me close.

"I never got to tell you how glad I am that you moved back here."

"Like you're even here all the time," I scoffed, though I was touched.

"I like knowing that I'll see you when we're back on the island and that Connor is back with his mom." When he pulled away, there was laughter in his voice. "Besides, I need you to write some features for *The Chronicle* if it's going to survive."

Chapter Seven

I hummed as I drove to the general store. Spending time with my brother always lightened my spirits. Perhaps it was because I admired how Wayne always managed to do what he liked while staying close to both our parents and maintaining an abiding attachment to Dickens Island. A trait I wish I had. My family thought I was the voice of reason simply because I came across as calm and practical when the truth was, I was often conflicted about issues. Was I too strict or too lenient with Connor? Should I tell my father I had no business interfering in my aunt and uncle's marital disputes?

I turned on the local music station and caught the tail end of a report. "And now we'll hear from Police Chief Fanning."

There was a crackling sound, then Gregg Fanning came on. "The body of Melissa Faraday was discovered at seven thirty this morning when I went to her home at 17 Clydesdale Road at the request of her employer, Jodie Reinking. Mrs. Reinking had called the precinct because she was worried when Miss Faraday didn't show up at work at seven o'clock."

I gasped. Missy was dead! So that was the reason for the siren. I pulled over to the curb. "'. . . never missed a day of work at the bakery. Never arrived late. When Missy didn't answer her phone, I knew something was wrong.' I went to check on Miss Faraday. She didn't respond to my knocking or to my phone call, so I entered the premises and found her lying on her living room floor. She had been shot twice in the chest. Forensics will tell us more."

My heart was pounding as I turned off the radio. How could Missy be dead when I'd just seen her last night? She'd told us about the near miss she'd had with the black car that had tried to run her down. At the time, I thought she was mistaken or exaggerating. Or downright lying. But now I knew someone really had been after poor Missy, and now she was dead.

I inhaled deep breaths until I grew calmer, then drove slowly to the police station. Lettie Trisk, the gray-haired sixty-something dispatcher, sat behind the counter of the small room.

"Hi, Delia. What can I do for you?"

"I need to talk to Gregg."

"He's still talking to the press outside Missy's house." Lettie shook her head. "Terrible what happened. Poor girl. Someone shot her in her own home. I can't think of the last time someone was murdered on Dickens Island."

"I know. Missy was frightened. She told my Uncle Brad and me that someone in a black car deliberately tried to run her down on her way to get her car after work."

Lettie was already jabbing buttons on the phone. "Gregg will want to hear all about it."

To my surprise, she managed to get him. In a few words, she told him why I'd come to the station. After listening a minute, she said. "Got it. Will do," and set the phone down.

"Gregg said he's about done there and should be back here in fifteen minutes or so. Care to wait? Or he'll catch up with you if you gotta leave."

I knew my father would take Missy's murder to heart, given the fact that she'd just been a guest in his house and he regarded every Dickens catastrophe as his personal concern. "I'm expected at the general store. Gregg can talk to me there whenever he's free."

"I'll let him know," Lettie said.

The parking lot behind the Dickens General Store was full of cars, a lot more than usual this early in the day, and I was lucky to find a spot behind the All Day Breakfast Café half a block away. The general store was crowded with customers when I walked in, though very few seemed interested in shopping. Most stood in small groups, deep in conversation, as they tried to make sense of the disturbing event that had shattered our usually crime-free island. This didn't surprise me since the store also served as the village hub. My parents and their employees were always kind and welcoming, and the variety of merchandise of tried-and-true styles and products were comforting in an old-fashioned way.

I returned customers' greetings and waved to Meg and Derrick, our two full-time employees, as I made my way to the office. I found my father sitting at his desk, agitated as I knew he would be.

"Did you hear what happened?" he demanded.

"I heard it on the radio on my way here after seeing Wayne." Mentioning that I'd gone to the police station would only upset him more.

"Who on earth would want to kill a gentle soul like Missy Faraday?"

"I can't imagine," I said.

"I've been trying to reach Brad, but he's not answering his cell. I called his office in Mineola, but his secretary said he didn't come in this morning."

A chill snaked down my spine. "Why do you need to talk to Uncle Brad?"

"I even called Reenie," my father said, ignoring my question, "but she hasn't spoken to him. She agrees with me that we need to have a memorial service for Missy. The poor girl has no family to honor her."

"Did you see Uncle Brad after he dropped Missy off last night?" I asked.

"I was asleep when he came in."

What time was that? I wondered. "Would you like me to make you a cup of tea?" I asked.

"That would be nice. I could sure use one."

I went into the small kitchen off the storage area and filled the electric kettle with water. As soon as the water boiled, I poured it into a mug over a lemon-flavored teabag. I added a bit of brown sugar, stirred, and brought it to my father's desk.

"Who would kill someone like Missy?" he mused again.

"Did you know her parents well?" I asked, more to stop him from dwelling on her murder than from curiosity.

"I wouldn't say I knew them well, but I make it my business to know everyone who lives on Dickens Island. Frank and Essie moved here over forty years ago when Missy was a toddler. From Pennsylvania, I believe. They were in their forties then. Essie worked here for a while—shortening trousers, doing simple alterations. She was a wizard with the sewing machine until she got sick. Poor woman, she died about thirty years ago.

"Frank was an accountant and continued to work at home and in his Riverhead office until he retired. He was on the town council for the past few years, till he got sick and died in September."

"And Missy took his place," I said.

Dad sipped his tea. "She did."

We were silent for a moment, thinking about Missy. My father finished his tea and stood. "I'm going out to chat with our customers. The murder has upset them a lot."

"Good idea," I said, though I wished he didn't consider it his job to comfort our fellow islanders.

"Let me know if Brad calls."

"Will do."

I reached for one of the gift catalogues I'd been wanting to go through. Gifts were an important part of our business, and having a selection of really nice choices that were reasonably priced would be a great addition to the Updated General Store, as I secretly called it. And I knew the exact place to put the display.

I only got as far as page ten when there was a knock at the door.

"Come in," I called out.

Gregg Fanning walked in. He looked frazzled. "Hi, Delia."

"Hi, Gregg. I heard you on the radio." I gestured to my father's chair behind his desk. "Have a seat."

"Glad to." Gregg sank back in the chair and stretched out his legs. I noticed his usually smooth cheeks were stubbly because he hadn't had a chance to shave. It gave him a kind of rugged look, actually.

Gregg caught me staring at him and suppressed a smile. I felt my face grow warm. He was two years older than me, and in high school I kind of had a crush on him. Not that he knew it. Like me, Gregg had been away from Dickens Island, first to attend college in the Midwest, then to work on a police force in Ohio that included two years in homicide. I knew he'd been divorced before moving back to the island five years ago.

Now he crossed his arms and gave me his undivided attention. "So, you were with Missy yesterday. Tell me about it."

"Don't you want to take notes?" I asked, suddenly nervous.

"Maybe when you come down to the station and make an official report. Meanwhile, let's just talk. I have a very efficient retentive memory."

"Okay." I thought of Uncle Brad and wished I hadn't stopped at the police station earlier. Whatever I had to say would put him in a bad light. "Missy came to dinner last night at my father's house."

"Were the two of you good friends?"

"Not really. She always said hi to me when I came into the bakery for my morning chocolate chip muffin."

Gregg grinned. "That's my favorite muffin too, though the pistachio is also great. You should try it sometime."

"Maybe I will."

"Did your father invite Missy to dinner?"

"Uncle Brad did. She was upset because she said someone tried to run her down as she was crossing Duxbury on her way to get her car. So she called him, and he invited her to dinner at my father's."

Gregg's eyes lit up at this piece of information, but his tone remained calm when he said, "I expect they were good friends, both serving on the town council."

I released a deep breath. "I guess."

"Did Missy herself tell you about the incident?"

"Yes. We were at my father's house when she told us—my father, Connor, and me."

"Tell me everything you remember Missy saying about that incident—time of day, location, color of the car."

I repeated what Missy had said about the black sedan barreling down on her the moment she started to cross Duxbury Street to get her car in the lot across the street from where she usually parked.

"Did she call the precinct to report the attack?"

"She didn't." I grimaced. "She called Uncle Brad instead. Connor asked her why she didn't call the police. Missy said since she had no proof of what had happened, she didn't think the police would believe her."

"Uh-huh."

"Frankly, it sounded . . . I thought she might be exaggerating."

"Instead, she called your uncle."

I nodded.

"Who invited her to dinner at your father's house." It wasn't a question.

"Yes."

"Who was at dinner last night?"

I squirmed. "My son, Connor, my father, Uncle Brad, Missy, and me."

"Not your Aunt Reenie?"

"No."

"She was otherwise occupied?"

"I—Er, I don't know."

"I see." Gregg nodded slowly, getting the picture. "What else did Missy talk about last night?"

"She mentioned her parents—that they were older when they had her and she was an only child. When she left, Missy said I was lucky to have my family."

"That's understandable since both her parents are gone."

"Maybe." I thought back to the secret looks that had passed between Missy and my uncle. "Dad said Frank and Essie were in their forties when they moved here, and Missy was really young. That's kind of old for first-time parents, don't you think?"

"So?"

"Do you think Frank and Essie kidnapped Missy because they couldn't have a child of their own? And decided to move to a small island where no one knew them?"

Gregg burst out laughing. "Maybe you should start writing novels like your brother."

"It was just an idea," I said.

"Let me assure you, in all the years they've lived here, no one's ever accused the Faradays of having kidnapped Missy. Is there anything else you remember?"

I shook my head. Mentioning the looks Missy and Uncle Brad had exchanged would only bring on more laughter.

"How did Missy get home after dinner?"

"Uncle Brad drove her."

"Remember what time they left?"

"About eight thirty."

"Have you spoken to your uncle since last night?"

"No, I haven't. Dad—" I stopped.

"Your dad tried to reach him and couldn't?"

I nodded, feeling miserable.

"No problem. I'll have a chat with Brad eventually, and with your father as well. Do you have any thoughts regarding who might want to murder Missy?"

"No! None at all. Do you know what time Missy was murdered?"

"Not yet." Gregg stood. "Thank you, Delia. You've been very helpful. I'll be in touch."

I watched him leave the office, hoping I hadn't said something that incriminated Uncle Brad. But I'd needed to tell the police about the black car that had come close to hitting Missy. Because it seemed the driver had succeeded in killing her after all.

Chapter Eight

My conversation with Gregg Fanning had left me too unsettled to continue browsing through catalogues and websites in search of new inventory. As I exited the office, I spotted my father conversing with four or five customers in the small seating area where, until a few years ago, people used to wait while Essie Faraday or another seamstress did simple alterations. More recently, shoppers often gathered there to rest, relax, and chat with neighbors. My parents, following dad's habit of leaving things as they'd always been, had never considered repurposing the space into one where a new type of merchandise could be sold. But maybe I could put it to good use.

Dad waved to stop me from leaving the store as he hurried over. "Delia, what on earth did Gregg Fanning want with you?"

"I thought he should know what Missy told us about the car that had tried to run her down."

"Of course. Of course. Did he ask about Brad?"

"He wanted to know if I'd heard from him today. Has he called?"

Dad shook his head. "I spoke to Reenie again. She promised to let me know if he contacts her."

"He probably went to see a client before stopping at his office and forgot to charge his phone. It wouldn't be the first time," I said.

"I suppose." Dad looked pensive. "Did Gregg say anything to you about the murder that he didn't mention in his public statement?"

"No. Hopefully, the forensic pathologists will find evidence in the room where Missy was shot. And the autopsy might turn up more information."

"People are scared," Dad said. "Fred Kraus thinks we should set up a neighborhood watch, with members taking turns driving around the island at night."

I laughed. "Right. That's sure to stop any potential murderer."

"Delia! It's nothing to joke about."

"I know. Sorry, Dad. Did anyone you talked to hear the gunshots?"

"Fred lives a few houses from the Faraday house. He said he heard two shots a little past midnight. Charlene, Sadie Alvarez's daughter, said she heard two shots closer to two o'clock in the morning"

"I heard the siren when Gregg went to check on Missy."

Dad nodded. "I heard it too."

My cell phone buzzed, and I fished it out of my pocketbook.

"Hello, Delia, it's Mavis O'Hara calling from the high school."

Instinctively, I walked several paces away from my father. "Yes, hello, Mavis."

"Is Connor ill? He wasn't in school today."

An icy chill ran down my back. "Er, yes, I know," I said, my words taking on a life of their own.

"Oh, he's sick? Sorry to hear that."

"Yes, well, it's nothing serious. A cold. He's just sleeping it off."

"Which is probably why he didn't answer the phone when I called the house."

"You called the house first?"

"Yes. Just checking."

"It's good that you do. Goodbye."

My father strode over to me. "Was tha—?"

"No. Just . . . Nothing."

My father had enough to upset him; he didn't need to worry and wonder why Connor had skipped school today. I wished *I* didn't have to deal with Connor cutting school. My heart was racing madly. I needed to be on my own so I could figure out how to deal with this latest problem.

"Dad, I gotta go. Let me know if you hear from Uncle Brad, and I'll call you if he happens to call me." I reached up to kiss his cheek.

"Of course." He shook his head. "Honey, I feel like everything around me is falling apart."

So do I, I thought. *So do I.*

I ran to my car and called Connor's cell phone only to get his voicemail. During school hours, he was supposed to use the phone only for emergencies, but I was sure he called and texted friends. But what friends did he have besides Trevor Sykes?

Next, I texted my son. Connor, call me when you get this.

Nothing.

A shot of panic spiked through me. Where was Connor? There was a murderer on the loose. Should I call Gregg? And say what? That my son played hooky and I wanted him to find him? No. I wouldn't do that. I remembered how cheerful Connor had been that morning. He'd obviously already had everything planned out then. Maybe he and Trevor had decided to take the ferry to Long Island and spend the day there. I put my car in gear and drove out of the parking lot. At least I could check on that possibility.

At the ferry office, I asked the young woman behind the desk if she knew if one or two fifteen-year-old boys had taken the eight thirty or nine o'clock ferry to Hollowdale, the small town near Riverhead, that morning.

"Not that I noticed," was her not very helpful answer.

"Did one or two boys that age buy tickets this morning?"

"Nope. During the week, it's mostly commuters with monthly tickets who take those ferries."

"Thanks," I said. At least now I could assume Connor was on the island.

Next, I called the Sykes' home. The word was that Thelma and Eddie Sykes were rough around the edges and let their two kids run wild. Thelma was five years older than me and worked as a nurse at a Long Island hospital. We'd exchanged pleasantries the few times she had come to pick up Trevor. Her husband was a long-distance truck driver and away much of the time. They had an older daughter named Madison. Thelma usually worked the evening shift, so there was a good chance that she was home now. But no one answered the phone.

Of course, the boys could be at Trevor's house and simply not answering the phone. I decided to drive there and ring the bell. The house was almost at the opposite end of the island, one of a group of bungalows that had been built as summer vacation homes about fifty years ago without much regard for the strong winds that blew there. I pulled up in front of the weather-beaten bungalow. A few of the unpainted shingles were hanging loose, and a rusted bicycle lay on the sandy lawn. I rang the bell and knocked on the door. Finally, a girl of about nineteen wearing an oversized sweatshirt that hung to midthigh and jeans came to the door rubbing her eyes.

"Yeah?"

"Hello, are you Trevor's sister? I'm Connor's mom, and I was wondering if he was here."

"Nope." She turned and started closing the door.

"Wait! Do you know where they might be?"

"Trevor said something about digging for treasure. He didn't say where."

"Digging for treasure?" I echoed. "Is he with my son?"

"Maybe. Probably." The girl yawned without bothering to cover her mouth. "That's all I know."

"Thank you," I said, but she closed the door so fast, I doubted that she heard me.

I sat in my car and shook my head. The day was getting weirder and weirder. First, Missy Faraday was found murdered and Uncle Brad was missing, then Connor skipped school to dig for buried treasure. I suddenly remembered the questions he'd asked last night about Captain Kidd. What on earth had turned him on to digging for treasure that a pirate might have buried centuries ago?

Since I was on the other side of the island, I decided to drive back along the outer road that circled the island instead of cutting across on Sedley. Because wouldn't a pirate bury his treasure near water? I drove half a mile and saw no sign of the two boys. Oddly enough, the dog that had visited us yesterday was trotting along the road as though he had somewhere to go. He stopped as I passed him. I braked the car and backed up. Our gazes met.

"Want to go home with me?" I asked.

For a moment, he remained still. Then he walked toward the car. I got out to open the back door, and he leaped onto the seat. I drove slowly along the shore road, keeping my eyes peeled for Connor as I headed back to the village and the general store.

I turned to the dog in the back seat. "I'll only be a few minutes."

He looked at me, then curled into a ball, which seemed to be his favorite position.

"You're back," Derrick said.

"Just to pick up a few items." I continued on to the grocery section and took three cans of dog food from the shelf. I added a bag of kibble and a chew toy, then went behind the counter for a bag. I returned to my car and drove home.

"Who do you belong to?" I asked the dog.

Instead of answering me, he gazed out the window.

"Okay, keep it to yourself, but I need to call you something, so your name—when you're with Connor and me—will be Riley."

"Arf," was Riley's comment.

I pulled into the driveway and got out of the car. I opened the rear door for Riley, and he followed me into the house. I gave him half a can of dog food. He finished it off and drank most of the water I'd set down beside his food. Then he curled up in the corner next to the stove and went to sleep.

Riley's presence had a soothing effect on my nerves. I was agitated. I was upset. A woman I'd spent the evening with had been murdered. My son had cut school and was probably out digging somewhere, searching for pirate gold. My aunt and uncle were fighting, and now my uncle was off the grid. But there was nothing I could do about any of the above. I stretched out on one of the living room sofas that flanked the bookcase and called my mother.

"Hello, Cordelia. How are you?"

I smiled. Except for a few rebellious teen years when I'd disobeyed her every chance I got, I found my mother to be the most understanding and supportive person I knew. "Not great. How are you?"

"I heard the sad news about Missy Faraday. Who would murder such a sweet woman?"

"That's what everyone's wondering. It's especially upsetting since Missy spent last evening with Dad, Uncle Brad, Connor, and me."

"Interesting. How did that come about?"

I told her. When I was finished, my mother said, "So Reenie tossed him out. I wonder if she'll actually file for divorce."

"So you know all about it. Dad asked me to talk to each of them to try to get them to kiss and make up—as though anything I say would have an impact."

"He did, did he?" My mother's tone had turned to ice. "He's still meddling where he has no business, and now he's dragging you into it."

"Mom, Connor cut school today. Trevor's sister said the boys went digging for pirate gold."

"Did they? There have always been rumors that Captain Kidd buried some of his gold on Dickens Island."

"Aren't you worried about Connor?"

"Because he cut school for one day? Didn't you? More than once, as I remember."

"I wish you'd come home. I don't know what to do about Connor. I've tried to talk to him, but he's still angry because I left him with you and Dad. And Uncle Brad is off somewhere. No one can reach him, and Gregg wants to question him about Missy."

"Delia, honey, you need to separate what's your responsibility from what isn't. Don't let anyone tell you what to do, and that includes your father. Trust your own judgment. You have a good head and a loving heart."

"But, Mom—"

"I have to go. My art class is about to start. Talk soon." And with that, she was gone.

Chapter Nine

Even though my mother hadn't given me any specific advice regarding how to deal with the issues going on in my life, I felt more centered after our chat. Mom was a dreamy sort of person who didn't quite float through life, but she had a gentle presence. She was easy to talk to, and all of us in the family went to her for solace and support.

She'd worked with Dad in the general store and, until recently, had gone along with most of his decisions. My brother, Wayne, told me this past year that she'd started offering suggestions to update the store, all of which Dad ignored, nor was he eager to go on any of the trips abroad that she'd mentioned. He'd also brushed aside the idea of moving off the island, even for a few months of the year. It was a shock to all of us when Mom announced she was going to live in the city for a while and do a few of the things she'd been wanting to do for years. Of course I'd offered to let her stay at my apartment.

Had we exchanged places? I wondered. I certainly hoped not. I called Dad to see if he'd heard from Uncle Brad, but he hadn't.

"Gregg called. When he found out that Brad was staying with me, he asked what time he came in last night." Dad sighed. "I had to tell him I didn't know." He sighed again. "I can't believe he considers my brother a suspect."

"We don't know that he does. But Uncle Brad was with Missy last night. I'm sure Gregg wants to get as much information about her last few hours as he can."

"And you still haven't had a chance to talk to Brad about that other matter."

I drew a deep breath. "Dad, I don't think it's my place to do that."

"Well, someone has to talk some sense into them. Brad's off somewhere doing God knows what. Meanwhile, Reenie is starting divorce proceedings."

I gulped. "She told you."

"Yes, the second time I called to ask if she'd heard from him. Or was it the third?"

I opened my mouth to offer to call Aunt Reenie, then closed it again. My mother's words rang in my head, and I knew she was referring to this very subject.

"I have to go, Dad. I'll see you tomorrow and work on what I was planning to take care of today."

"Goodbye, Delia. Love you."

"I love you too."

Riley came over and nuzzled my hand. I petted his unkempt coat, making a mental note to buy a brush and do something about the tangles. Or should he get a haircut? Or have a bath? Maybe all of the above.

He padded to the front door. I opened it to let him out. Then I realized I was hungry, so I went into the kitchen and made myself a tuna fish sandwich and a cup of coffee.

There was no point in driving all over the island to search for Connor. Now that I was calmer, I took stock of the situation and realized my son would come home when he was finished digging for the day. How much trouble could he and Trevor get into? It was interesting that my mother hadn't seemed concerned that he'd cut school and had reminded me of the few times that I had.

I chuckled as I remembered taking a morning ferry and the train into the city with Amanda, my best friend in high school. We'd heard that the actor we both had a crush on was filming a movie on Fifth Avenue near the Metropolitan Museum of Art. Of course, we never got within twenty feet of where they were shooting. And our parents found out about what we'd done and grounded us for the rest of the month.

I wandered back into the living room and plopped down on the sofa to the left of the bookcase. My thoughts traveled back to my earlier conversation with my brother. Wayne wanted me to write a series of articles about Dickens Island that would draw attention to the newspaper. From the way he'd put it, I had free range of topics. Of course, history was always a big draw, but including anecdotes along with descriptions of historical events would add a personal touch.

My father, Uncle Brad, and Helena had told Wayne and me countless tales—some true and some apocryphal—about the island's history. The truth was, I didn't know the actual history of Dickens Island, except that sometime in the late 1800s, my father's great-grandfather settled here with a group of friends and relatives. At that time, the island was an uninhabited forest.

My curiosity piqued, I studied the shelves of books in the built-in bookcase to see if my grandmother had any books on the history of Dickens Island. Helena had been a voracious reader, and she was interested in all sorts of subjects. In fact, I had found it a bit odd not to have discovered more books in the house aside from those in the bookcases in the upstairs hall and in the bookcase I was perusing right now.

Most of the books were novels and mysteries in no particular order, with a few nonfiction books scattered among them. I felt a stab of excitement when I came upon a history of Long Island that looked promising. I sat down with it and began to read.

Some minutes later, I put the book aside, disappointed because the little information that it had about Dickens Island was what I already knew—that it had been virtually uninhabited even when Gardiner's and other islands were occupied. It had remained mostly covered by trees and bushes, though it was believed a local Indian tribe had used part of it as a cemetery. The tribe's sachem sold the island to an Englishman in the mid-nineteenth century. Some thirty years later, he or his son sold it to James Nathaniel Dickens.

Someone must have written a book about Jamie Dickens. He was a well-known frontiersman who had spent his younger years in the wilds of Kansas before returning east and buying the island. I made a mental note to stop in at our small local library as well as one of the bigger libraries on Long Island. Even if there was nothing much written about my ancestor, I was sure to find information I could use for other articles for *The Chronicle.*

I gave a start when the front door opened and Connor came into the house with Riley.

"Hi, Mom." He surprised me by bending over me and kissing my cheek.

"Hi, Connor. I see you brought Riley inside with you."

"Riley?"

"Uh-huh. Since he's here so often, I decided to give our canine friend a name."

"Cool." Connor was on his way to the kitchen to get something to eat when I called out to him. "Where were you today?"

He turned. "In school. Where do you think?"

I joined him in the hall. "Mrs. O'Hara called to tell me you were absent. You never answered my calls or texts. I was worried; I didn't know where you were. There's a murderer on the loose, in case you've forgotten."

Connor didn't answer.

"Where were you?" I asked, hoping he wouldn't lie.

"Around," he mumbled.

"Trevor's sister said the two of you were out digging for pirate treasure."

Still nothing. I let out a huff of exasperation. "I don't like your skipping school, Connor, and I certainly don't like you wasting time and energy searching for an imaginary treasure."

Connor's face lit up. "It's not imaginary, Mom! Captain Kidd was a real person who turned pirate and stockpiled a fortune. And he buried treasure on Dickens Island, just like he did on Gardiner's."

Though I was angry that he'd cut school, I couldn't help smiling at his enthusiasm. I'd never seen Connor this excited about any of his school subjects. "Buried treasure on Dickens Island is an urban legend that was propagated to stir up interest for the tourists. I've seen the book that Farley Kriss carries in his bookstore. *Captain Kidd's Lost Treasures.* He wrote it."

"Yeah, I read it. Trevor has a copy and loaned it to me. It's all made up stuff."

"Okay . . . so?"

I glanced at my son. He looked like he was about to explode with a secret.

"I swear it's real, Mom. He made a map and tucked it inside one of his logs."

"You mean the record that ship captains used to keep?"

"They still keep logs, Mom."

"Where did you see it? In the library?"

"Nope. I found it." He gestured toward the living room. "I'll show you."

I followed him back inside. Connor stepped close to the bookcase. He pulled out the two books at the left end of the middle shelf, then reached inside to press a rectangle-shaped button that protruded from the back of the bookcase. I heard the sound of cogs, then stared in amazement as part of the bookcase began to move. The left side turned toward the wall as the right side jutted out into the living room.

"Awesome, isn't it?"

"I had no idea!" I exclaimed as I peered inside. "Helena never mentioned a secret room."

The small area had an odd shape. The longest wall faced the door while the two shorter side walls curved gently toward the door. All three walls held bookshelves from floor to ceiling. The bottom shelves were twice as large and were filled with coffee-table books, magazines, and what looked like ancient journals of various sizes. An armchair beside a reading lamp occupied an interior corner.

"I found it last week when I was checking out the books on the living room shelves, looking for a history book for a class assignment. I knew Helena had a library of all kinds of books, but I wasn't finding anything really helpful." Connor grinned. "That's 'cause she kept the good ones here."

I pointed to one of the bottom shelves. "And that's where you found the log?"

"I almost didn't see it because it's not very big. See?" Connor reached for a well-worn leather-bound book and opened it. Inside were what appeared to be six or seven tan pages that looked fragile to the touch. They were filled with charts and lists in old-fashioned cursive writing in ink that had faded with age. I could barely make out the words.

"And you managed to read this?" I asked.

"It wasn't easy. The esses look like effs. I couldn't make out every word, but I got the gist of it. It's a record of one of his journeys. The last page has a list of islands and their locations and a few notes about each of them. That's where he buried some of his treasure!"

I glanced down at the log. "Somewhere in here it actually says he hid treasure on Dickens Island?"

Connor shifted his shoulders. "Kind of. He mentions the island, calls it by its Indian name and describes a specific spot on the northern shore in nautical terms. And look!" He turned to the last page and removed a loose, stained piece of paper that had been folded in quarters. Connor opened it carefully and pointed to the curved line that had minor but definite irregularities. There were two icons of some sort and an X below the line.

"That curve is the exact shape of part of Dickens Island's shoreline facing Connecticut. I figured the X is the treasure—the spot in the log that Kidd described in nautical terms. It's located in what's now the bird sanctuary. The number here has to stand for the number of paces from this symbol that looks like a tree." He gnawed at his lower lip. "The trouble is, there are so many trees in the sanctuary, we weren't sure which tree he meant."

"So the log doesn't mention anything about hidden treasure."

Connor released a huff of exasperation. "Not in so many words. In case the log fell into the wrong hands."

I stared at my son in disbelief. "Connor, even if this log was really written by Captain Kidd, you can't assume that a curved line and a few symbols point to buried treasure here on Dickens Island."

"Why not? You can see for yourself how old this log is." Connor turned to the first page. "And there's his name, plain as day!"

"So based on this, you and Trevor cut school and started digging for treasure?"

He shrugged. "There's always the chance that someone already dug it up, but why not give it a try?"

I wasn't getting anywhere by pointing out how farfetched his idea was, so I tried another tack. "You can't go digging in the bird sanctuary, Connor. That's island property."

"We're Dickenses, so it's ours, right?"

"Not exactly." Something unpleasant occurred to me. "Does Trevor know all about this?" I asked. "I hope you didn't bring him into this room."

"I didn't. I swear," he added when he saw how the idea of Trevor invading this secret, sacrosanct place offended me. "I told him I came across the info in the library last week when I was in Riverhead, and I made a copy of the map." Connor looked down at the ground. "I mean, I like Trevor and all, but this belongs to our family."

"It does," I said, greatly relieved. "Now let's leave Helena's secret room. Later, we'll talk about your punishment for cutting school."

We stepped back into the living room. Connor closed the door and replaced the books on the shelf, then we headed for the kitchen with Riley following behind.

"I hope you'll take into account that it's the first time I ever cut school," Connor said. "Anyway, I'll probably get detention."

"I don't think so. I said you were home sick."

Connor shot me a look of pure amazement. "You did?"

"Just don't ever do it again," I mumbled as I fed Riley some more of the dog food I'd bought and reminded myself to buy a few doggie dishes. Connor sat down to a snack of cookies and milk. As I made myself a fresh cup of coffee, it hit me that we'd just had our longest conversation since I'd moved back to the island.

Chapter Ten

Connor started up the stairs to his room to work on a school project. When Riley followed, Connor paused and called down to me. "Can Riley come upstairs with me?"

"He really should have a bath before he jumps on your bed or a sofa." *And gets a flea and tick treatment*, I thought.

"Okay. I'll give him a bath."

"You're going to bathe him?" I asked, surprised.

"Sure. Don't you think I can? I'll use some of your shampoo. Later we can buy him some doggie stuff of his own."

"Hold on a second. I'll get the dishwashing detergent. Use that instead of shampoo."

Connor burst out laughing. "Come on, Mom. Dishwashing detergent?"

"Believe it or not, it's gentler on a dog's coat. My neighbor in Manhattan has a labradoodle. She used dishwashing detergent when she ran out of Mitzi's shampoo."

I handed him the plastic container of detergent. "Would you like me to help?"

"Nah. I can manage." After a pause, he said, "I'll call down if I need you."

I smiled as I wrapped my head around the shift in Connor's attitude toward me. No doubt it was because I hadn't gone berserk when I found out he'd cut school to search for pirate treasure. And having Riley around seemed to be having a good effect on both of us, though that would only last until we located his owner.

I let a few minutes pass before I went upstairs to see how the bath was going. Connor was standing in the bathtub in his underwear, rinsing the suds off Riley with the hand nozzle while the dog remained remarkably still. This had to be quite unusual for any animal, let alone one that was a virtual stranger to us. It was hard to imagine that someone wouldn't be missing him.

"Mom, could you please get me a couple of towels?"

"Sure."

I grabbed two old towels from the linen closet just outside the bathroom and handed one to Connor. I unfolded the other one and we both rubbed Riley dry. "I think you can finish drying him with my hair dryer. I'll pick up a brush tomorrow and work on the tangles in his coat."

"And get some flea powder. Just in case."

I grinned when the dog licked Connor's cheek. "He likes you," I said.

"I love him! I hope we don't have to give him back."

"I'll call Dr. Morrison tomorrow," I said, "to find out if Riley's his patient and if he knows who he belongs to."

"I suppose we ought to do that," Connor said, not sounding happy. "Though Riley likes living right here, don't you, boy?"

"I'll go start dinner. It should be ready in half an hour."

I popped last night's leftovers in the microwave and put handfuls of salad in a large bowl. I mixed in some dried cranberries and pieces of pecans, dressed it with oil and vinegar and a few seasonings, then I called my father.

"Hi, Dad. Have you heard from Uncle Brad? Is there any news about Missy's murder?"

"Brad's still on Long Island having dinner with a friend." My father chuckled. "We got all bent out of shape worrying where he'd gone. Turns out he was in court most of the day. It's your Aunt Reenie I'm worried about. Gregg brought her in for questioning."

My heart jumped to my throat. "Regarding what happened to Missy?"

He sighed deeply. "I'm afraid so. When Gregg and his deputy, Billy Watson, were searching Missy's house, they came across one of your aunt's signature scarves in Missy's bedroom."

"Oh!" Aunt Reenie's colorful silk scarves had RDs printed all over them. They were her trademark. "I wonder how it got there."

"Obviously the police are wondering that too."

"But you can't for one minute suspect that Aunt Reenie killed Missy Faraday. I know she—" I stopped short.

"You know what, Delia? Now isn't the time for secrets."

"Aunt Reenie suspected that Brad and Missy were having an affair."

"That's ridiculous. Missy looked to Brad as a mentor. And I'm certain my brother would never betray his marriage vows."

"Who told you that Gregg questioned Aunt Reenie?"

"Gregg did. When he called to find out if I'd heard from Brad."

"Where's Aunt Reenie now?"

"I have no idea. I tried calling her, but my call went to voicemail."

"I'll try her after Connor and I have dinner."

"Why did Chief Fanning question Aunt Reenie?" Connor asked as soon as we sat down to eat.

I hesitated. Was it a good idea to tell a fifteen-year-old details of a crime investigation? Then I thought *Why not?* Word was bound to get out anyway, and Connor had been with Missy hours before she was murdered. "To talk to her about Missy's murder."

Shock and excitement shone in Connor's eyes. "He thinks she offed Missy because she and Uncle Brad were smashing?"

I frowned. "We do not know they were . . . smashing. The police found one of Aunt Reenie's scarves in Missy's house."

"Maybe Aunt Reenie went over there to tell Missy to keep her hands off her husband and things got weird."

"Let's not assume the worst. Missy did say someone tried to run her down yesterday."

Connor shrugged. "That could have been a made-up excuse to call Uncle Brad. A trick to get him to be her protector."

"That was my thought too," I admitted, "until she ended up dead this morning."

"Mom, there was something cringe about her," Connor said, his expression serious.

"Translate, please."

"Missy was clueless. The built-in alarm that warns us when something's off or weird was missing." He shook his head. "She didn't have it, so she came off cringe."

I beamed at my son in admiration. "You put your finger on the piece of Missy Faraday I could never quite put into words. It kept her naive. Almost childlike. In certain ways, anyway."

"You think that's what got her killed?" Connor asked.

"Could be. Could very well be."

We finished eating, and I got up to clear the table. As Connor was leaving the kitchen, I called out, "I haven't forgotten about your punishment for cutting school. You have five days to clear your things out of the garage. Take what you want to keep up to your bedroom or let me know if it's too big and needs storing somewhere else. Make a pile of what you want to throw out. And no more digging for pirate treasure."

"Mo-om! Please! We're not hurting anyone. And think what great publicity it would be for the island if we did find gold."

"Sorry, Connor, you can't just go around digging holes on public property. I expect you to fill in the holes you and Trevor created so no one falls and twists an ankle. Once that's done, I want you staying close to home. There's a murderer on the loose, after all."

Connor made a face and stormed off. So much for an improvement in our relationship.

* * *

When the kitchen was in order, I sat down and called Aunt Reenie.

"I did not kill Melissa Faraday," she declared by way of a greeting.

"Hi, Aunt Reenie. I'm just calling to see how you're doing."

"How do you think I'm doing, accused and interrogated of murdering that nincompoop by someone who should know better than to even imagine I had anything to do with her death?"

"You know Gregg has to do his job."

"Then he should look at the people involved with Missy Faraday and who might have reason to kill her. Like your Uncle Brad. The way I heard it, he was the last person to be seen with her. It seems he invited her to dinner at your father's house. A real family affair."

I ignored the accusatory tone. "Do you have any idea how one of your scarves happened to turn up in her house?"

"As I told Gregg, she must have stolen it. How many times did Brad drive her home? I may have left the scarf in his car and she took it for some crazy, bizarre reason."

"That's possible," I agreed.

"It's the only thing that makes sense. Certainly, Brad wouldn't have given it to her as a gift, not with my initials all over it. I have to go, Delia. Katie's texting me. The poor girl is devastated because I'm divorcing her father."

"Talk to you later," I said and hung up. *Poor Katie* was right. My cousin was getting bombarded with news bombshells of her parents' lives, none of them good.

I'll catch up with Uncle Brad tomorrow, since he's still on Long Island, I thought. Besides, I'd had enough tumult today to last me a month. Instead, I'd spend some time in my grandmother's secret reading room. It was the perfect cozy spot to relax in as I rummaged through books and old journals. It would help take my mind off murder.

Chapter Eleven

I called upstairs to Connor to tell him I was going to spend an hour or two in the secret room. "I'll text you if I get trapped inside and can't get out."

Connor laughed. "You won't get locked in. You saw how the door opens when you're inside."

"I did. See you later," I called back, glad that he wasn't still angry because I told him he could no longer dig for treasure.

As soon as Riley heard my voice, he came trotting down the stairs and followed me into the living room. There was something uncanny about the way he sensed that I'd appreciate his company seemingly even before I knew it. I stroked his head, and he gazed back at me through the fringe of hair covering his eyes. How did the poor dog manage to see? I made two mental notes: to bring him to the veterinarian's office for the first available appointment and then to a groomer ASAP.

Facing the bookcase, I removed the same two books Connor had, then pushed the white rectangular button. I marveled at the way the bookshelf slowly pivoted ninety degrees then stopped, allowing me access to the hidden room. I stepped inside. Riley didn't follow.

"Coming in?" I asked.

He tilted his head one way, then the other. I waited for him to decide. Finally, he crossed the threshold and joined me in my grandmother's inner sanctum.

Now that the shock of learning about the room's existence had worn off, I took my time checking out the contents of the shelves. I scanned the titles, many of which were familiar to me. They were mostly mysteries, mainstream, and women's fiction. I chuckled when I caught sight of a few racy novels

An idea had been brewing in my mind, and seeing all these books brought it to the forefront. I'd told Dad my thoughts about setting up a Book Nook in the general store, a quiet haven with a seating area and a selection of books where people could relax and take a break from shopping. I had the perfect spot in mind—the area where people used to wait while they were having an item of clothing altered. There was a sofa already in place. Now all I needed were more chairs, a small table or two, and books. I started pulling out books I'd already read to bring over to the store.

That taken care of, I selected a few mysteries I wanted to read, then focused on the lower shelves that were filled with reading matter of various sizes and shapes. I was intrigued to discover a few centuries-old books and another log like the one Connor had discovered.

I brought the log over to the chair and turned on the standing lamp. The log had been written by a sailor who had spent years on whaling ships. It was difficult to make out the words because the spelling and letters were very different, as was the sentence structure. The ink was faded in places and completely blotted out in spots. The entries only filled three pages, leaving the remaining pages blank. Unfortunately, there was not enough information, as far as an article for *The Chronicle* was concerned.

I returned it to the shelf and opened another journal with stiff cardboard covers that had been written by a sixteen-year-old girl who had lived on Dickens Island in the early 1900s. Victoria Watts wrote pages and pages about her family, her day-to-day life, and finally about her betrothal. I felt a stirring of excitement. This journal might be useful as part of a historical article. Where had Helena gotten these old journals? Or had they been here when she'd inherited the house from her parents?

When I looked up, Riley stood facing the door, patiently waiting for me to let him out.

"Sorry, boy. I lost track of time." Indeed I had. An hour and a half had passed while I'd been reading about life on a whaling ship and courting in the 1920s.

When I exited the secret room, I found Connor in the kitchen eating a piece of leftover pie. He bent down to pet Riley, who made sounds as if he were speaking. Clearly, he was telling Connor something.

"Okay." Connor stood and walked with Riley to the front door.

"Do you think he'll want to come back inside?" I asked.

"I'll go out with him and see if he does."

I put Connor's dish in the dishwasher, wondering if the dog had a place to go home to. Minutes later, Connor and Riley were back in the house. My son was grinning.

"He wanted back in. Mom, I think we got ourselves a dog."

* * *

The following morning, I was up at seven thirty to make Connor breakfast and watch him walk down to the road to wait for the school bus. The junior-senior high school building was in the center of the island. It was an easy walk or bike ride to our house, but on the days Connor brought home heavy textbooks in his backpack, he preferred to take the bus. I was glad to see he seemed cheerful enough. Today he had baseball practice, the first of the season, which meant he'd be taking the late bus home. I hoped baseball would take his mind off Captain Kidd and his phantom treasure.

I straightened up the kitchen, poured myself a second cup of coffee, and reached for my cell phone.

"Here goes nothing," I told Riley, who had come over to rest his head on my knee.

I was nervous about calling Jack Morrison for a few reasons. I was duty bound to find out if Riley belonged to someone, someone who had managed to misplace a dog of his size and amazing temperament. Didn't the owner miss him? Aside from the emotional attachment, Riley must have cost a good deal of money. He wasn't the type of dog to race out of his owner's house the moment the front door opened. It made me wonder if Riley's owner deserved to have a dog like Riley—a dog Connor and I were growing very attached to.

Jack and I had dated when I was in high school. In fact, he was my first real boyfriend. It all began the second week of July when he came into the general store where I was working. I had just turned sixteen and would be starting my junior year of high school that fall. Jack was three years older than me and a sophomore at Cornell. He was home for the summer and had a job at a veterinary hospital on Long Island.

Our romance was hot and heavy even after he went back to Ithaca, and we got to see each other most weekends. But just before Thanksgiving, he sent me an email telling me it was over. He'd met someone, and she was going to be a vet too.

Devastated, I cried for days. There was no way I could compete with a girl older than me who was going to be in the same profession as Jack, a girl who saw him every day and night. Eventually, I got over being dumped and dated a few guys. But I didn't get emotionally involved again until I met my husband in college.

I knew Jack had married at one point—not the classmate he'd left me for—and had become a partner in a veterinary practice near Riverhead. At some point, he got divorced and ended up buying the small veterinary practice on Dickens Island while continuing to work a few days a week at the Riverhead location.

We had run into each other a few times since I'd moved back to the island, and while he still looked good, still had that killer smile, I was no longer susceptible. I'd forgiven him for ending our relationship all those years ago. Considering how young we were, we probably would have broken up at some point. Yet, once in a while, I wondered what my life would've been like if we'd stayed together and eventually gotten married.

"No, I haven't heard that anyone's missing a Beardie or a dog resembling what you're describing, Delia," was Jack's response when his receptionist put him on the phone and I explained why I was calling.

"Could someone have brought him over on the ferry and lost him somehow?"

"Always a possibility, but in that case, Gregg would have been notified, and he would have called me. You can always look to see if someone's posted a note on the bulletin board in the general store." Jack laughed. "You should know. People post anything and everything there."

"Good idea," I said. "I'll check. This dog's very obedient, so I can't imagine him running off."

"Tell you what. When I'm at my Riverhead office tomorrow, I'll have my receptionist contact other Suffolk County animal hospitals to see if anyone's gotten a call about a missing Beardie or a look-alike. Meanwhile, there are places you can call or contact online like HomeAgain, Fido Finder, and Pet Amber Alert."

"Thanks. I will. Meanwhile, I'd like to bring Riley in so you can look him over. I'm afraid his coat is badly matted. I'm going to have a tough time getting out the tangles."

"He'll need a haircut," Jack said, "and a short one at that. Long-haired dogs require constant attention. You're in luck. Charlene is the only pet groomer on the island, and she happens to be working here today."

"Can you fit Riley in, then hopefully Charlene can give him a haircut?"

"Give me a minute to check my schedule and Charlene's." When Jack got back on the phone, he told me to be at the animal hospital at three for Riley's examination and grooming. "I'll also scan him to see if he has a microchip. If he does, that means he's registered with a microchip company. They will have his owner's information."

"Thanks, Jack. Much appreciated. See you later."

I glanced over at Riley, who was curled up fast asleep at my feet. "Now what do I do with you until your appointment at three o'clock?" I wondered aloud. I was hesitant about leaving him alone in the house while I ran errands, and at the same time hesitant about letting him run free. He could take off and not come back here by a quarter to three, which was when I planned to leave for his appointment.

For a moment, I wondered if I was being ridiculous for bringing him to have a checkup and a haircut. If his owner showed up, he or she might be outraged that I'd gone so far as to have his matted hair cut or shaved. But then any savvy owner would know it was necessary. And any savvy owner would be overjoyed to have his or her missing dog back.

I sighed as I looked up the apps Jack had mentioned and called to find out if any dog resembling Riley was missing. Forty-five minutes later, I got my final no.

"Okay, you're mine, at least for today," I told Riley. "Let's go for a walk."

I opened the front door and breathed in the fresh air that held a whiff of the Sound. I shivered inside my parka. It was a chilly, windy late-March day, despite the sun shining brightly above the bare trees. Riley sprinted down and around the curve, and I followed him. I had yet to start an exercise regimen since my move here, and it felt good to stride on the path that ran along the outer road. When I'd gotten as far as my father's house, Riley came bounding toward me. It was the first time I'd seen him run toward me, and it was a lovely sight. I wished I had something to throw so he could fetch it. Another time.

"Let's go home, Riley," I called to him as I turned around. I had no idea if he'd follow me.

For a minute or two, there was no sign of him, but then he came tearing past me. He finally turned to check on me, and when he was sure I was following him, he slowed down to match my gait.

"I hope Jack doesn't find your owner," I told him.

Was that a smile I detected on his hairy face?

I realized the only way I could keep an eye on Riley until his appointments was to have him accompany me while I ran my errands. As he'd done before, as soon as I opened the rear door of the car, Riley jumped right in. I drove to the village and parked in the lot behind the stores. We entered the general store together as if we'd been doing it for years.

Riley caused quite a stir among the browsing customers.

"Is that your dog, Delia?" someone asked.

"I'm taking care of him," I answered.

Though we walked briskly in the direction of the bulletin board, a few people dashed over to pet Riley. He tolerated their attention almost as though he knew he should. The discolored bulletin board was full of pin holes, and one corner was torn. Time to replace it, I decided, and made a mental note to order a new one. Aside from an ancient sign someone had posted looking for a summer rental, there were a few assorted messages, their corners curled up. No one had posted anything about a lost dog.

In the pet area, I selected a leash, a collar, a container of doggie shampoo, and a squeaky toy. Riley allowed me to put the collar around his neck. I clicked on the leash and headed for the office.

My father looked up from his desk. "Hi, Delia. This must be Riley." He got up to pet Riley. Riley responded in his usual friendly way.

"Connor told you about him," I said.

"He texted me and sent me a few photos. He's crazy about the dog. I only hope he doesn't get his heart broken when you find his owner."

"I've been making calls and Jack's going to contact vets on Long Island. Nothing so far."

My father returned to his desk chair and sighed. "Your uncle's in the hot seat today. Gregg's questioning him over at the precinct."

"Why are you surprised? Uncle Brad was with Missy the night she died. And for a good part of yesterday, no one knew where he was."

"My brother had no reason to murder the poor woman."

"Do they know what time she died?"

Dad shrugged. "Either they don't know yet or Gregg wouldn't say when he interviewed me yesterday."

"Did Uncle Brad tell you what time it was when he got back to your house Tuesday night?"

My father squirmed in his chair. "He said around midnight."

"That late? I thought he was only driving Missy home."

"He told me he dropped Missy off and then went to his office to do some work."

"Did he happen to run into anyone?" I asked.

My father frowned. "No one."

I racked my brain for something comforting to say. "Surely Gregg can't arrest someone if there's no evidence that he's committed a crime."

"Of course he can't!"

The phone rang. Dad answered it. From the relief on his face, I knew it was Uncle Brad. After a few exchanges, he said, "That's ridiculous! He has to know you're not a flight risk." Pause. "I'll try to make the meeting tonight." Then. "Okay. See you later."

As soon as he set down the receiver, he let out a groan. "That was Brad. Gregg finished questioning him—for now. He instructed him not to leave the island."

"And Uncle Brad's clearly not taking it very well."

Another groan. "He's offended that someone he considers a friend, someone who knows him so well, is treating him like a suspect in a murder investigation."

I chuckled. "Aunt Reenie had the same reaction."

"It can't be easy for Gregg, working this homicide with just Billy Watson and his part-time deputy. And everyone he questions is a friend or neighbor. Maybe he should ask the Suffolk County Police to take over the case."

"Gregg's too proud to do that," I said. "Besides, he's worked homicide. It sounds like Uncle Brad is still determined to be at tonight's council meeting."

"More determined than ever. It's an open meeting, and they'll be discussing the purchase of the VanPatten Farm. My brother has very definite ideas regarding how the property should be used."

"I think I'll go to the meeting," I found myself saying.

"Really?" Dad lit up. "I'm glad you're finally taking an interest in the dynamics of our island community."

"Wayne roped me into writing a few articles about the island. Attending a council meeting will give me a good sense of how Dickens Island residents are thinking."

"Maybe you'll get the chance to talk some sense into Brad and Reenie."

"I doubt it. If anything, I expect fireworks. Their stands on this issue are diametrically opposed."

After my father left the office, I turned my attention to the catalogues I couldn't focus on yesterday and succeeded in finding several clothing and summer-related items I thought would appeal to my fellow island residents as well as the day trippers who would show up in droves as soon as the weather turned warm. Riley dozed at my feet, as comfortable as if stopping at the general store was something he did several times a week. The next time I glanced at my watch, it was close to one o'clock.

I decided to have a quick lunch at the All Day Breakfast Café, which was dog-friendly. I almost changed my mind when I noticed all the tables and booths were occupied.

Bennie Davos, the seventy-something owner, approached. "Hi, Delia. I'll have a table for you in a minute."

"Thanks, Bennie."

He glanced down at Riley. "I see you got yourself a canine companion."

I smiled. “He found us. Came by the house two days ago and hasn’t left. You hear of anyone missing a dog like Riley?”

Bennie scratched the back of his neck. “Can’t say that I have. He’s a Beardie, right? A Bearded Collie?”

“I think so,” I said.

“You know, your grandma had a Beardie.”

I felt a surge of excitement. “I had no idea. Did you ever see it?”

“Sure. She got Duncan when she and her family moved to the island full-time. She used to tell us stories about him when she was my teacher. How she loved that dog!” Bennie grinned. “According to your grandma, he was the smartest dog alive.”

“I had no idea,” I said. “She never mentioned Duncan.”

“That’s surprising,” Bennie said. “Your table’s free. Follow me.”

I followed him to a small table against the wall and waited while he removed the remaining dishes and wiped down the tabletop.

“Need a menu?”

“No. I’ll have a tuna on rye and a glass of sparkling water.”

“And some water for Riley,” Bennie said before rushing off.

Chapter Twelve

I pulled into the animal hospital's parking lot at five minutes to three. I figured Jack was squeezing us in between appointments, and I didn't want to be late, even if it meant Riley and I had a long wait before us. But after the receptionist took some basic information from me, a college-aged assistant approached. Smiling, she said her name was Keira. She weighed Riley on the scale in the corner of the hall, then led us into one of the two examining rooms. She spoke to Riley as she checked his ears and teeth, then took his temperature. Riley remained calm and seemed to be taking the examination in stride.

"Good boy." Keira stroked his head when she finished looking at his paws. To me, she said, "Clearly, this isn't his first visit to the vet. Except for the poor condition of his coat and the fact that he's a few pounds lighter than he should be, Riley appears to be in fine physical condition."

"That's good to know," I said.

"Jack will be with you in just a few minutes," Keira said, and left.

The wait stretched out to fifteen minutes. Riley lay down with his face between his paws, and after gazing at the animal photos, Jack's veterinarian diploma, and a few awards he'd been given, I paced up and down the small room. Finally, Jack charged in, a large grin on his face, with Keira at his heels. To my surprise, he kissed my cheek.

"Sorry for the delay, Delia. I was out treating a horse that has colic and expected to be back sooner."

"That's all right," I said. "I'm glad you were able to fit Riley in."

"My pleasure." Jack turned to study Riley. He felt his belly, then looked over the rest of him.

"He's a beauty, all right, despite his badly matted coat. I'm surprised no one's claimed him, but maybe we'll have better luck once I scan his microchip."

"How old do you think he is?" I asked.

"I'd say around three years old. His adult teeth are all in and in good shape, and his paws are somewhat callused.

"He's been running around in the woods."

"Which means he needs a few shots to make sure he doesn't get Lyme or any other diseases. Along with flea and tick medicine. I'll check his titers to see if his CORE vaccines are in effect." He turned to Keira and told her which shots to prepare for Riley.

When she left, he turned to me. "So how does it feel to be living on the island again? I'd imagine it's quite a change from Manhattan."

"It sure is different," I agreed, "but it's a nice change from having a nine-to-five job that ran into overtime three out of five days."

"Whoever thought someone would be murdered here on our island? Poor Missy. I heard she was over at your dad's for a family dinner the night she was killed."

"She was."

"Was your father performing one of his kind deeds?"

"What do you mean?" I asked.

"Inviting her to dinner." He looked at me questioningly. "Or were you and Missy friends?"

"Oh, I didn't invite her. My Uncle Brad did."

Jack chuckled. "Why am I not surprised?"

"What do you mean?" I bristled.

"Hey!" Jack raised his hands. "No reflection on your uncle, but Missy served on the council with Brad and liked to play the helpless female around men. She was manipulative that way."

"Some people thought so," I said, remembering what Aunt Reenie had told me about Missy. "Did she come on to you that way?"

"A few months ago, we were both at a local meeting. I knew her father had recently died, so I went over to offer my respects. I ended up sitting next to her when the meeting began. Every so often, she'd make a comment to me and nudge me like we were buddies. I didn't know what to make of it. Then she asked if I'd drive her home. I said sure, since there wasn't much else I could do. She invited me in for a drink and simply shrugged when I said I had to get home. But she called three or four times after that to ask me the silliest questions. I admit I wasn't very friendly by the fourth call."

"Even Connor noticed there was something odd about her. She told us at dinner that someone driving a black car had tried to run her down that afternoon. I thought she'd made the story up for attention, but now I believe it really happened."

"I wonder why someone would target *her*," Jack said.

"Good question," I said. And it was. Why would someone want to murder Missy Faraday?

Keira returned, and Jack gave Riley his shots and scanned the area between his shoulder blades for a microchip.

"Yep. He has a chip."

"Oh." Somehow I hadn't expected this. Or didn't want to know he had a chip.

"I'll see if I can track down Riley's owner and let you know what I find."

"Thanks, Jack."

"Meanwhile, you can return to the waiting room until Charlene's ready for him."

* * *

Poor Riley wasn't happy about getting all his hair clipped, and who could blame him? Not only did he look emaciated, which he really wasn't, but the poor dog stood shaking from the cold. And we were indoors. Riley was used to spending time outdoors. It was near the end of March, and the weather was often chilly and almost always windy. Charlene mentioned she sold many dog items, including clothing. I was happy to find a navy coat that fit Riley. He squirmed as I buckled him in.

"Sorry, boy. You'll have to wear this till your coat grows in. At least when you go outside."

He yowled pitifully in response.

At home, I put a load of laundry in to wash and started dinner. I figured that Connor and I would eat around six. The council meeting began at seven thirty, and I hoped to get there early enough to have a word with Uncle Brad. My mind was crammed with the events of the past few days, and it changed from subject to subject as I did household chores.

My thoughts often returned to Missy and how sad it was that her life had ended. From what Aunt Reenie and Jack had told me, she had been manipulative and probably had come on to Uncle Brad. And I wouldn't be surprised if she had swiped Aunt Reenie's scarf. But I remembered her cheerful greeting every morning I came into the bakery. She'd had her whole life ahead of her, until someone had seen fit to cut it short. Why? What had she done that made someone angry enough to murder her?

My cheeks grew warm when I thought of Jack Morrison, and I told myself not to fall into nostalgia or rekindle old emotions. Our time together was long past. Sure, he'd been friendly, but that didn't make up for how badly he'd hurt me.

He had refused to let me pay for Riley's visit, and he promised to let me know if he got a lead on Riley's owner.

Riley. I was going to have to tell Connor that he had a microchip and an owner somewhere. As though he knew I was thinking about him, Riley ambled over to me. I took off his coat and rubbed his flank.

"Your hair will grow back real fast," I told him.

Connor came home from school, his cheeks red from the outside chill.

"Look at you!" he said when he spotted Riley. A minute later, the two of them were roughhousing.

I told Connor that Riley had an owner after all.

"He does? Don't you think it's strange that the guy never went looking for his lost dog?"

"I do," I said. "Dr. Morrison's going to look into it."

"Maybe he decided he didn't want Riley anymore."

"Maybe," I agreed.

While we ate dinner, Connor told me a few things that had happened during the school day, including that the subject of Captain Kidd had come up in his English class.

"I have to write a paper about someone famous who lived in this area," Connor said. "Maybe I'll write about him."

"I'm going to be writing an article for your uncle's newspaper," I said. "We have plenty of books here for our research and more in the library."

"And in the secret room," Connor added. We both laughed.

He helped me clear the table, then when Riley walked to the front door, he put the dog's new coat on him and took him out for a walk. I was grateful that Connor's resentment toward me seemed to be fading, but I'd be naive if I thought that a child's sense of being abandoned by his mother could really disappear this quickly. Perhaps the weekend would be a good time for us to have that talk.

At ten past seven, I got in my car and drove the short distance to our village hall, located just past the building that housed our police department, post office, and the town manager's office. It was a white wooden building that had been constructed in the 1950s after the old village hall had burned down. It was used for meetings and the occasional marriage reception. A small area had been designated the site of the island's Historical Society, but except for a few aged pamphlets and a book about Long Island's history, with a chapter on Dickens Island, the Historical Society had never gotten off the ground.

All hopes of having a chat with Uncle Brad prior to the meeting vanished when I saw the parking lot was almost filled to capacity. While the monthly council meetings were open to the public, except for the few civic-minded residents who showed up regularly, islanders only attended meetings when there was something under discussion that affected them directly. Had Missy Faraday's murder drawn them here tonight, or was it the VanPatten Farm and people wanting to know how the land would be put to use?

I opened the back door to the sounds of a contentious conversation. I heard my aunt's and uncle's names mentioned, but not much else because all three men were speaking at the same time. They fell silent as I approached. We exchanged nods, and I continued on my way to the meeting room.

Rows of chairs took up two-thirds of the room. Many of the seats I passed were already occupied, though a few clusters of residents stood conversing in hushed tones. Uncle Brad chatted with Sadie Alvarez, George Simon, and Pete Osbourne, the other members of the council, on the raised platform at the front of the room. My aunt and her aide, Chet Thomas, sat to their right.

I found an empty seat at the end of the first row and waited for the show to begin.

At precisely seven thirty, Uncle Brad called the meeting to order. "Thank you all for coming tonight. It's a pleasure to see so many of you interested in an issue that impacts the quality of our lives here on Dickens Island.

"Before we open our meeting to discuss tonight's scheduled agenda, I want to express my personal grief and outrage along with the council's that Melissa Faraday, a council member and life-long resident of Dickens Island, was murdered two nights ago. I know that Chief Fanning and his department are doing everything possible to find and apprehend the person responsible."

Most heads turned as Uncle Brad looked at Gregg sitting in the last row.

"There will be a graveside ceremony for Missy at the Dickens Cemetery at eleven o'clock tomorrow morning and a reception afterward in the Interfaith Chapel next door. Coffee and tea will be served. Feel free to bring a cake or batch of cookies to share with friends and neighbors."

A large, beefy man well over six feet tall stood. He was Ralph Caccini, a loudmouth troublemaker and one of the men who had been arguing when I'd entered the hall. "Any suspects besides you, Brad?"

There was a burst of laughter from some in the audience.

"Thanks for your interest, Ralph. For your information, I'm not a suspect, but I was with Missy earlier that evening along with some members of my family."

I glanced at Aunt Reenie to see her reaction. Her face was as rigid as a mummy's.

"Moving on," Uncle Brad said, "we have a few small matters to take care of before we open our discussion to the main topic of the evening."

I paid scant attention to the announcement that a traffic light would be installed at a corner where two accidents had taken place or the treasurer's report on the cost of repairs to the ferry building. A few people made comments.

"Which now brings us to the matter of the VanPatten Farm purchase and how the land will be used."

There was a low rumble of voices as residents exchanged comments with their neighbors.

"The situation is this: Tim and Velma VanPatten have decided to sell the farm that's been in their family for generations. The council and the town manager agree that acquiring the property will benefit Dickens Island and all its residents. What remains is to decide how to best make use of the land. We have a few ideas, and we're eager to hear your thoughts regarding these possibilities.

"Regarding the specifics: the VanPatten Farm is almost rectangular in shape and covers an area of ninety-two acres. It's situated mid-island and extends north as far as the Sound and has ten acres of shoreline between the bird sanctuary and Marley's Beach. The VanPattens have raised cows, pigs, and chickens along with various crops, though not in recent years. The homestead and two barns are in poor shape and will have to be repaired if we decide to turn the place into a model farm where we raise and sell flowers, pumpkins, and perhaps corn. Or we can vote to rezone the property and repurpose it for an entirely different kind of project."

This time, the exchange of residents' comments almost reached a roar as Aunt Reenie came to stand at the front of the platform. She and Uncle Brad shot glances at each other. Aunt Reenie looked furious; he merely smiled.

"As your town manager, it's been my duty to investigate and research the proposed purchase as well as our community's needs in order to recommend what would be the best use of the land now known as the VanPatten Farm. With this in mind, as soon as my office and the council agreed to purchase the farm, I created a committee to explore and recommend which kind of enterprise would bring the most growth and prosperity to Dickens Island."

A shout rose from the residents sitting around Ralph Caccini. "Progress, yes! Progress, yes!"

My aunt smiled as she raised her hands, instructing the audience to tone down their enthusiasm while at the same time allowing it to continue for a minute or so. "We came up with a few workable projects that would bring vitality and financial profit to our community and appeal to present and future residents as well as potential tourists. During the process, we discovered that several businesses are eager to work with us. They consider Dickens Island a fresh and attractive rustic setting a short distance from the city.

"In the spirit of transparency, I will share with you that we looked into the two offers the VanPattens received when word got out that they were selling the farm. Both are suitable to our needs. One is for the construction of a community of townhouses; the other for a hotel-casino enterprise. My office finds both proposals very attractive."

"What about putting in a ferry to Connecticut?" Ralph called out. "It's long overdue."

"Ferry! Ferry!" several voices shouted.

My aunt beamed, clearly pleased at this outburst. "I'm of the opinion that a ferry line between Dickens Island and Connecticut is long overdue. Hopefully, whichever enterprise we choose to undertake will encourage more visitors to Dickens Island. In which case, a ferry line must be considered a necessity. Creating a new ferry line comes under the auspices of Highway, Ferry, and Transportation, but given the fact that talk of a new ferry line never goes any further than discussion, perhaps it's time we put it to a referendum vote."

Ralph Caccini and his group burst out in cheers.

Uncle Brad's face was the color of a boiled lobster when he came to stand beside his wife. I could almost see the flashes of animosity pulsating between them.

"Before you continue, Madam Town Manager, I am obliged to address and correct a few of the factual errors you've put forth."

My aunt opened her mouth to speak. Did I just see Uncle Brad poke his elbow in her ribs to warn her to be quiet?

"First of all, it's the job of the Highway, Ferry, and Transportation Department to determine whether or not a new ferry line would be in our best interest. It's not something that can be done simply because a few residents think it would be a good idea. Creating a new ferry line brings many expenses—building a ferry house, purchasing ferries, hiring people for various positions. And, of course, working closely with the state of Connecticut."

He shrugged. "After all, we don't even know if Connecticut is at all interested in setting up a ferry line with us."

"Liar!" my aunt said softly, but loud enough for the first few rows to hear.

"And what you consider proposals, Reenie dear, are only ideas. Possibilities. We're still in the talking stage of what to do with the property."

"If it were up to you, *Bradley dear*, we'd never leave the talking stage. My committee has come up with viable uses for the land under discussion." She quickly segued into proposals, figures, and rich tax revenues that would benefit the island.

"Sounds lovely on paper," Uncle Brad commented when Aunt Reenie paused to draw breath, "but there's one possible use for the property that I believe you and your committee have overlooked, and that is keeping the VanPatten Farm a farm. We are an island rich in history, and now we have an opportunity to show how farming on Dickens Island has evolved through the years when farmers provided food for residents and neighboring communities. This could be a year-round attraction for tourists and school visits. A site of island festivals and craft fairs. As I mentioned before, we could even continue to raise a few crops and flowers that we would sell. The Hallockville Museum Farm in Riverhead could be our inspiration."

Aunt Reenie burst out laughing. "The Hallockville Museum Farm may be thriving, but my committee has inspected the VanPatten property. It hasn't been a functioning farm in years. Sad to say, the barns and part of the farmhouse are in serious disrepair and in danger of collapsing. As is the chicken coop. All structures would require a complete overhaul, which is quite an expense."

Tim VanPatten got to his feet. He was a large, deliberate man in his eighties and moved slowly. "It's my understanding that the council and the town manager voted to buy the VanPatten Farm last month, yet the sale has yet to go through. Velma and

I don't care what use you make of the property. We don't give a fig if you tear down all the buildings, but we would like to finalize the sale so we can move ahead with our retirement plans."

He glared at Uncle Brad. "I'd like to remind you that we've had several offers for the property, but we wanted to show our loyalty by selling the farm to the island for the benefit of its residents."

"Much appreciated, Tim, and I'd like to remind you that the land is zoned as farmland and farmland only. The offers you received were based on plans to use the property for other purposes."

"Which is what your wife is proposing!" Tim retorted.

One after another, residents expressed their preferences regarding how the farm should be used. Most sided with Aunt Reenie and agreed that the land should be used to make money for the island, but there were some who liked Uncle Brad's plan to turn the property into a museum farm, exhibiting the changes in farming over the years, or into a working farm with crops and livestock. Someone even suggested turning it back into a working farm that would be run by students from an agricultural college.

Which plan did I prefer? I could see the land being used for summer cottages. I could see it being turned into a model working farm. I didn't much like the idea of a hotel/casino.

Uncle Brad allowed the conversation to go on for almost an hour. Finally, he said, "Thank you all for your input regarding this matter. Sadie has made a note of your suggestions and opinions." He cast a quick glance at Aunt Reenie. "We will meet with the town manager and her committee and reach a decision, if not at the next meeting, surely by the following one."

Grumbles rumbled, too low for me to make out words, as Dickens residents expressed their disapproval, but I wasn't sure of what. Tiny, white-haired Rose McCauley stood and drew back her shoulders.

"Bradley Dickens, you'll take your sweet time chewing over the future of that property until it goes your way. How about filling us in on a more important matter? Bring us up to date on the investigation into Missy's murder. Are the police any closer to finding her killer?"

Chapter Thirteen

Uncle Brad beamed at his former elementary school teacher, who was over ninety. "Miss Rose, I think the best person to answer your question is Chief Fanning. Gregg, would you be so kind as to share with us what you can about the case?"

Gregg rose to his feet, his pursed lips a clear sign he was not happy to have been put on the spot. My uncle's grin told me he was thoroughly enjoying this moment, a bit of payback for having been questioned for hours like any other "person of interest."

"Right now, the DIPD is talking to everyone who spent time with Missy Faraday the day she died. We're also learning everything we can about Missy Faraday's life, especially over the past few months. So if you've seen or heard anything about her that you think might be a link to her killer, be sure to contact me or the precinct. We want to know what you know."

Several hands shot into the air while at least three people started talking at once.

"Sorry, I can't answer any questions at this point," Gregg said firmly.

When more voices joined in, Uncle Brad called for order.

"Asked and answered," he said. "Missy's homicide is an ongoing investigation, and the police have their reasons for not sharing information. Anything else you'd like to bring up?"

I slipped out of my seat and headed for the back door as someone asked Brad who would be filling Missy's seat on the council. The meeting would end shortly, and I wanted to beat the mass exit. I called my father as I drove home and filled him in on the meeting. He wasn't happy to hear that, once again, I hadn't found an opportunity to talk to Uncle Brad.

"Dad, why don't you talk to him? After all, he's staying with you. It's only natural to ask what's going on."

"I would, Delia, only no matter how I ask, my brother's going to take it the wrong way. He'll get angry and tell me he's a grown man and can take care of his private life. He doesn't need his older brother looking out for him. Then he'll storm out and go God knows where. I want to be the safe haven for him, and I can't do that by questioning him.

"Believe me, honey. I wouldn't ask you to do this if I could do it myself. And I'm especially worried because Reenie claims she wants a divorce. That's bound to come out if Brad and I talk. He'll be so hurt to find out she told you and me before telling him. You wouldn't want that, would you?"

"Of course not." I sighed. "Okay. I'll give it a shot tomorrow."

When I got home, I found Connor watching TV in the family room. Riley lay stretched out on the sofa beside him. He jumped down and ran to greet me.

"Hi, Connor!" I called out as I rubbed Riley's haunches with both hands.

"Hi, Mom. Good meeting?" he asked when I came to sit beside him.

"Interesting. Your great aunt and uncle were at it again, this time over the farm they're buying for the island."

"I finished off the food we brought home from Gramps's house and gave some to Riley."

"I don't think it's a good idea to give him people food," I said. "Especially chocolate."

"I know chocolate can be killer. And never give a dog chicken with bones in it. I've been reading up on it."

"Did you let him out?" I asked.

"I will when this show is over."

"Okay. I'm going upstairs." I leaned over to kiss his cheek." Please don't forget to lock the door when you come back in again."

"I know. There's a murderer lurking around." Connor grinned to let me know he wasn't annoyed by my reminder

I smiled as I headed for the stairs, pleased at the progress we were making. Riley's appearance had been a godsend.

"I almost forgot," Connor shouted. "The vet called on the landline. He said feel free to call him back up to ten thirty."

My heart zinged up to my throat. I turned around. "Did he find out something about Riley's owner?" I asked.

"Yeah." Connor looked at Riley. "Turns out his owner is d-e-a-d. He said he'll explain everything to you. Call him on his cell."

"I'll do that right now," I said, and flew up the stairs.

I had my cell phone in one hand and Jack's business card in the other as I entered my bedroom. I thumbed in Jack's number then held my breath as his phone rang once, twice, a third time. Disappointed, I was about to end the call when he picked up.

"Hello, Delia. Sorry I missed you earlier."

"Hi, Jack. I was at the council meeting. Heard lots of residents weighing in on what they think should be done with the farm the council is buying."

"Ah," was all Jack had to say about that. "I did some investigating on your pooch and his owner. Turns out his owner, an elderly gentleman named Aaron Spiegel, died suddenly of a coronary last week. Aaron lived alone in a small cottage near Mattituck, a few blocks from the Sound. I managed to contact his daughter, Vicki, who lives in Riverhead. She said her father never went anywhere without his Beardie whose name, by the way, is Samson."

Samson! "How does she think the dog got to Dickens Island?"

Jack chuckled. "On the ferry, same as everyone else. Vicki said her father often brought Samson to Dickens Island for long walks. The dog loved coming here. Aaron had a tough time getting him back on the ferry to go home.

"The day Aaron died, he'd been shopping on Love Lane and collapsed in the street. The EMS came and took him to the hospital, where he was pronounced DOA. They found Vicki's name in her father's wallet and called. She hurried to the hospital. By the time anyone thought to look for Samson, he was nowhere to be found. He must have run off and made his way to the ferry and to the island."

I swallowed. "I suppose she'll be coming here to get Riley." I couldn't bring myself to think of him as Samson. "Anyone would."

"So you'd think," Jack said. "I told Vicki that you and Connor were taking good care of him. At which point, she asked if there was any chance you'd consider keeping him. She's a single mother, and one of her sons is asthmatic. She felt guilty admitting that having a large, active dog was the last thing she needed in her life."

I exhaled the gallons of air I hadn't realized I'd been holding. "Thank you, thank you, thank you!" I thought a moment.

"I hope she wouldn't mind signing a document to that effect and making it official."

"I doubt it, since she offered to hand over whatever doggie supplies her father had in his cottage. She said she'll be calling you over the weekend to make arrangements. And she gave me the name of his vet. I'll text you her number."

"Thanks so much for doing this, Jack! Connor will be thrilled. I don't know how we can ever thank you properly for going this extra mile."

"How about having dinner with me?"

My body jerked, suddenly on guard. Despite my joy that Riley was now ours and feeling a bit fluttery from Jack's attention, the memory of the deep pain he had once caused me made me wary.

"I don't think we have to go to such extremes as dinner," I said.

"Would lunch be better? Or breakfast?"

I squirmed. I was tired after putting in a long, emotional day, and I didn't feel like blurting out exactly what I was thinking—*you hurt me once. I won't let you hurt me again.*

"Okay. I get it," Jack said. "Good night, Delia." He hung up.

"So that's that," I said aloud, wondering why I felt deflated.

Connor appeared in my bedroom doorway. "Mom, what did the vet say?"

"We can keep Riley."

"Wow! That's lit!" He grabbed me in a hug. Riley poked his head between us. "Hey, what's wrong? Aren't you glad?" he asked when he saw my expression.

"Just some grown-up stuff," I said.

"About the vet?" my intuitive son asked.

I shrugged. Something else I had to tell him when the time was right.

* * *

I arrived at Missy's gravesite in our small cemetery at a quarter to eleven. John Knowles, our part-time nondenominational cleric, was a stickler for starting every service on time. I was surprised to find twenty or so people already milling around. My aunt and uncle were there, standing as far from each other as two people could and still be part of the same gathering. At the same time, they each looked up from their conversations to wave at me. Not wanting to choose sides, I smiled and waved back and remained standing on the outskirts of the group.

At five to eleven, John, a tall, rangy man in his mid-forties, shouted out a general greeting as he strode past us to take his place beside the open grave. I had no idea what denomination or church Missy had belonged to. Not that it mattered. Unless a rabbi or a priest was called in, John's services ran pretty much the same. And they were always short, which suited most of us.

He'd finished the religious segment of the ceremony and had begun to say a few words about Missy when I became aware of a stocky guy—about forty-five and wearing a red plaid jacket, jeans, and work boots—walking toward us. Staggering, actually. As he drew near, I wrinkled my nose at the strong smell of liquor and the stream of blue language he mumbled to himself.

John stopped midsentence to address him. "Have you come to join us as we say our final goodbye to Melissa Faraday?"

"Yeah. Why else would I be in this godforsaken place?"

Missy's ex-boyfriend? I wondered. His eyes were bloodshot, and he had a week's growth of facial hair. Just my luck, he came to stand beside me.

John eyed him, then continued speaking about Missy—the fact that she'd always lived on Dickens Island, that she'd recently lost her father and had taken his place on the town council, and finally how sad it was that her life had ended so tragically when someone broke into her home and shot her.

"Godawful bad luck," the stranger next to me shouted. "The police better get the bastard who killed her."

Gregg, who had been standing near Aunt Reenie, walked over to him. "Watch that mouth if you want to stay here."

The man grinned, showing a missing cuspid. "Aye, aye, sir."

John said a prayer, then asked if anyone would like to say a few words. My uncle raised his hand to be recognized.

"Though Missy was on the council for a short time, she did her utmost to learn about the island's infrastructure and various committees in order to make herself a knowledgeable member."

My aunt nodded as he spoke, an "if you believe that, I'll sell you the Brooklyn Bridge" expression on her face. And I wasn't the only one who noticed. A few people laughed knowingly.

"Thank you, Brad. Would anyone else like to say a few words."

I found myself raising my hand. "Missy always had a cheerful smile and was very welcoming when I came into the bakery."

Though people nodded in agreement, it was only after I'd spoken that I realized how lame that had sounded. I was about to add something, anything, when the guy next to me spoke.

"Missy was real good at a few things too personal to mention." He giggled in a knowing way. "She should have listened to me and moved in with me, instead of burying herself on this island. And now she's dead!"

Gregg and Billy moved in on the man and led him away. I wondered if they were going to interview him at the precinct or simply escort him to his car or the ferry.

No one else had anything to add. We all threw a spadeful of dirt onto the grave. Then John announced that the reception would be held at the Interfaith Chapel. People started walking in that direction.

Aunt Reenie, deep in conversation with her aide, was the last to leave the cemetery. Surprisingly, Uncle Brad was on his own as he headed for the chapel. I decided that now was as good a time as any to have that chat with him, and then I'd have fulfilled my obligation to my father.

"Wait up, Uncle Brad," I called as I ran to catch up with him.

He halted, and I linked my arm with his. "I'd like to talk to you before we go into the reception—if that's okay with you."

"Of course, Delia. What is it, honey?"

I almost felt guilty as I moved off the path and stopped at a bench. Uncle Brad thought I had a problem and, as always, was willing to be there for me.

We sat down facing each other.

"It's my dad," I said.

Uncle Brad rolled his eyes. "Figures. Why doesn't he just talk to me if he has something to say, like any normal person would? I'm staying at his house, for God's sake."

"He's worried about you and Aunt Reenie. The fact that you're fighting."

He drew back. "Not my doing. I have my opinion regarding how best to repurpose the VanPatten Farm, and my dear wife has hers. Can I help it if we aren't in sync?"

"No, of course not. But I'm worried too." I hesitated, then went on. "Aunt Reenie plans to start divorce proceedings."

Uncle Brad waved away that thought with a flick of his wrist. "Reenie's just pissed that I won't go along with her plans. She should be used to it by now."

"And she thinks you were having an affair with Missy."

He laughed. "Does she? Just because I spent time with Missy, trying to help her? I could accuse Reenie of having an affair with Chet Thomas. She spends more time with him than with me."

I ignored that, largely because we both knew that Chet had no interest in women. Uncle Brad was refusing to realize his marriage was in trouble. From what I'd seen last night, he was making a big mistake.

"Aunt Reenie's really angry with you. She threw you out of the house."

Uncle Brad smiled. "That's Reenie. Emotional to the core. She'll get over it."

I didn't know what else to say. He was refusing to see reality.

He stood. "Delia, honey, please don't worry yourself about my marriage. If your father's so concerned, tell him to talk to me instead of sending you as his emissary. You have enough to take care of." He put his arm around me and drew me close. "Let's go inside. I could use a good cup of coffee."

Chapter Fourteen

The aroma of good coffee and baked goods greeted us as we entered the chapel. The assembly room with its panel of windows on opposite sides made up most of the building. Out of view were the small kitchen, bathrooms, and the few classrooms downstairs in the finished basement that the elementary school and the few homeschoolers sometimes used. John officiated at nondenominational services here most Sunday mornings. Otherwise, it was in frequent use for parties, celebrations, receptions, and meetings.

The number of people filling the room was now double those of us who had attended Missy's burial, which was usually the case when it came to services and food. Uncle Brad made a beeline for the long table laden with desserts and urns of tea and coffee on the far side of the room. I made a detour to use the ladies' room and ran into my aunt. I wondered if she was waiting to speak to me or needed to use the facilities.

"Did you manage to talk any sense into your uncle?" she demanded by way of a greeting.

I laughed. "Regarding what, Aunt Reenie? Getting him to agree with you on future plans for the VanPatten Farm? Or did you want me to convince him you're serious about filing for divorce? Actually, I did try to talk to him about *that* and got nowhere."

"Of course you got nowhere," she snapped. I recoiled, though I knew her anger wasn't directed at me. "Right now my main concern is how he rhapsodizes in public over that poor unfortunate woman who got herself murdered. Letting everyone figure out what went on between them. Not considering for a minute how *humiliating* it is for me."

She turned away so I wouldn't see the tears welling up in her eyes.

I longed to put my arm around her but knew her pride wouldn't allow it. "Aunt Reenie, I'm sure that's not the case at all. Really. Uncle Brad was just being kind to Missy."

"Delia, there's no need to put on an act to spare my feelings. I ***know*** he was sleeping with her. You'd think he'd consider my feelings and stop acting like her savior. Ha!" She let out a bitter laugh. "Her savior who couldn't save her."

"Was that guy who crashed the funeral Missy's ex-boyfriend?" I asked to change the subject.

"Yes. His name is Peter Maris. Missy had an order of protection out on him. Gregg had been trying to locate him since the murder. He was glad to haul him into the station to question him. That's where he is now."

"I'm glad Gregg's following up on it," I said.

Aunt Reenie's expression was severe. "You might want to tell your uncle I have an appointment with a divorce lawyer tomorrow. I've already informed Katie and Eric."

Aunt Reenie stormed off, and I mulled over our exchange as I used the facilities. She was angry and hurt, believing that

Uncle Brad had betrayed her, and she was taking steps to go through with her divorce plans. If only he'd talk to her, explain that he was only being kind to Missy. Because observing them together the other night, I was certain now that was all it was.

I reentered the assembly room, eager to see what goodies were being offered before they all disappeared. A few of the women always baked for occasions like this, and I knew the bakery where Missy had worked was going all out to honor one of their own.

I made up a plate of mini pastries for myself and filled a paper mug with coffee from the urn. I turned and almost collided with Jack Morrison.

"Oh, sorry," I said automatically.

"No, it's me who should apologize," Jack said.

I stared at him. Now wasn't the time or the place to delve into our past. "Okay," I said, for want of a better answer. I headed for one of the empty tables on the other side of the room. I sat down. Jack slid into the chair beside me.

"Look, I don't mean to be a stalker, but after we spoke last night, I realized I had no right to assume you'd forgotten what an ass I was when we were younger."

I bit into a chocolate cream-filled pastry. *Yummy*. Jack waited while I chewed and swallowed. "You mean the way you broke up with me in an email and crushed my teenaged heart?"

He nodded. "It was a dumb thing to do. Totally heartless."

"And cruel," I added. "So why did you?" I finished off the pastry.

"Lianne and I were in a lot of the same classes. We started hanging out, talking about the time we'd both be vets." Jack sighed. "We had so much in common—or so it seemed."

"I get it. She was there in the flesh. I suppose getting dumped would have hurt no matter how you did it. But your note sounded so—impersonal."

He grimaced. "I'm sorry about that. I was trying to make a clean break, and that was the only way I could manage it. And then a month into our relationship—Lianne and mine—I realized I'd made a mistake."

"Oh? She wasn't smart and pretty and confident, or really planning to become a vet?"

"Yeah, she was all of the above. She was also competitive and manipulative and self-centered. I saw it. But it was too late. We were thrown together. Everyone thought we were the perfect couple. Somehow I couldn't bring myself to split and tell our small group of friends it was a mistake—for both of us, it turned out."

"I heard about the break up," I said. "Did it come from Lianne?"

"The final words, yes. But by then we'd both had enough of each other."

"Okay, you're forgiven." I sipped my coffee, then reached for another pastry on my plate.

Jack put his hand on my arm. "That's not all."

His touch sent a quiver to my heart. I met his gaze and waited for him to continue.

"You must have thought I was pushing you away when I sent you that email."

A bitter laugh escaped. "What else was I supposed to think? To feel? Yes, we were very young, but I was in love with you. And I thought you loved me."

"Oh, I did. Very much." He said it so softly, I barely heard the words.

"You never said."

"I know I didn't. The idea terrified me. I was nineteen years old. In college with years of school ahead of me, and I was in love with someone three years younger than me. A kid in high school."

I was too shocked to speak. I'd assumed Jack had fallen out of love with me because I was too young and inexperienced to know how to keep someone interested in me. It had eroded my self-confidence and made me vulnerable, the perfect patsy for my ex-husband. And *that* awful experience had kept me from forming another close relationship.

"I can't tell you how many times I thought of calling you, writing a letter, sending you a card just to say hi."

"Instead you got married."

"You saw how well that turned out."

We sat in silence. Jack had said everything he wanted me to know. The next move was up to me.

"Okay, Jack. I'll go out with you," I said calmly.

"You will?" He opened his eyes wide in astonishment.

"Yes, not as your old girlfriend, but as someone you've known and haven't been in touch with for many years. We'll be two people getting to know each other."

"I can do that." He hesitated. "Is Saturday night okay?"

"It is."

"Pick you up at seven?"

"Sure."

Jack grinned as he stood. "See you then. Now I have to get back to my patients."

I watched him stride off as several thoughts and emotions played bumper cars in my head. Some of the old feelings rammed against a caution alert and memories of the pain I'd gone through to get over Jack Morrison in the first place. Knowing he had run from our relationship because of the deep feelings he'd had for me made me smile. *So I did leave an impression on him after all!*

Now we were older and very different people. We were both divorced, and I had a teenaged son. Going on a date with Jack was going to be a strange kind of experience. We'd once been so close, but we'd experienced twenty years of living apart since we'd last been together.

His revelation touched the very essence of my core. I planned to pore over every exchange of our conversation later when I was calmer, but right now I needed the cozy comfort of my everyday life. I bit into my last pastry.

"I see someone isn't worried about watching her figure."

I groaned silently as I looked up and saw Peggy Philian, Amanda's mother, staring down at me. "Hello, Peggy."

"Hello to you, Delia. I was surprised to see you sitting with your ex-boyfriend. Don't tell me you're thinking of dating him again after what he pulled."

When I didn't answer, she asked, "How does it feel, living again in the boondocks of society?"

"I'm happy to be here," I said stiffly. I knew from experience to keep my answers short and innocuous when talking to Peggy. She was a gossipmonger, always sniffing around for news.

"I suppose you were missing your son. How old is he now? Sixteen?"

"Fifteen."

"Amanda's two are fourteen and sixteen. Talk to her recently?"

"Not lately."

"And how is dear Gillian? I haven't seen your mother in—it must be weeks now."

As if you didn't know she's staying in the city. "Mom's fine." I stood, eager to make a quick escape.

Peggy drew a deep breath as she rested a hand on my arm. "I miss your mother's voice of reason. I don't suppose she could have stopped Missy from getting killed, but somehow she'd manage to get Reenie and Brad to work together instead of pulling the town apart."

I squeezed her hand because this was the first genuine comment of our conversation. "I'll tell Mom you've been missing her," I said as I walked away.

But Peggy had to have the last word. "Give Amanda a call. She'll love hearing from you."

Maybe I would call Amanda, I thought as I tossed my debris and joined the cleanup crew. Unlike her mother, Amanda respected another person's privacy, and as my father often said, she had a good head on her shoulders. So, she'd be a good person to talk to about Jack. She knew very well what I went through when he dumped me, and I wondered what she'd say when I told her we had dinner plans this Saturday night.

Connor texted me while I was driving home to say he'd be going to Trevor's house after school, so I had a free afternoon before me. I was eager to return to my grandmother's hidden room and examine her treasure trove of books and historical pamphlets and journals at leisure. I was also on the lookout for actual journals like the one Victoria Watts had written and the log Connor had discovered, supposedly written by Captain Kidd. I hoped to find one that would spark my interest enough to start me on the first article in the series Wayne wanted me to write.

Riley greeted me enthusiastically when I got home. I took him for a long walk, fed him a few treats, then made myself a cup of coffee.

I went into the living room and opened the panel to the hidden room. As I stepped across the threshold, I felt a twinge of anxiety for fear that I might get locked inside. Of course I could leave the door open, but the room lost much of its space with the door jutting into it. Besides, I was being silly.

Riley surprised me by joining me as I was closing the door.

I came across a few centuries-old journals, but unfortunately, none of them had more than a few pages of entries. It was almost as if someone who had once lived here had collected old journals but couldn't afford to buy any really good ones except for the log Connor had found and Victoria Watts's diary.

The bottom shelf had a variety of pamphlets of historical places from all over the country, places Helena must have visited over the years. I felt a surge of excitement as I removed them and found a pile of four journals behind them in the far corner. I opened the cover of the journal on top and saw the familiar bookplate with my grandmother's name. I took all four journals out. The one on the bottom, its blue cover faded, its edges ragged, was the oldest. The name on the bookplate was Helena Catherine Whitcomb. I carried it to the chair and began to read.

Chapter Fifteen

Helena had started the journal in September of her sophomore year of high school. The previous summer she, her parents, and her younger sister had moved from Great Neck to live on Dickens Island year-round. The house I was now living in had been built as a vacation home and required a heating system and upgrades in the kitchen and bathrooms.

In those days, the elementary school was the only school on the island. Older children took the ferry to attend junior and senior high school on Long Island. The first two months of entries were mostly complaints—how Helena missed her friends; how she hated the new school; how boring it was to live on an island; how lonely she felt. The only good thing was her parents got her a dog, a Bearded Collie she named Duncan.

Was this whiny teenager the same person I had always admired for being the capable, take-charge woman who had accomplished so much in her life? I skipped pages and began reading again when Helena wrote about visiting her VanPatten cousins who lived on a farm.

Riley, who had been snoozing at my feet, started to tremble and whimper in fear. Stunned, I watched him huddle to the ground and creep behind the chair.

"I didn't mean to frighten you, boy."

I knew that voice well, yet it couldn't be! I was inside a small closed room with Riley. My mouth fell open as my grandmother appeared before me. She was almost translucent, not as solid and three-dimensional as a real person. But then she wasn't a real person, was she? This . . . thing I was gaping at was Helena's ghost!

Riley released a mournful cry and ran to the door. *Good idea! Let's get the hell out of here!* I yanked open the door and had one foot outside the room when I heard my grandmother's plea. "Please don't leave, Delia. We have to talk."

My instinct was to follow Riley, who was halfway to the kitchen, when the ghost figure said, "I'm here for a reason. There's so much I need to tell you."

I turned around slowly and stared. As usual, Helena wore a long skirt and a sweater, with a silk scarf draped gracefully around her neck. Her short, wavy gray hair framed her lovely oval face. Only my grandmother was dead!

"You have a new dog," she said, smiling. "He looks exactly like the Beardie I got when I was in high school."

"I know. Duncan."

She gestured to the journal. "You must have read about him."

I nodded. "Bennie Davos said you used to tell your students stories about him."

Helena gazed off into the distance. "Duncan used to bring home items he snatched from other houses. How that dog loved to get into mischief. How I adored him."

She sounded exactly like Helena. She looked like her. I blinked. I was having trouble accepting that my dead grandmother was actually speaking to me.

"Why are you here when you're . . . ?" I struggled to find a kind way of putting it.

"Dead?" She smiled. "It's all right to say it. I realize seeing me this way must be shocking to you. I do apologize."

This had to be the weirdest experience of my life. Though I was in shock, I didn't feel threatened in any way, and so my heart slowed down to a mere gallop.

"Vibrations of dangerous proportions are emerging from Dickens Island and are having far-reaching effects in the atmosphere. I've been sent to find the cause of the discord and to help resolve the problems and restore peace and order."

Helena gestured to me. "Delia, I'm relying on you to fill me in on what's been happening."

"For one thing, Missy Faraday's been murdered. Someone broke into her home a few nights ago and shot her."

"Ah, Missy." My grandmother released a deep and mournful sigh. "An innocent caught up in old transgressions. The evil runs deep."

"What do you mean?" I asked.

She only shook her head. "Tell me more. I know there must be more."

"Things have been really contentious between Aunt Reenie and Uncle Brad. Worse than ever. She's talking divorce." I grimaced. "My father expects me to play peacemaker and marriage counselor—as if they'd listen to me."

"Your father shouldn't be asking that of you," Helena snapped.

"Their squabbling is causing a rift among the residents. The islanders are taking sides. Splitting into two camps."

"Heavens! We can't have that!"

I reached out to take her hand like I used to and instead encountered a cold rush of air. I reared back.

"Sorry about that," Helena apologized. "It would be helpful if you could catch me up with the details of everything that's been happening here on the island, starting with Brad and Reenie's latest spat.

I spent the next half hour telling Helena about my aunt and uncle's quarrel over the future of the VanPatten Farm, Aunt Reenie's suspicions that Uncle Brad was having an affair with Missy Faraday, and everything that had transpired the evening of Missy's murder. She listened carefully, only asking an occasional question. Her expression was grave when I finished.

"Now I understand why I was sent here. So much of the problem has its roots in the past, a past that no one knows about and is closely connected to the VanPatten Farm."

"Really? In what way?"

"Delia, honey, it's too complicated to go into right now. You'll find out some of the background of the situation by reading my journal. I'll be back later, and we'll talk some more."

I had at least five questions I wanted to ask Helena, but she was already fading. For a moment, I wondered if I'd imagined the entire scene because I'd been reading her journal. Then I remembered Riley's reaction, and I knew it had been real.

* * *

Connor came home in time for dinner. He seemed to be in a good mood. We were finished eating when he asked, "Mom, do you think some of those old logs and journals in that hidden room are worth anything?"

I startled when Connor mentioned the room where my grandmother's ghost had paid me a visit. I had no intention of telling him I'd just been talking to Helena's ghost. "I have no idea. Why do you ask?"

He shrugged and looked guilty. "Trevor's sister said they could be worth thousands of dollars."

"Connor! We talked about this. I don't want people knowing that we have old logs and journals."

"I'm sorry, Mom. Trevor kept at me, asking where I got the information about where to dig for the pirate treasure. His sister overheard and got real interested. Don't worry. I kept it vague."

I felt a quiver of unease. Rumor had it that Trevor's thieving habits came from his father, Eddie. And who was to say that Trevor's sister, Madison, didn't go in for a bit of larceny herself? "What do you mean you kept it vague? I asked you not to talk about it."

"I just said we had some old books and papers about Captain Kidd. They lost interest pretty quickly, and we talked about other things."

So much for keeping it vague! I pursed my lips. Antiquarian books and ephemera might be valuable, but it was farfetched to think that Trevor and his sister's curiosity meant they were planning to rob us. I had too many important things on my mind to consider such a possibility.

I cleaned up the kitchen. Connor took Riley out for a walk and then went upstairs to do his homework without my having to remind him. Riley was back to his calm self and seemed none the worse for having seen a ghost. Aaron Spiegel's daughter, Vicki, called, and we had a long chat about her father. She was overjoyed that Riley, as we now called him, had a good home with Connor and me. She readily agreed to sign a document saying that we were now his rightful owners and offered to bring over all the doggie paraphernalia from her father's house on

Sunday afternoon, if that was okay with me. I told her it was and said I was looking forward to meeting her.

That taken care of, I decided to spend an hour or two reading my grandmother's journals. I was curious to find out what had happened on the VanPatten Farm all those years ago that was impacting events playing out on Dickens Island today.

Chapter Sixteen

I read late into the evening, managing to get through two-thirds of the first journal. It covered Helena's teen years from fifteen to nineteen. She mentioned visiting the VanPatten Farm for the first time a month before her sixteenth birthday. The VanPattens were distant relatives on her mother's side of the family. Helena's mother's cousin Claudia was married to Joseph VanPatten. They had three children around Helena's age. William was the oldest, Gloria was three years younger than him and a year older than Helena, and Tim was three years younger than Helena.

By the time summer was in full swing, Helena was a frequent visitor to the farm. She often stayed over and helped with the chores. I smiled as I read about the four teenagers' activities—parties with friends, movies on Long Island; hayrides at night, swimming at the beach, and picnics on weekends. This continued into the fall, with Halloween costume parties, followed by day trips into Manhattan around Christmas.

The journal took a turn after the new year. Something secretive had crept in, and by February, Helena was often alluding to The One. She went into great detail about her feelings for this person and her conviction that The One felt the same way she did, only to be convinced two days later that The One was only being kind and didn't feel what she was feeling.

I shook my head, puzzled by the sudden change in the tone of the journal, which was now guarded and reserved, when previous entries had been open and candid. Who was The One? Helena rarely mentioned the names of the boys in school except in the most casual way. Since she had spent most of her free time with her cousins, I assumed The One had to be one of them.

Was it William, the oldest? Handsome, responsible, and energetic despite his withered leg from a childhood case of polio, William saw to it that the four of them had fun while everyone stayed safe. Was it mischievous Tim, who kept coming up with daredevil plans? And why keep it secret? Because whoever The One was, he was a cousin? Or was it because Helena wasn't sure that The One shared her feelings? In which case, she wasn't about to reveal his name, not even in her journal.

It was close to eleven o'clock when I went upstairs to bed. Reading my grandmother's journal had filled me in on life at the VanPatten Farm in the fifties. Helena alluded to problems concerning the farm but avoided details. Were they financial problems, I wondered, or family issues? And did these problems have anything to do with the fighting over the use of the farmland today?

As soon as Connor left for school Friday morning, I took Riley for a long walk, and then I returned to Helena's secret room, hoping she would appear again. I had so many questions to ask her. First and foremost, who was The One? Did she ever find out if he cared for her? And if he felt the same way she did and they were only distant cousins, why didn't she marry him?

I called to her, to no avail. Maybe she could only come here at certain times. I had no idea how her visits were regulated.

I paged through the rest of the first journal, looking for clues. The One appeared often but never with a name. By the time Helena was in her first year of college on Long Island, she was spending afternoons and evenings with The One. They often engaged in serious discussions, though Helena never included any details or the subjects of their conversations.

Maybe the answer was in the next journal. But glancing through it, I saw very few references to the farm or mention of her cousins. Or even of The One. Perhaps her great passion, never having been reciprocated, finally died away. Disappointed, I put the journals back on the shelf and came to the conclusion that my only chance of learning the identity of her secret love was to ask her the next time she appeared. Whether or not she told me was up to her.

Having reached a temporary dead end regarding that mystery, I decided to put my efforts into gathering books for the Book Nook. I retrieved three of the empty cartons I'd stowed in the garage after my move from Manhattan and started taking down books from the living room shelves.

I pulled out novels, mostly mysteries, and a few nonfiction general interest books as well. I even added a few cookbooks that I knew I'd never use. As I packed the boxes, I realized I liked the idea of hosting monthly meetings for island residents who loved to read. However, the format of the Book Nook meetings would be less rigid than that of a typical book club, where everyone read the same book whether they liked it or not.

I'd heard of the Silent Book Club concept, where people gathered to read in silence in the company of other people and then shared what they'd read with the group. Of course some people might choose to listen to a book instead. Another way of doing it would be to have everyone read a book of their choice about a specific topic, such as families or a period in history.

Then we'd spend the meeting sharing what we'd read. Maybe I'd serve cookies and tea and coffee. This would be a wonderful way to bring islanders together to talk about what they've been reading instead of squabbling about local issues like how we should repurpose the VanPatten farmland.

The Book Nook could also be a great draw for summer people, I decided, as I reached for a few popular beach reads. Maybe I'd set up a "take one, leave one" shelf. I chuckled, thinking that once the weather got warmer, we could hold our meetings on the beach or inside a small canopy tent there and call it Books on the Beach. But first things first—I needed to set up the Book Nook in the general store and get out the word.

When the three cartons were well filled with books, I piled them in my car and drove to the village. I parked behind the general store and went inside to ask Derrick to help me carry in the boxes.

My father came by as Derrick was setting down the third carton in the Book Nook area. "What's all this?" he asked.

"It's for the Book Nook I'm creating. The sofa's fine, but we'll need more seats. I'll bring over a few folding chairs from the house."

Dad stared at me. "The Book Nook?"

"I told you about it the other day. You said it was a terrific idea."

"Well, sure. I meant it was something we might consider at a future date—as long as we don't need the area to display merchandise. And bringing over cartons of books and leaving them in the middle of the store on a busy shopping day simply isn't good for business, Delia."

I glanced down at the sofa that had been there for ages, then I looked around the nearly empty store. It was time to take a stand.

"Dad, you've asked me to update the store and bring in new concepts, yet you give me a hard time about every proposal

I make. The new merchandise I finally got you to okay is selling well, but you still fight every one of my suggestions. I'm getting the feeling you want to keep things exactly as they have been for the past thirty years."

"Delia, believe me, I want to renovate the store," he insisted. "It's just that you want to make so many changes all at once."

I bent down to pick up one of the cartons. "Fine. I'll take these back home with me and leave you to run the store as you always have." I was speaking low, but Meg and Derrick and the few customers in the store had come close enough to get the gist of our argument. All eyes were on us. "I'm beginning to feel like I'm only in the way."

"That's not true, Delia. The Book Nook is a terrific idea. So are your other suggestions. It's just—I have a hard time adjusting to new ways of doing things."

And to letting me make decisions. I set down the box and exhaled. "I can't work in the general store if you reject every improvement I come up with."

"You're right," Dad said.

"If you genuinely don't care for a suggestion, don't think you can work with it, that's one thing. Shooting down every idea is another."

Dad frowned. "So your mother told me."

Now wasn't the time to bring up my mother. "Yes or no, can I move ahead with setting up the Book Nook?"

My father's lips moved as though he was trying out the words that would delay the project. Finally, he said, "Sure, honey. Go ahead with your Book Nook. You have my blessing."

"Thanks, Dad. I'll bring over a few bookcases, maybe set up one as a 'take one, leave one' kind of lending library. It should go over big with the summer crowd."

"That's a terrific thought. Make it nice and cozy."

"I will, Dad."

Our spectators, realizing that whatever we were having words about was over, moved on. I figured that now was as good a time as any to tell my father about my talk with Uncle Brad. I sat down on the sofa and patted the cushion beside me.

"By the way, after the service for Missy, I managed to chat with Uncle Brad."

Dad sat down. "Finally. What did he have to say?"

"He doesn't believe Aunt Reenie's serious about going ahead with the divorce."

"Well, maybe she isn't," Dad said. "Your aunt can get pretty emotional about a subject, then calm down."

"She insists she means to go ahead with it. She told me she has an appointment with a divorce lawyer. She's convinced Uncle Brad had an affair with Missy. I told her I didn't get the sense there was anything like that between them, but she thought I was just trying to spare her feelings."

My father looked troubled. "For all his smarts, sometimes my brother is an idiot! Maybe if you tell him to call Reenie and convince her he had nothing to do—"

"Dad, I'm sorry their relationship is in trouble, but I've spoken to both of them, and nothing I said made any difference." I met his gaze. "Why don't you talk to Uncle Brad? He's still staying at your house, isn't he?"

My father shot me a look of disappointment, as if I'd let him down. I supposed he was so used to my mother being an agreeable helpmate that my refusal to get further involved in my aunt and uncle's marital problems came as a big surprise. I suddenly understood that he always relied on my mother to handle family disagreements because he hated confrontations.

"I'll have to think about that," he finally said. "Brad hates it when I pull the big brother act, as he calls it. And you did try to get him to see reason. Maybe we should just let things ride and see how they play out."

"Good idea," I said, though what I really thought was that Dad had come up with a good excuse not to talk to his brother. I stood. "I'm going home now."

Some of my disapproval must have come through, because my father suddenly looked worried. "You're still going to help me update the store, aren't you?" he asked.

"Only if you promise to let me actually do it," I said firmly.

I drove home slowly, thinking about my parents' marriage. Mom was flighty in some ways, but like her sister, she was far-sighted and rock-solid practical. If something needed attention, she was ready to set about fixing it ASAP. My father had a deep sense of responsibility for Dickens Island and its residents, along with an abiding need to keep things as they were. He claimed he wanted to modernize the general store and turn it into a thriving business, yet he balked at each suggestion I made, and probably whatever ideas my mother had offered as well. And he expected her to be the bearer of bad news because he hated to disappoint or confront anyone. No wonder my mother had felt the need to take a breather from their marriage.

Aunt Reenie had great plans for the island's growth and economy, and Uncle Brad stopped her at every project. Their polarization came out in council discussions—a far more active and colorful version of my parents' disagreements. They fought verbally over every important issue. And now their marriage was in jeopardy.

Was this the route of all marriages? I wondered as I turned into my driveway. My own marriage had started out well. I'd met Mitch Garvey during my junior year of college. Though he was a year ahead of me, we were in two business classes together. One day, he'd asked to borrow my notes. That led to our studying together, dating, and eventually living together. He got a job in Boston my senior year, and we saw each other on weekends. We got married the week after I graduated.

I found a job and added a few decorative touches to the small apartment Mitch had rented the previous year when he was living on his own. We were happy, both engrossed in our new jobs and in each other. And then I got pregnant.

I stepped out of the car and walked up the exterior steps to my house. I didn't want to dwell on the deterioration of my marriage and subsequent divorce. I would have to share some of it with Connor eventually, but I didn't have to think about it now.

Riley was excited to see me. He barked and raced around me, which I took to mean he wanted to go out. He stood still while I buckled him into his coat, and we went for a long walk across the island to Marley's Beach. As soon as we hit the sand, Riley dashed ahead, straight into the Sound, getting his paws wet. I started running along the shore. Riley ran beside me, barking as he went. It was as though he knew he'd found his forever family and was free to gambol and no longer had to be on his best behavior.

Back at the house, I washed the sand off his legs and paws, then fed him some treats. I made myself a cup of tea, which I carried into the hidden room. Riley must have forgotten his earlier fright when he'd encountered Helena's ghost, because he followed me inside and stretched out beside the chair. I was eager to read more of my grandmother's journals. I was even more eager to talk to her and learn what evil she was alluding to regarding the VanPatten Farm.

Chapter Seventeen

I started reading the second journal, then put it aside. I checked all the journals to make sure they were in order. Sure enough, I had arranged them properly in chronological order. What puzzled me was the four-year gap between the first and second journal. The only entries covering those years were one that mentioned Helena's transfer to a college in Ohio after her freshman year, and another stating that after graduating from college she started teaching in the elementary school on Dickens Island.

Then a few months into her second year of teaching, without ever having mentioned their courtship, Helena was engaged to marry my grandfather, Ellery. I never knew my grandfather because he had died in his forties when my father and Uncle Brad were young boys. He was twelve years older than my grandmother. Helena never said much about him; neither did Dad or Uncle Brad. From what Great-Aunt Sarah, my grandfather's sister who lived in Arizona, told me, he was taciturn and kind of a loner. Not the kind of person I imagined Helena, who was lively and loved being with people, would choose as a mate. She hadn't even mentioned my grandfather in her first journal, which made me wonder if she'd known him then, or rather, if she'd known him well, since island residents all knew each other to some degree.

Once again, the entries sounded cagy, as if Helena were skirting around issues of the utmost importance to her at the time and was reluctant to put them down on paper. In several places, she wondered if she was doing the right thing by marrying my grandfather. This was often followed by a list of his traits that she admired: being steadfast and caring, even-tempered and kind. And he loved her and promised to take care of her.

She also included a list of negative habits that he didn't have: gambling, drinking, cursing, and meanness. But she said nothing about her feelings for him. She mentioned her parents were happy about her upcoming marriage. The only allusion to The One was a comment that she hoped marrying Ellery would put an end to her romantic yearnings that would never be fulfilled.

Riley jumped to his feet and yowled as he raced to the closed door.

"I do wish he wouldn't carry on every time I show up," Helena said as she manifested before my eyes. "It makes me feel like some kind of a monster."

"You have to understand. Seeing a ghost takes some getting used to."

I went over to Riley and held his quivering body close. "No need to be frightened. It's only my grandmother," I cooed. Eventually, his heart rate slowed. I opened the door, but to my surprise, he didn't run out as he had the first time she'd appeared.

"That's good. He's getting used to my presence," she said.

I went back to my seat while Riley stayed by the door.

"How much of my journal have you read?" Helena asked.

"I finished the first one and started reading the second. I was surprised there was such a large time gap between the two."

Helena shrugged. "Not much happened in those years."

"Why? You were young. In college. You didn't write about how you and Grandpa met, though I suppose you knew each other since you both lived on the island."

"We'll talk about that another time. Now I want to tell you about the people who lived on the VanPatten Farm."

"You didn't mention them in the second journal."

She paused, then said, "What I'm about to tell you isn't in any of my journals. I didn't include this information because it doesn't concern me personally."

I nodded. Though I was now totally confused, I decided to keep quiet and let Helena tell her story the way she wanted to.

"As you read in my first journal, my family came to live on the island full-time when I was fifteen. We had to sell our home in Great Neck because my father lost his clothing business and had to go to work for a former competitor. I started out my sophomore year in high school thoroughly miserable. I had to leave my friends and get up early every morning to take the ferry to a school in Suffolk County. I complained and carried on, blaming my parents for ruining my life."

Helena shook her head. "My poor mother and father. Looking back, it's amazing they didn't disown me. They were going through financial difficulties and were forced to hear their older daughter tell them what awful parents they were. When my mother told her cousin Claudia how unhappy I was, Claudia invited me to come out and spend a day at the farm. I refused to go to any smelly farm, of course, until one sunny Saturday in April, I agreed to do them a favor and pay them a visit."

Helena smiled. "That visit changed my life."

Now I had at least thirty questions I wanted to ask but had the good sense to keep quiet.

"As arranged, my father dropped me off at ten in the morning and told me to call him when I wanted him to pick me up. I was nervous but also excited because I'd only met Claudia and her husband, Joseph, a few times. They were practical, hardworking people. They were also kindhearted. They greeted me with hugs, then sat me down in their large kitchen to have some of Claudia's leftover-from-breakfast Dutch baby pancake smothered in fresh fruit.

"I'd no sooner finished eating when all three VanPatten kids came into the kitchen. William, the oldest, was a sophomore at one of the colleges on Long Island. Gloria was a year older than me. I'd noticed her in school because she was so pretty and always had a bevy of girlfriends around her, but I'd had no idea at the time that she was my cousin. Tim was a seventh grader. I'd noticed him on the ferry because he and his friends were always running around and getting into trouble.

"Their mother made the introductions and asked them to show me around. They took me into one of the barns and the henhouse, then out in the fields where cows grazed. I was amazed by all that I saw. Meanwhile, their questions never stopped coming. What was it like to live in a town like Great Neck? How did I like living on Dickens Island? What did I think of the high school? They were easy to talk to, so I asked how they liked living on a farm. They all said it was okay, though they didn't like getting up early to do chores before school.

"And suddenly I was helping them clean the pens and the chicken coop and putting down mulch in some areas. It was work, but it didn't feel like work, with us all talking and laughing and making jokes. Then the goats needed milking, and William showed me how to do it. I was so excited when I filled my first pail without losing too much milk.

"Joseph came by as we were bringing the cows into the barn. 'Helena, your dad called. He wants to know if he should come fetch you now.'

'Yes. I guess so.' I was surprised that the day had gone by and it was already time for me to go home.

"'Of course you're welcome to stay and have dinner with us,' Joseph said.

"'Stay!' Tim said. 'Mom's making her famous meatloaf and mashed potatoes.'

"I'd already tasted Claudia's outstanding cooking. It was far better than my mother's sad attempts at gourmet cooking.

"'Yes, stay,' my cousin Gloria implored. 'Then we'll have even teams for charades.'"

My grandmother's smile was bittersweet. "I stayed for dinner, and I stayed overnight and the following day. It was close to six o'clock Sunday evening when my father finally came to pick me up.

"'Have a good time?' he asked as we drove home.

"'Uh-huh. Great. They've invited me to come again next weekend.'

"My father was glad to see me happy. 'That's real nice, Helena. I'm glad you enjoyed visiting your cousins.'"

Helen smiled. "I loved going to the farm. Staying there was like being away on a vacation. I helped with the chores, and when they were done, we had fun. We went to the movies, on hay rides, to parties. Sometimes we just stayed home and played games. This continued well into my first year of college, when I went to school on Long Island, and while I stayed in the dorm during the week, I came home most weekends."

"You sound so sad."

"Do I? I suppose it's because all wonderful times come to an end."

I waited for her to explain. When she didn't, I asked, "Why did they come to an end?"

She made a scoffing sound. "Why do you think? We grew up."

"Will you tell me which cousin was The One? The person you loved?"

That drew a deep sigh, loud enough to make Riley stare at Helena.

"That's not important. I need to tell you what happened on the farm. What I didn't write about in my journal." She started to fade.

"You can't leave now!" I exclaimed.

"Sorry, Delia." Helena was transparent now. "I'm new at this and haven't figured out how long I can remain on this plane. I'll return soon to tell you more about the VanPatten family. It will help you deal with the island's current problems."

Help me *deal with the island's problems?* I stared at the space where my grandmother's ghost had been a minute earlier and saw shelves of books instead. How frustrating not to hear the rest of the story! Disappointed by her sudden departure, I paged through the second journal again, hoping to read something about her VanPatten cousins I might have missed, but the names William, Gloria, and Tim rarely appeared and only in relation to something regarding island news. There was nothing personal. How odd that after spending years in her cousins' company, she hardly mentioned them. Her friendship with them must have ended, including her relationship with The One.

It dawned on me that Helena had probably chosen to leave when she did because she couldn't bring herself to talk about the cousin she'd loved. Even now, after all these years, the subject was too painful to discuss.

Chapter Eighteen

Connor arrived home from school and told me my father had invited him to dinner and to play video games afterward. "Gramps said he'll bring me home if it's okay with you."

"Sure, text him it's fine," I said.

A minute later, he was grinning when he looked up from his phone. "I'm going over there at six thirty. He said it's okay if I bring Riley."

He and Riley disappeared inside his bedroom, and a minute later, I heard music muffled by the closed door. Connor was happy, and I knew that having Riley was a big part of it. I settled down on the living room sofa and skimmed through the history books I'd pulled from the shelves for my article on the history of the island.

When Connor and Riley left, I defrosted a few slices of frozen pizza and made myself a salad for dinner. The house was strangely quiet without them. I went into the family room to watch TV. Connor arrived home at ten o'clock, flushed and happy, having won most of the games he'd played with my father.

* * *

I woke up Saturday morning in a great mood. The sun was shining, and the temperature was unusually warm for the fourth week of March. I found myself singing in the shower, which I rarely did. I told myself it wasn't because I had a date with Jack that evening. I was no longer a sixteen-year-old who was vulnerable to his easy smile and good listening skills. I refused to put myself in the position of letting him hurt me again. Though he'd apologized for breaking up with me all those years ago, it could never erase the pain he had caused. My grandmother and I had something in common. We'd both lost our first love, and it had impacted the rest of our lives.

When I went downstairs, I found Connor playing with Riley. I was surprised to see him up so early.

"I took Riley for a walk. I figured he'd want to go out first thing," he said.

"Would you like an omelet for breakfast?" I asked.

"Yeah! With mushrooms and Swiss cheese."

"You got it," I said, glad that I'd bought a dozen eggs the day before.

I made an omelet large enough for the two of us, put bread in the toaster oven, and made myself coffee.

"So what are your plans for today?" I asked as Connor, who'd finished eating before me, was putting his dish and milk glass in the sink.

"I'm going over to Trevor's house. We're going bike riding around the island."

"Okay." I paused, then added, "As long as you're not out digging for pirate gold."

"Mo-om," he complained. "I said I wouldn't. But . . ."

"But what?"

"Do you mind if I bring Captain Kidd's log over to Trevor's house? His sister, Madison, is dying to see it. And what's the harm, since she knows about it already?"

Warning bells went off in my head. "I don't think that's a good idea, Connor. The log is very old. For all we know, it's worth a lot of money. It's not something you should be taking out of the house, much less while you're riding your bike."

"I promise I'll be very careful. I'll put it in my backpack."

I wavered. Connor and I were getting along so well. I hated to say he couldn't do something, but taking a centuries-old log to Trevor's house so his sister could see it wasn't a good idea.

"I'm sorry, but the answer's still no."

"I knew you'd say that!" His face took on the closed look I had seen so many times over the past few months, the one that had seemingly disappeared a few days ago.

If you knew how I'd react, you shouldn't have brought up the log in the first place, I thought but had the good sense not to say aloud. "Where is the log now?" I asked as Connor clamored up the stairs to his room.

"In my bedroom," he shouted. "Want me to bring it down so you can lock it up in a safety deposit box in the bank?"

I knew he was being sarcastic, but the log was old and needed to be treated with respect. "Please bring it down. The log is very old and might be valuable. I feel better keeping it in Helena's reading room. You can look at it there whenever you like."

A minute later, he came tramping down the stairs, the log in his hands and his backpack slung over his shoulder. "Here." He held it out to me.

"Thank you. Are you going to Trevor's now?"

"Yes."

"Do you know when you'll be coming home?" I asked. "I don't like you riding your bike in the dark."

"I know. You've told me that a hundred times."

We were back to where we were a week ago. One step forward, two steps back. "I'll be at the general store most of the afternoon. And I'm having dinner with an old friend."

"What friend?"

"Jack—Dr. Morrison."

"The vet?" Connor stared at me. "You never said you were old friends."

"Well, we are. There's frozen pizza you can defrost for dinner."

"I'll eat at Trevor's. Or at Gramps's."

What kind of mother am I? I was awash with guilt when I realized I'd agreed to have dinner with Jack without having arranged dinner plans for my son. "Or you can have dinner with Jack and me," I added lamely.

Connor burst out laughing. "I don't think so. If I stay to eat at Trevor's, I'll ask Madison to drive me home, and you can drive me there tomorrow to pick up my bike. Or Gramps will be happy to have me. He said to come over anytime I wanted."

"That's great," I said, relieved. "Don't forget to text me and let me know what you're doing"

"Sure." Connor bent down to rub Riley's haunches and whisper something in his ear. "See ya," he said, waving casually to me as he headed for the door.

I brought the log into my grandmother's reading room and sat down to study it. *Captain William Kidd* was written on the brown card stock cover, which was water-stained in spots, its top corner rubbed raw. Inside, the tan-colored lined pages included lists, sketches, and notations about harbors, weather, and gales.

A modern bookmark jutted out between the last two pages—Connor's, no doubt. I opened the folded page and for the second time studied what could possibly be considered a line roughly resembling a section of Dickens Island's shoreline that faced Connecticut. If this *was* meant to represent Dickens Island, then the X beside a tree about half an inch below the line would be located where the bird sanctuary was now. There were arrows pointing in four directions with numbers above each arrow. Since the ink was barely visible, I could barely make out the numbers. Aside from not knowing how much the shoreline had changed over the years, I had no idea what the standards for length and distance were in Captain Kidd's day. This was before the metric system was invented.

I closed the log and placed it on the shelf beside the other sailor's log. Though I could understand how a fifteen-year-old boy could get carried away by the idea of finding pirate loot, as far as I could tell, it was pure fantasy. I had done the right thing telling Connor not to do any more digging. Just as I'd been right not to let him bring the log to Trevor's house. It wasn't easy to suddenly step into the parenting role when the last time I'd been responsible for my son was when he was a toddler. Deciding I wasn't a terrible mother after all, I went into the garage where I knew I'd find two bookcases that would be perfect for the Book Nook and stowed them in my car.

* * *

"Looks pretty good, Delia," Derrick said proudly. "Nice and cozy. Maybe I'll take a little snooze here when no one's looking."

"You will do no such thing," Meg said as she joined us, sign in hand. BOOK NOOK it said, in large letters. The bookcases, now filled with books, stood against the wall facing the sofa and four chairs. "Where should we put the sign?" she asked.

"I have it!" Derrick exclaimed as he dashed off to get whatever he had in mind. He returned a few minutes later with a wrought-iron stand.

"Perfect!" Meg and I said together.

"Finally have a use for this," Derrick said.

The Book Nook did look cozy. We added a small table between two of the chairs and voilà! We had launched the reading area in the store.

"Shoppers will love this Book Nook of yours," Meg said.

Derrick twisted his lower lip from one side to the other in thought. "They sure will. I hope they don't just plop into a seat to read and forget about shopping," he finally said.

"We want them to feel at home in our store," I said. "At the same time, we want to perk up their shopping interest."

"How do we do that?" Meg asked.

"I was thinking we could try a few selling lures to find out what works. For example, a twenty-minute flash sale in a designated section—not to be revealed until that day."

"Revealed how?" Derrick asked.

"I was thinking we could have a daily printout with just three or four items on it for shoppers to read when they enter the store: new merchandise; what's on sale. A joke. What's going on in the Book Nook."

Derrick frowned. "Who would write it?"

"I will. Easy enough to do. I'll run it off on my printer. Maybe forty copies to start off with."

"That many?" Meg asked.

I looked at Meg and Derrick, both of whom were over sixty and had worked in the store for the past two decades. They'd skated by the last few years, doing less and less as sales dwindled down. I had to know if they were amenable to change.

"Right now, the general store is barely holding its own. As you know, I've started updating our inventory to keep us out of the red. The appearance could use a complete overhaul, but I'm afraid that requires a large outlay of money. Meanwhile, I'm trying my best to come up with ideas to attract more shoppers."

I waited for one of them to ask me a question. When neither of them spoke, I took the bull by the horns. "So, are both of you up for it? Willing to deal with changes and innovations? There will probably be a learning curve, and you'll be busier than you are now, or so I hope."

Meg's eyes lit up. "I sure hope your plans work. It gets downright boring without customers to help."

"That's for sure," Derrick agreed. "I didn't want to say anything, but I miss all the traffic we used to get. A chance to chat with neighbors. Advise them what to buy."

I grinned. "So you both are up for working in a busier store?"

"Things have been so slow this winter, I thought for sure your father was going to fire one of us," Meg said.

"Graham kept the two of us on out of the kindness of his heart," Derrick said.

I nodded, knowing it was true. "I'll keep you up to date regarding any changes I'll be making."

"If the store gets busy, do you think you'll be hiring more salespeople?" Meg asked.

I laughed. "Let's wait and see how my plans play out."

"I'm asking because my granddaughter's coming to spend the summer with Andy and me. I bet she'd love to work here."

"I'll keep it in mind."

Pleased with how things were moving along, I went into the office to spend an hour or two poring over catalogues. I thought I might google a few display designers, though I knew my father wouldn't agree to spending money on reconfiguring the store. But maybe we could keep the old-fashioned feel and simply update some of the décor. I felt a sense of excitement. I really was going to institute changes, changes I hoped would pay off.

I ate a quick lunch in the All Day Breakfast Café, then stopped in at Maggie's Hair Salon to see if she could fit me in for a quick trim, wash, and blow out. My hair was past my shoulders and getting a bit straggly. I let Maggie convince me to get highlights, so it was close to four o'clock when I arrived home.

I was glad my busy, productive day had kept me from thinking about both my grandmother and Jack Morrison. Dwelling on either of them was a fruitless endeavor. Curious as I was, I had no way of guessing what Helena was about to tell me regarding the VanPattens and the love that went nowhere. And Jack—we were simply going out for dinner. Nothing more. No emotional entanglement. Our young love affair was in the past.

Connor texted me to say he'd be having dinner at Trevor's house. My father would pick him up at eight, and he'd spend the night there. That was fine with me. Connor had lived with my parents for most of his life. I'm sure he missed their company as much as my father missed Connor's, especially now with my mother living in Manhattan.

I walked Riley, took a quick shower, put on makeup, then spent some time deciding what to wear. I finally chose a pair of black leggings, a V-neck red silk tunic, knee-high boots, and my favorite gold pendant and earrings. Feeling a bit nervous, I sat down in the living room to wait for my date to show up.

Chapter Nineteen

Jack arrived at seven on the dot. He greeted me with a hug and a kiss on the cheek, rubbed Riley's flanks until the dog all but swooned in delight, then slowly turned his head to take in what he could see of the hall, the family room, and part of the kitchen.

"This was my grandmother's house," I said. "She left it to me."

"I remember being here. We stopped by once before spending the day on the beach. Your grandmother gave us blueberry cobbler and lemonade."

"Yes, she did," My cheeks grew warm as I remembered the evening that had followed that day on the beach. "Where are we eating?" I asked abruptly to cut off such dangerous thoughts.

"I made reservations at the Hathaway Inn. Okay with you?"

"Why not? I loved the place when I was young, though I haven't been there in years. I remember it being nice and comfy, if a bit old-fashioned."

"The new owners renovated the restaurant and brought in a great chef. I thought it would be a good place to catch up."

Jack helped me into my parka, and we walked outside to his Jeep Grand Cherokee. A flash of déjà vu filled my head of another time, a different car, and a younger Jack. It felt surreal being with him now when he'd been such a large part of my past.

"It looks like Riley's made himself totally at home with you and your son," he said as we drove to the restaurant.

"Actually, he chose us. Riley followed Connor home one day and took a nap on our porch."

"That's interesting."

"Even more interesting, it turns out my grandmother had a Beardie when she was in high school when her family came to live on the island all year round."

"It sounds as though Riley is a spirit descendent of your grandmother's dog."

His comment sent shivers down my spine. I couldn't imagine what Jack's reaction would be if he knew I'd been in communication with Helena's ghost. To keep the subject from getting too personal, I told him about Connor coming across Captain Kidd's log from one of his last voyages, and that Connor was convinced the map he'd found folded up in the log showed where Kidd had buried treasure on Dickens Island. I finished by saying, "Connor and Trevor Sykes cut school the other day to dig for pirate booty in the bird sanctuary."

Jack laughed. "Can't say that I blame them. Finding treasure is a boy's fantasy."

"If it was ever buried there in the first place," I said. "Anyway, I told Connor to stop digging for pirate booty."

"Forget the booty. If the log actually belonged to William Kidd, it could be worth a good deal of money."

I frowned. "Which is why I told Connor not to tell anyone about it. But Trevor wheedled the information out of him. And his older sister, Madison, wanted Connor to bring the log over to their house so she could examine it. I nixed the idea."

"That was smart. I'd keep the log in a safe place if I were you."

"That's where it is," I said.

We turned onto a road that ran beside a brook in the center of the island and pulled up in front of the Inn. A young man came dashing up to the car, and I realized the new owners must have instituted valet service. Jack handed over the car fob and ushered me inside.

I recognized the narrow hallway, only now it opened up to dining rooms on both sides of the hall instead of just to the room to the right. The tables, most of which were occupied, were covered in crisp white tablecloths and spaced well apart for the diners' comfort and sense of privacy. Both rooms led to a dining room beyond.

A smiling young woman told us where we could hang up our jackets, then, menus in hand, she led us to a table next to a fireplace that had a few logs burning. The oil paintings of various sizes and subjects adorning the walls caught my eye. Each had a small price tag beside it.

"The owners feature local artists," Jack said. "They're scheduling a few art-related events in the summer when the tourists arrive."

"Smart move. It's good for everyone involved." I opened the large menu. The offerings were similar to the dishes they used to serve at the Hathaway Inn, but these came with an interesting sauce or roasted vegetable. "Is there anything you recommend?" I asked Jack.

"Their fish dish of the night is one of my favorites, but I'm also a huge fan of their meatloaf, which is chock full of mushrooms. And their steaks can't be beat."

I looked up. "You must eat here often."

"Often enough."

Our waitress arrived and told us the specials, then took our drink order. Jack and I each ordered a glass of wine.

"How does it feel to be living on Dickens Island again?" he asked.

"I like it," I said. "I have great plans for improving the general store." I paused, then found myself adding. "Most of all, I'm happy to be living with Connor. He'd been staying with my parents while I worked in Manhattan."

Jack nodded slowly as he digested what I'd just told him. No doubt it was something he already knew, since islanders were well informed about each other's lives. Just as I knew he'd been married and divorced, he must have known that Connor had been living with my parents.

"It must be an adjustment for both of you," he finally said.

"Oh, it is. Though Connor and I saw each other here or in the city, it was always on weekends or vacations. Living together day to day is different. Suddenly I'm raising a teenager on my own and hoping I'm doing it right."

"Does Connor get to see his dad?" Jack asked.

"Never!"

I was grateful that our waitress showed up with our drinks. I took a deep sip.

"Have you decided what you'll be having?" she asked.

"Not yet," Jack said easily.

"I'll give you a few minutes then," she said with a smile and left us.

I studied the menu, recalled what the specials were, and chose a shrimp dish with roasted asparagus and rice pilaf with apricots and almonds.

"I'm going to have the fish special," Jack said. "Care to share a salad? They're big enough for two."

"Sure." We decided on the beet salad.

Our waitress returned and took our order. When she left, Jack said, "Delia, I'm sorry I upset you. I didn't mean to hit a nerve."

I grimaced. "I never want to see Mitch Garvey again. I'm grateful he's living somewhere on the West Coast, far from Connor and me."

"That bad?"

I nodded, surprised to find myself wanting to tell him about Mitch, a topic I usually avoided. "We started out fine, happy and in love like other couples. We met in college, got married as soon as I graduated, and lived in Boston, where Mitch was already working. I got a job, and everything seemed fine.

"Then I got pregnant. It wasn't planned, but I was happy to start our family a bit earlier than scheduled. Mitch turned moody. He tried to convince me to have an abortion, but I wouldn't. He didn't seem especially worried about money, so I couldn't understand what the problem was.

"He was always good to me, but then I had always doted on him. I supported him when he fell into a bad mood, when he was convinced someone was using him to get ahead at work. I never thought much about it, but it reached a breaking point when Connor was born."

I grimaced. "There was an incident involving Connor when he was three months old. It frightened me. I brought my son to the island, and we stayed with my parents for two weeks. I was thrilled with my perfect son and figured that Mitch was just feeling a bit miffed because he was no longer my number one concern. But I must have said something that made my mother believe things weren't right in my marriage."

I met Jack's gaze. "For a year and a half, I tried being the perfect wife while tending to my son's needs as my narcissistic husband grew angrier and angrier. Yes, he went to couple's therapy with me, where he charmed our counselor into thinking I was the one at fault. Finally, I couldn't take it any longer. I grabbed Connor and went to my parents' house. Mitch showed up the next day and turned violent. The police got involved. It was awful."

I shook my head, remembering. "I filed for divorce. First, Mitch pleaded with me to come back home and have my parents raise Connor. I refused. He got ugly and started doing scary things. I left Connor with my parents, and I went to stay with a friend in Manhattan. I got an order of protection and a divorce."

I sipped my wine. "I rented an apartment in Midtown close to my new job and brought Connor to live with me. I was happy to have him with me, but something was always disrupting his care. First the daycare facility I loved closed unexpectedly, and I couldn't get him in anywhere else. I tried babysitters, but they often disappointed me, arriving late or not arriving at all. My mother offered to take him for a month. And that month turned into another. Connor was happy with my parents, so I concentrated on my work, which was demanding and enjoyable."

Jack listened intently, the way he always used to when we were dating, which was probably why I asked him the question I'd never put to anyone else: "Do you think I'm a terrible mother for abandoning Connor all those years?"

He reached out to take my hand. "You were traumatized by the way your marriage turned out."

"I loved Mitch, and I'd planned my future with him. Then suddenly he was a threat to me and my baby. How did I not seen the signs? Or if I saw them, why did I ignore them?"

"It's difficult acknowledging when someone you love and put your trust in isn't the person you thought they were."

"It is. Afterward, I was devastated. I no longer trusted myself to make important decisions." I bit my lip. "If I'd made a mistake in choosing a man who was so flawed, so narcissistic, how could I be sure to do the right thing for Connor?

"Raising him involved so many decisions. When something went wrong, like when the daycare closed, I was sure it was my fault. I should have been aware that it was in financial straits." I gave a little laugh. "Leaving Connor with my parents seemed the wisest, safest thing I could do for my son at the time."

Jack's grip tightened. "Has your ex ever tried to contact you?"

"Twice after the divorce went through, but not recently."

"That's good." He released my hand.

I smiled. "I didn't mean to go into the sad story of my marriage. It's not something I talk about or even think much about now. Somehow I could always talk to you. About anything."

Our waitress brought our salad, and we ate it without speaking. When our main course arrived, Jack offered me a taste of his fish, and he sampled a bite of my shrimp. Both were delicious.

"Is everything satisfactory?" our waitress asked.

"Very much so," I said.

"My compliments to the chef," Jack said.

Our waitress smiled. "I'll tell her."

As we ate, Jack told me briefly about his marriage and its ending, which was nowhere near as dramatic as mine. "We simply grew apart, each of us focusing on work and different sets of friends."

"Did you want children?" I asked.

"Yes, but Claire learned she couldn't have any."

I refrained from asking more questions because I sensed Jack didn't want to go into the subject any further. Soon he was telling me about his present life—practicing in two offices and working with one of the animal shelters near Riverhead.

"It's some of the most rewarding work I do, bringing sick and injured dogs and cats back to health so they can be adopted. I'm happy to say that most of them are placed in forever homes."

"Do you ever end up adopting some of the animals yourself?" I asked.

He laughed. "I have two cats and a dog right now. You'll get to meet them."

I was saved from answering because at that moment our waitress arrived and asked if we'd like to have dessert. She handed us small menus listing the selections.

"They're all good, but the chocolate cake in a flowerpot with fruit on top is to die for," Jack said.

"Sounds delicious, but I can't eat an entire dessert."

"Let's share it," Jack said.

We ordered coffee and one dessert. A few minutes later, a beautiful young woman in a white apron brought us our order. She beamed at Jack when she said, "How nice to see you! Dessert is on the house."

"Thanks, Margot." Jack stood to hug her. "Everything was superb, but I didn't mean to pull you out of the kitchen. Margot, this is Delia Dickens. Delia, Margot Tedesco."

"Not to worry. Everything's under control." Margot turned her attention to me. "How nice to finally meet you, Delia. Jack tells me you used to eat here when you were a girl."

"I did, but I enjoy your cooking more."

That pleased her. "Thank you. It means a lot coming from a Dickens. But please, enjoy your coffee before it gets cold." Margot spun around and disappeared behind the kitchen doors.

"How did you get to know Margot?" I asked, telling myself I was simply curious, not jealous.

"Her ragdoll rescue is my patient."

"Oh." I took a teaspoon of the rich chocolate dessert and nearly swooned from the warm, rich flavor.

"Like it?" Jack asked.

"Like isn't the word I'd use for perhaps the tastiest, yummiest dessert I've had in years."

He laughed. "Gwen, Margot's wife, makes the desserts. Last month, she was written up in one of the most prestigious food magazines."

"Deservedly so," I said, grinning. I took another taste, then sipped my coffee.

Driving home, Jack played some music at a low volume. "So, any regrets that you agreed to have dinner with me?"

"None at all." I was sated and relaxed as I reclined against the back of my seat. "The food was delicious and the company good."

"My thoughts exactly." Jack rubbed my forearm.

We didn't talk much as we drove the short distance back to my house. I had no idea what would happen next. What Jack would do. How I'd react. It felt good to be in his company again, but that didn't mean I was ready to fall back into his arms. He had ended our relationship in a hurtful way, and it had taken me years to get over it. Besides, I had no idea what he was feeling. Maybe he just felt guilty for the way he'd treated me and wanted to make amends, nothing more. After all, his divorce was more recent than mine. He could still be hurting and working through unresolved issues.

Jack pulled into my driveway and turned off the motor. "I'll see you safely inside," he said as he stepped out of the car.

I laughed. "You don't have to. This is Dickens Island."

"Where someone was murdered a week ago."

"True."

We climbed the steps to the front door. I put the key in the lock and stepped inside. The lamp I'd left on the hall table cast enough light to show me the family room was in disarray. One of the chairs was knocked over. Magazines and newspapers were scattered across the floor. Riley's barking sounded muffled. It was coming from the downstairs bathroom.

A frisson of fear ran down my spine. "Someone broke in," I said. "Thank God Connor wasn't home."

Jack nodded. "The intruder might still be here."

"I think he's gone. We would have seen his car or truck."

"Still, we need to be careful." Jack switched on the overhead hall light and took out his phone. A minute later, he was telling Gregg what we'd discovered. "Got it," Jack said and disconnected.

"Gregg's on his way over. He wants us to wait for him outside."

My mind was on Riley, who hadn't stopped barking. The intruder must have shut him in. "I'll just set poor Riley free," I said as I started for the bathroom.

Jack grabbed my arm. "Delia, wait! If the burglar's still here, the dog will go after him. We don't know if he has a weapon."

He was right. I followed Jack outside. Minutes later, Gregg pulled up behind Jack's Jeep. He and Billy Watson jumped out of the car and ran over to us.

"What happened here?" Gregg asked. I was aware of the gun in his holster.

"When we went into the house, my dog was barking. Whoever broke in locked him in the bathroom and ransacked the family room. I don't know what else he did."

Gregg nodded. "Okay. Stay out here until I give you the all-clear to come inside."

I shivered as he and Billy drew their weapons and entered the house. After what seemed like an hour but was really only a few minutes, Gregg opened the front door. "There's no one here. I'm afraid your burglar made a mess in the two bedrooms."

"How did he or she get inside?" Jack asked as we entered the house.

"There's no broken glass or jammed doors, so I suspect they used the old charge card trick," Gregg said. "You might want to get stronger locks tomorrow."

Riley, happy to be freed, jumped on me, then on Jack. I went into the kitchen to give him a few treats. The three men followed me and sat down at the table. I noticed it was the one room left untouched.

"Do you have any idea who did this?" Gregg asked.

"Not really," I said.

"Or what they were after?" Billy asked.

Instead of answering, I said, "I'd like to see what damage they did upstairs."

"Would you like me to come up with you?" Jack asked.

I shook my head and climbed the staircase, dreading what I'd find. Drawers were pulled open, items tossed on the floor, the mattresses in both rooms were half-yanked off the bed. Connor's room was more of a mess than mine.

I was furious! I was sure that whoever had invaded my house had been after the log. Part of my anger was directed at my son. Connor had told Trevor and Madison about the log after I'd told him not to. Either Madison had come for it, or she'd sent someone to do her dirty work.

Thank God Connor was spending the night at my father's. I called his cell and he answered, sounding annoyed.

"Hi, Mom. Can't talk. We're in the middle of a game."

"Okay. Just making sure you got there safely."

"Mo-om, why wouldn't I?"

"See you tomorrow."

"Right. Good night."

Greatly relieved, I went downstairs and joined the men in the kitchen.

"I have an idea who was here and what they were after."

Billy pulled out his phone, asked if he could record me, and when I nodded my assent, he made an official request for information. I told them briefly about Connor finding the map in Captain Kidd's log, the boys digging for pirate's treasure, and Madison's sudden interest in the log.

I finished by saying, "She wanted to see the log for herself, but I convinced Connor not to bring it over there tonight. Good thing I hid it in a safe place." I glanced at Jack. "Madison knew I was going out for the evening. She could have left Connor and Trevor and come here, knowing no one would be home."

Gregg's eyes widened. "Your son is over at the Sykes' house now?"

"No, he's at my dad's. I just spoke to him."

"That's a relief," Jack said.

"I'll talk to Connor tomorrow," Gregg said. "No point in upsetting the rest of his evening." He stood. "Now we'll have a chat with Madison Sykes. See what she has to say for herself."

Chapter Twenty

When I closed the door behind Gregg and Billy, I realized my hands were trembling.

"Are you okay?" Jack asked.

I shook my head. "No, I'm not okay. I thought I was, but . . ."

"Would you like me to stay the night?"

I burst out laughing. "Your idea of the perfect ending to our date?"

Jack chuckled. "I meant in the guest room. Or on the couch in the family room."

I found myself nodding. "Actually, I'd like that, even though I have Riley for company."

Hearing his name, Riley's ears perked up.

"Let's do that. But first, I have to go home and take Baron out for a run. The cats are fine once I give them their late-night snacks." Jack put his hand to his forehead. "But what am I thinking? Do you want to come with me so you won't be alone? Or even stay at my place? It must be a mess upstairs."

"It is a mess, but I need to be here whenever Connor comes home in the morning." I petted Riley, who gave me a Beardie smile. "I'll be fine until you return." I had an idea. "Bring Baron with you, if you like."

"Really?"

"Sure. I'll feel safer with two dogs, especially since one let himself be trapped in the bathroom."

Jack laughed. "Don't be too hard on Riley. The burglar must have lured him with food."

"Which tells us two things," I said. "The intruder knows we have a dog and knows dogs well enough to have brought treats or meat or something."

* * *

Jack returned half an hour later. At his side was Baron, who turned out to be a giant mastiff. One day, he'd look ferocious, but for now he still had the soft lines of puppyhood. He greeted me by jumping up and latching on to my shoulders.

"Down, Baron," Jack said. The dog obeyed immediately. He turned to stare at Riley, who was keeping his distance. Riley barked twice. If I could translate, I imagined he was saying, "Stranger, this is *my* house."

Jack spoke softly to Baron. I stroked Riley, who looked petite next to Baron. Then Jack was offering Riley something to eat. Riley hesitated, then took the treat. Jack fed one to Baron, all the while speaking softly to both dogs. I had no idea what he was saying, but after the dogs finished their treats, they sniffed each other. Five minutes later, they were running through the house together, playing.

"Baron comes from a long line of English champions. I'm considering breeding the line."

"He's friendly," I said. "I see how quickly he took to Riley."

Jack laughed. "You should see Baron with the cats. They climb all over him, and more often than not, the three of them sleep together."

I asked Jack to go through the house with me as I set items back in place and checked to see if anything was missing. We started in the family room, which had been superficially searched, moved onto the living room, then headed upstairs.

"I'll put Connor's room in order," I said as we climbed the steps. "but he'll have to go through his things to check if anything's missing."

"Were Trevor and Madison's parents home when Connor was having dinner there?" Jack asked.

I stopped at the landing and turned around. "They were out for the evening. Have you ever met them?"

Jack frowned. "Suffice it to say, I've had my dealings with them."

"Didn't pay their bill?"

His humorless laugh told me I was right.

"I heard they weren't a family I'd want to associate with, but Connor likes Trevor. There are so few teenagers living on the island. I couldn't very well tell him to have nothing to do with him."

We put Connor's mattress back on his bed, then I picked up the items that had been swept off his desk, including his laptop. I turned it on to make sure it was functioning. Thank goodness it was fine.

I left my room for last. Seeing the half-open drawers of my bureau made me cringe at the idea that a stranger had gone rifling through my clothing, including my underwear. After we placed my mattress back on the box spring, I changed the linens. I glanced in the drawers of both night tables and saw that nothing was amiss. Not that I kept anything of value there. The clothes hanging in my closet appeared to have been skipped over, though shoes had been tossed off the shoe rack and out of shoeboxes.

I took down the jewelry box I kept on the top shelf of my closet, hoping it had escaped the intruder's interest. I didn't own many good pieces that were worth much, and I was wearing my favorite gold earrings, matching pendant, and gold bracelet. My jewelry, mostly silver, was scattered about the top level of the box. My fingers separated rings and earrings as I took inventory. Nothing appeared to be missing. I pulled open the bottom level, which held a few larger pieces, and gasped.

"Damnit, it's gone! They stole it!"

"What?" Jack asked.

"My grandmother's pin." I sank onto my bed as tears welled up.

Jack sat beside me and put his arm around my shoulders. "I'm sorry."

I sniffed. "I never wear it because it's much too ornate—an antique pin of a bird on a branch. It's made of gemstones and gold." I swallowed. "And worth a lot of money."

Suddenly, I was furious. I shot to my feet. "Whoever broke into my house and stole from me is going to regret it."

Jack stared at me. He'd never seen me riled up before. But then, he'd only known me when I was a lovesick teenager and always on my best behavior.

The two dogs, sensing something was happening, came bounding up the stairs to investigate. Watching them sniff everything in sight, then seek our attention was a balm to my ragged nerves.

"What a night this has been," Jack said. "I'm sorry whoever broke in stole your pin. Want to call Gregg and tell him?"

"I do."

We went downstairs, and I called Gregg from the kitchen and told him about the theft, describing the pin in great detail.

"I'll get this to property crimes units in New York and Connecticut ASAP," he said. "I'd like you to stop by the station tomorrow, around midmorning, and fill me in on anything else you've discovered is missing. We'll put it in writing, and you'll sign it so we'll have your official statement."

"I will," I said. "What did you find out from Madison?"

Gregg exhaled loudly. "She was lying every which way. Insisted she never left the house, until her brother Trevor said she did—I think they'd been fighting and he ratted on her to get back at her. Suddenly, Madison remembered she'd gone out for a walk but didn't realize that meant *leaving* the house.

"I asked if she used her cell phone. She balked at that until I reminded her I could track her calls, which was when she mentioned talking to her boyfriend. 'Yeah, like five times,' Trevor said. The boyfriend's name is Guy Lovett. He's twenty, lives in Riverhead with his father, and is currently unemployed. Lovett's well known at his local precinct for shoplifting but has yet to be charged with anything major."

"Do you think he's the one who broke into my house?" I asked.

"Possibly, but it's too early to say for sure. I've called his cell, and he's not answering."

"Can't you track him through his cell phone?" I asked. "Find out if he was on the island tonight?"

Gregg laughed. "It doesn't work that way. Madison insisted she hasn't seen Lovett since last night. She claimed he's out with friends tonight. That will be easy to check once we find him."

I thanked Gregg and said I'd see him tomorrow. In the living room, I poured a healthy Scotch on the rocks for Jack and me. We talked until I caught myself yawning, then went upstairs to bed.

* * *

Maybe it was because I knew I was being watched over by one able-bodied man and two good-sized dogs, but I slept deeply and soundly until seven thirty when the ring of my cell phone woke me.

"Mom, why didn't you tell me we were burgled last night?"

"Connor? Why are you calling so early?"

"Why didn't you tell me? I bet I know who did it. What did he take?"

I sat up and blinked. "How did you find out?"

"Uncle Brad told Gramps last night, but he only told me just now. I'm not a baby! I have the right to know these things."

"How did Uncle Brad—?" For some reason, Gregg must have told him. "Forget it. I'm not trying to leave you out. I only wanted you to enjoy your evening. I planned to tell you everything when you came home."

Instead of answering, Connor was busy talking to someone—my father, I assumed. Then he got back on the line. "Gramps is driving me home now. He said to put on a big pot of coffee. He'll make breakfast."

And what were my son and my father going to think when they discovered Jack had slept over? There was nothing for them to discover, I decided. "See you in ten," I said, and hung up.

I dressed quickly and went downstairs. Riley and Baron came bounding over to greet me. Jack was still sound asleep on the living room sofa, gently snoring. I shook him.

"Sorry to wake you, but my son and my father are on their way over here."

Jack sat up. He had, I noticed, stripped down to his underwear. "I'll get dressed and walk the dogs," he said.

"Great. Thanks. Do you have to go to the animal hospital?"

"There are no hours today at either hospital, and I don't have any patients staying over, so no. I can get to the cats later on. I put out kibble for them last night."

"I'll start the coffee," I said as I rushed off to the kitchen and Jack headed for the bathroom.

He was staying. I felt nervous, wondering what Connor and my dad would say when they found him here. Dad especially, since he knew how badly I'd taken our break up. But that was twenty years ago. Still, I was concerned about Connor. I didn't want him thinking I was involved in a romantic relationship.

Am I involved in a romantic relationship? I wondered as I filled the carafe to the top—all ten cups. The way today was going, I had no idea who else might stop by for breakfast.

As it turned out, Connor and my father arrived just as Jack returned from walking the dogs. The three of them were in the middle of a conversation as they entered the house.

"So," my father said after he kissed me, "Brad told us you were burgled. Is anything missing?"

I grimaced. "A beautiful pin Helena gave me. How did Brad find out?"

"He ran into Gregg and Billy at the All Day Breakfast Café last night."

I turned to Connor. "Whoever was here tossed both our bedrooms. I put yours back in order, but check to see if anything's missing."

"I will. Good thing you hid Captain Kidd's log. It's safe, isn't it?"

"I haven't checked," I admitted, "but I will."

Connor dashed up the stairs to his room. A minute later, he was flying back down. "Mom, he took the map!"

"The map's in the log," I said. "I saw that myself."

Connor's face scrunched up, and I knew he was on the verge of crying. "It's the copy of the map I made for when Trevor and I went digging. I put it in my desk drawer. It's gone."

"I'll tell Gregg," I said.

"I know who took it," Connor said. "But he's not getting the treasure. I'll make sure of that!"

Chapter Twenty-One

After breakfast, Jack and my father went home. A minute later, Connor headed for the front door

"Where are you off to?" I called after him.

"To get my stuff out of the garage. My punishment, remember? Or did you forget?"

Before I could respond, Connor slammed the door behind him. I was concerned about his state of mind. Should I go after him and rebuke him for taking that tone of voice with me, or should I act the supportive mom? In the end, I decided to do neither. Connor was furious that someone—probably Madison's boyfriend—had stolen the map he had traced and was planning to dig for the treasure himself.

I doubted there was anything to dig up, but Connor felt Trevor, whom he considered a friend, had betrayed him. Though from what Gregg said regarding his interview with Madison, I got the impression that Trevor had nothing to do with the break in. Still, Connor hadn't listened to me when I told him not to tell anyone about the log. He had, and the result was the house got burgled and the copy of the map was taken along with a valuable pin that had great sentimental value for me.

I cleaned up the kitchen, then stopped by the garage to let Connor know I was going out.

"Lookin' good," I said, gesturing to the three small piles of items arranged at the front of my now less cluttered garage.

"Thanks. The middle pile is stuff I don't want anymore but is good enough to give away. The last one is junk." He pointed to the pile closest to him. "This is stuff I want. I should be done here in an hour or so."

"Good job. I'm going to the precinct to talk to Gregg."

"Tell him about the map."

"Oh, I will."

Since Aunt Reenie's town manager's office was in the same building as our small police station, I decided to pay her a visit while I was there. I knocked on her door and, finding it unlocked, walked on in.

She was sitting at her desk while Uncle Brad peered over her shoulder as they both studied the documents spread out before them. When they saw me, they drew apart as though I'd found them in a compromising position. Aunt Reenie was the first to regain her composure.

"Oh, hi, Delia. We're discussing an island issue that might turn out to be a problem. Brad told me you were burgled last night. I hope nothing valuable was stolen."

"Unfortunately, the thief stole a pin that Helena had given me."

"That's too bad," my uncle said. "Be sure to give Gregg a description of the pin so he can send it to all the nearby precincts. Hopefully, they can track it down to an antique shop or a local fence."

"I hope so," I said.

"I heard you were out with Jack Morrison last night," my aunt said, no doubt to deflect attention away from herself and Uncle Brad. "Do you think it's wise to get involved with him again, after the way he hurt you?"

"Aunt Reenie, are you saying you should never give a romantic partner a second chance?"

My aunt and uncle looked at each other. I grinned when I saw her ears turn red. I reached for the doorknob. "Have a nice day," I said as I let myself out.

I entered the section of the building that comprised our small police station. "Hi, Delia," Lettie greeted me. "Sorry about the break in."

"Thanks, Lettie."

She shook her head in dismay. "I don't know what this island is coming to. First a murder, now a burglary. Go on in. Gregg's expecting you."

I walked down the short hallway to the office that Gregg, Billy, and Sam Kettering, the part-time deputy, shared. Across the hall was an interrogation room, a kitchen, and a bathroom. At the end were two cells that were rarely occupied,

Gregg's desk was closest to the window in the far corner. He smiled and beckoned me to sit down. I was glad neither Billy nor Sam were there. Though I knew Gregg would share with them whatever I told him, I appreciated having a sense of privacy as I talked about last night's events.

"Now that you've had a chance to go through the rooms and put them back in order, did you come across anything that didn't belong there—an item, as small as a matchstick, that the burglar might have dropped?"

"I didn't find anything like that. I'm very upset because a valuable pin my grandmother had given me was stolen."

Gregg grimaced. "I'm sorry about that, Delia. I know how much you loved Helena." He pointed to the large pad of drawing paper on his desk. "Do you think you could draw a rough sketch of it?"

"I guess," I said, and set about drawing the pin as I remembered it.

"That's fine!" Gregg said when I was done. "Better than fine. And how big would you say it is?" he asked, holding his two pointer fingers up.

I measured the distance between my own two fingers.

"That's a little over two inches long," he said as he stood. "I'll have Lettie put this in our program and show you the results in a few minutes."

When he returned, Gregg said, "Let me know if you find that other items are missing. You may not discover what else was taken for some time."

"They took something else."

He shot me a questioning glance.

"Connor had made a copy of the map he'd found in Captain Kidd's log. He'd put it in his desk drawer, and now it's gone."

"You think that's what they were after?" Gregg said. "Madison knew the boys had gone hunting for the treasure so she got Guy Lovett to steal the map?"

"Could be," I said. "What did Madison say when you questioned her?"

"She denied knowing anything about anything. I'll be talking to her again."

"It's possible they were after the log," I said. "It might turn out to be genuine. If it really was William Kidd's log, it could be worth a lot of money."

"And since Lovett couldn't find the log, maybe he decided to make the break in worth his while. He looked further, found your pin, and took it." Gregg mused.

"Exactly. Have you found him yet?"

Gregg frowned as he sat forward. "Not yet, but I've put out a BOLO. We're thinking he's gone to his grandparents' home in Connecticut or to some cousins he's close to who live in Pennsylvania."

I stood. There was nothing else to discuss. "Please let me know when you find him, and if he tells you what he did with my pin."

"Of course."

Gregg stood and walked around his desk. "I'll walk you out. Lettie probably has the sketch of your pin ready. I'd like you to see it before I send it out to other precincts."

The pin looked amazingly like the one I'd roughly sketched. I made a few corrections that Lettie said she'd redo according to my instructions, then send it out to the police stations in the area as well as the ones near Guy Lovett's relatives. They would pass it on to antique stores, pawnshops, and fences in those neighborhoods. I thanked them both and left.

I drove to the general store to see if they could use another pair of hands for the next few hours. For some unexplainable reason, Sunday was often the busiest day of the week. We even got day trippers who took the ferry over, which was why I wanted to stock more appealing items, nautical in nature, that tourists might consider souvenirs. People were always in more of a buying mood when they were enjoying an outing, even if it was only a few hours' drive from home.

Every islander I ran into had heard about last night's break-in and tried to press me for details. I finally escaped to the office, where I perused catalogues and ordered some really nice summertime gift items. That accomplished, I told my father

I was leaving and stopped by the bakery for a cake before driving home.

Connor wasn't there when I arrived. He left me a note saying he'd finished sorting through his things in the garage and was out riding his bike. He'd walked Riley and fed him some treats. As I ate an egg salad sandwich for lunch, I worried about my son and hoped he was all right.

Aaron Spiegel's daughter, Vicki, came over on the two o'clock ferry as planned. When she arrived, I helped her unload the cartons of Riley's toys and paraphernalia from her car and carry them inside the house.

Riley greeted her warmly, then set about pulling his possessions out of the boxes. When he came to a large chewy toy that squeaked, he brought it over to a corner of the living room and got to work. We chuckled at his singlemindedness. I led Vicki into the kitchen for a mug of coffee and a piece of cake.

She talked about her father, saying he'd always had a dog that he loved to take for long walks. We chatted easily and discovered we both enjoyed watching foreign films and dining in ethnic restaurants. When I presented her with the paper of ownership I'd written and printed out, she read and signed it without a moment's hesitation.

It was close to five when Vicki noticed the time and had to dash off to catch the five-thirty ferry. We hugged and promised to keep in touch. As soon as she left, I took Riley for a long walk.

Connor returned home shortly after I did.

"Have a good ride?" I asked, relieved to see him. He'd been gone for hours.

"Okay."

I followed him into the kitchen, where he pulled a bag of potato chips from the pantry and started munching. "See anyone?" I asked as I cleared the table of the mugs and plates Vicki and I had used.

He made a scoffing sound. "Who would be out and about on this island on a cold March afternoon?"

"I just wondered if you stopped by the store to see Gramps. Or went to Trevor's house."

"Right! That's the last place I'd go after what they did." He stormed out of the room and up the stairs with the bag of chips. Normally, I'd say something about that, but I knew he was hurting. Again, I wished I knew the right words to make him feel better and to help take away the sense of betrayal.

Once again, I wondered if I'd made a mistake coming back to live on Dickens Island. I'd done so in order to make as few changes in Connor's life as possible. But maybe the better plan would have been to have him move to Manhattan. Of course, then he would have had to get used to a new school and new friends—in fact, to an entirely different lifestyle. But the city offered an array of activities and possibilities, a chance to develop various interests. If I had done that, this disastrous friendship with Trevor Sykes would never have happened.

I shook my head. I couldn't think that way. If only there were a handbook to help single mothers of teenagers! My own mother was involved in her personal journey and not available. The friends I had when I was living in Manhattan were mainly people I'd worked with. They were either childless or had older kids.

Amanda would know what I was going through. Her kids were close in age to Connor. She and her family lived in a beautiful home in Greenwich. Amanda had a part-time job as an interior decorator and spent the rest of her time being active in the PTA and chauffeuring her kids to their many activities. Even though our situations were very different, Amanda was clear-sighted. She'd be able to look at my situation and give me good advice.

The last time we had spoken was close to two years ago. But Peggy had said that Amanda would love to hear from me. Maybe I would make that call soon.

Chapter Twenty-Two

The following morning, I was getting breakfast for Connor and myself when I received a text.

"Special council meeting tonight at eight at the village hall. All Dickens islanders are encouraged to attend," I read aloud.

Connor looked up from his bowl of dry cereal. "What happened?"

"No idea."

"Maybe they caught Guy Lovett," Connor said.

"I doubt that would be a reason for a special meeting."

Connor scowled but said nothing. He gulped down the rest of his milk and grabbed his backpack.

"Have a good day at school," I said to his receding back.

He raised his arm in answer. A minute later, he was gone.

I spent part of the morning putting the books I'd amassed for the Book Nook in some kind of order. Shoppers stopped by to ask about it, and I told them I was creating a silent reading area and planning to eventually start a book club. Everyone loved the idea. One woman suggested setting up a monthly meet-up where people talked about a book they enjoyed reading or listening to. She was delighted when I told her that was exactly what I'd been considering. A few people offered to drop off books to add to the Book Nook's collection.

And of course everyone speculated about what the topic of that evening's council meeting might be.

Around midday, I went home, ate a light lunch, and took Riley for a walk. Thinking about my first article for *The Chronicle,* I was struck by the idea of writing about the women in Dickens Island's history. I went into Helena's hidden room to see what I could find on the subject. I came upon two books that might prove useful and sat down in the chair to skim through them. I was hoping Helena would show up, but she didn't.

Connor had baseball practice and didn't get home till almost five o'clock. He seemed cheerful enough when he told me about his school day. He didn't mention Trevor, and I didn't ask about him. He ate a large snack, roughhoused with Riley, then went upstairs to his room. I made meatloaf, mashed potatoes, and salad for dinner. At twenty to eight, Dad picked me up and we drove to the meeting.

"Half the island's population is already here," my father said as he pulled into one of the few empty spaces in the parking lot.

He joined a group of his buddies while I crossed the large meeting room and headed for the small kitchen where I knew coffee, tea, and hopefully cookies were set out. Midway there, I passed Aunt Reenie in animated conversation with Chet and Harlan Trott, a retired judge close to eighty. Up on the dais, Uncle Brad huddled with the other council members. I felt a sense of alarm. Were my aunt and uncle about to wage battle over another issue in front of the entire island population?

I forced myself to smile and greet neighbors as I waited my turn at the coffee urn. I added milk to my coffee, then studied the array of cookies.

"I'd go for the chocolate," a male voice said.

I turned and smiled at Jack. "My thought exactly."

I picked up a cookie and bit into it. "It is good. What brings you out tonight?"

"Same as you. I'm curious."

"I thought you were at the hospital in Riverhead at the start of the week."

"I am, but I finished early and decided to attend tonight's meeting." He gestured with his chin toward the large room. "Shall we?"

We found seats three rows from the front of the room. I waved to my father, who was sitting with his buddies. Jack asked me if there had been any progress on the burglary. Then he told me about the surgery he'd performed on a dog who had been hit by a car. By the time I finished telling him about Vicki's visit, Sadie Alvarez, the council's secretary, was calling the meeting to order. She and the other council members took their seats on the dais, as did my aunt and Chet Thomas.

When everyone quieted down and sat back in their seats, my uncle stepped forward. "We've called the meeting tonight because something unforeseen and disturbing has arisen concerning the purchase of the property known as the VanPatten Farm."

Uncle Brad had everyone's attention. His demeanor was somber, and I got a glimpse of the toughness that lay beneath his usual easygoing manner so familiar to me. It made me realize what a formidable opponent he must be in the courtroom.

"As many of you know, we were very eager to acquire this property. As a matter of course, I'd arranged for a title company to verify the chain of title, which is the history of who has owned the farm. We know this farm has been in the VanPatten family for generations. Still, we are obliged to do everything by the book.

"Bob Hastings, the title officer in charge of our case, called to tell me he couldn't find any record of deed of sale made to the present owner, Timothy VanPatten. William VanPatten is the last owner on record.

"I told all this to Tim, and he presented me with property tax receipts going back over forty years. Now I'm very pleased that Tim has been paying his taxes all these years, but that still doesn't alter the fact that he needs a deed to show that he indeed owns the VanPatten Farm."

Uncle Brad paused. "We cannot move ahead with the sale until we're presented with a legitimate deed showing that Timothy VanPatten owns the VanPatten Farm and has the authority to sell it to Dickens Island."

"That's a load of bullshit, and you know it!" came from the back of the room.

Every head turned to stare at Tim VanPatten, his face flushed with angry indignation.

"He's drunk again," Jack whispered to me.

"Bradley Dickens, you just said it yourself—the farm we're talking about is the VanPatten Farm, and I'm the VanPatten who owns it now."

Tim belched, which brought on knowing looks and chuckles from the audience. He laughed and apologized. "Sorry about that. I rushed through dinner to be here on time, and now I'm paying for it. Anyway, I've owned the farm and I've farmed the farm these past forty-something years, ever since my brother William left Dickens Island. At that time, William handed me a letter saying I was now the owner of the VanPatten Farm."

"And where is that letter now?" Uncle Brad asked.

"I honestly don't know. After I showed it to the people in the Deeds Office, or whatever they call it, in Riverhead, I must have misplaced it." Tim hiccupped, then let loose a false laugh.

"What's the big deal about an old letter? Everyone knows I own the farm." He looked around the room, scanning faces. "Most of you sitting here have bought corn and blueberries, peaches and pie from me and Velma over the years. Don't tell me you're gonna let some technical glitch bring the sale to a halt and keep Velma and me from moving to Florida."

"The Suffolk County Clerk's Office in Riverhead holds property deeds, and they don't have a copy of any letter from William VanPatten transferring the farm to you. The deed on record is in your brother's name. This isn't some technical glitch," my uncle said when Tim interrupted him.

"Yeah, that's exactly what it is, and you're the one who's holding up the sale."

Tim sat down. Residents turned to their neighbors and started talking. I heard fragments of sympathetic comments. After all, Tim was a Dickens Islander like they were, and his family had been here for generations. Others expressed concern and questioned Tim's honesty and wondered why the ownership was in question. Uncle Brad shouted for silence.

"We find ourselves in a difficult situation. Reenie, Chet, and a few others are combing our records for the letter Tim claims William wrote making him the owner of the VanPatten Farm. We've also asked the Suffolk County Clerk's Office to continue to search for said letter in their records. Until it's found, the council cannot, in good faith, move forward with the purchase."

Velma VanPatten called out, "And if you don't find the letter? Does that mean the sale won't go through? In which case, why should Tim and I continue to pay taxes on the farm if you say it isn't ours?"

Now Aunt Reenie stepped to the front of the dais. "Velma, let's not get ahead of ourselves. This issue will be resolved one way or another."

"Hey, Ms Manager, if we don't own the farm, who does?" Tim demanded.

"Your brother, William, perhaps. Or your sister, Gloria," my aunt shot back.

Tim waved his hand. "Contact them if you can find them. I haven't heard from either of them in the past fifteen years."

Uncle Brad went to stand beside Aunt Reenie. "Tim, we'll keep you and everyone informed of the latest developments. The meeting is adjourned."

Most people remained seated as conversations swirled around. Jack stood.

"I need to catch the next ferry. Talk to you soon." He bent down to kiss my cheek. "I'll text you," he said, and left.

I caught my father's eye. He jerked his head to one side to let me know he was ready to leave. We made our way past animated conversations. It was only when we were outside that he asked, "So what did you make of that?"

"I don't know," I said.

"Me neither. My mother never liked Tim. She said he was a lightweight compared to his brother and sister."

"I've known Tim and Velma all my life, but only to greet them when I ran into them at the store, or when I stopped at the farm for eggs or corn. They managed the farm well enough, didn't they?"

"They did, until a few years ago," Dad said when we were both in the car and he was starting the engine. "Tim's in his eighties and Velma's about seventy-eight. She's complained to me more than once that neither of their sons was interested in farming and couldn't wait to move off the island. And they both like their whiskey. Tim in particular can be a nasty drunk."

We were pulling into my driveway when Dad asked, "Has Connor settled down since the break-in?"

"It's difficult to tell. He doesn't seem as angry as he was yesterday, but he won't talk about it. I wish I knew what to do."

Dad sighed. "I'm worried about him. I've never seen him so excited about anything as he was when he came upon that log and what he considered an honest-to-goodness treasure map inside it. He loved the idea of digging for pirate treasure, though I suspect deep down he knew he wouldn't find anything."

"Worst than that, he's lost the only real friend he had on the island," I said.

"He's furious at Trevor and his sister." Dad shook his head. "I only hope he doesn't do something foolish."

"Me too." I kissed his cheek. "See you tomorrow."

My father patted my shoulder. "I'm so glad you're living here now. Connor needs his mother."

And you need your wife, I thought as he drove home to his empty house.

Chapter Twenty-Three

"I'm home!" I called out as I walked through the door.

No answer. I went upstairs and opened Connor's door. He was fast asleep in his jeans and hoodie with Riley beside him, rock music playing loudly. I turned off the sound. Riley jumped off the bed and greeted me with doggie affection. I left Connor sleeping and took Riley for a walk.

Back home again, I woke up Connor.

He sat up and rubbed his eyes. "I fell asleep," he said unnecessarily.

"I thought you'd want to wash up and get into your pj's before you're out for the night."

"I still have some homework to do."

"I'll be in the secret room if you need me," I said.

Connor laughed. "You really like that place, don't you?"

Downstairs, Riley followed me into the room, and I closed the door behind us. I didn't want Connor finding out that his great-grandmother's ghost stopped by from time to time to chat. At least not yet. Too many unexpected events were disturbing the peace of our island and the sanctity of our home.

I sank into the chair and closed my eyes while Riley curled up beside me. I hoped that Helena would show up tonight. I wanted to know more about the VanPatten Farm and why she'd taken a dislike to Tim. Was it because he could be an obnoxious drunk, or was it for some entirely different reason?

Please, please show up, I said silently, then finally said aloud. To my amazement, when I opened my eyes, my grandmother stood before me, and she was smiling.

"Hello, dear. I got the strongest impulse that you wanted to talk to me."

"I do want to talk to you," I said. "I just got back from an island-wide council meeting. Uncle Brad told us there's a problem regarding who owns the VanPatten Farm. Tim doesn't have the deed to the farm. He claims he had a letter saying his brother gave it to him, but he can't find it now. Uncle Brad's not buying it.

"So the way things stand, the sale can't go through. Tim and Velma are pissed. Tim says if he doesn't own the farm, who does? Aunt Reenie mentioned Tim's brother and sister. Tim says he hasn't spoken to either of them in years, and they couldn't care less about the future of the farm. What do you make of all this?"

Helena took her time digesting what I'd told her. I was kind of surprised when her first question was to ask me if Brad and Reenie were in agreement regarding the matter.

"Sure. They're both concerned about the irregularity that's holding up the sale of the farm. In fact—" I remembered them looking over documents together Sunday morning.

"Yes?"

"That must have been what they were discussing yesterday when I stopped by Aunt Reenie's office."

Helena was beaming. "Smart boy. He's finally making amends the best way possible—reaching out to Ravena in her role as town manager." She winked. "And how that woman loves to manage."

I made a scoffing sound. "Yeah, now they have the same goal—resolving the missing deed issue that's holding up the sale. But the minute that's worked out, they'll be back at each other's throats regarding what to do with the property."

"Don't be so negative," she chided me. "They've had a strong marriage all these years. It will take more than a disagreement over that farm to split them up."

It tickled me to see my grandmother still concerned about the state of my aunt and uncle's relationship. Then again, why shouldn't she still care? Uncle Brad was her son. I could only imagine how anxious she must be over my parents living apart.

"You told me Tim was the youngest of the three VanPatten siblings," I said. "Are he and Velma the rightful owners of the farm or not?"

"Hear what I have to tell you, then you can decide."

That's kinda strange, I thought. "Okay."

Helena leaned against the bookcase closest to me and cleared her throat. "I graduated from college and married your grandfather. We raised our family here on the island, and I taught at the elementary school. Meanwhile, both Gloria and Tim moved off the island, while William continued to work on the farm, helping his parents with the crops and the livestock. Though I saw Claudia and Joseph when I visited the farm to buy eggs and corn, I no longer knew what happened there from day to day, year to year. Claudia died. A few years later, Joseph got sick and died. He left the farm to William."

"Did any of them marry?" I asked.

"Gloria got married. Her husband was from Indianapolis, and that's where they raised their son. Tim moved around a lot, never settling down to any one job or place."

"What about William?" I asked, curious. "Did he ever marry?"

Helena let out a humph of exasperation. "You'd find out if you let me tell the story."

"Sorry," I said, now certain that William was the VanPatten she'd been in love with.

"A few years after William inherited the farm—he must have been forty-four at the time—Tim showed up with his fiancée, Adele." Helena closed her eyes and smiled as she remembered. "Adele was a beautiful young woman about fifteen years younger than Tim and perfectly delightful. My first thought when I met Adele was that she was too good for him. We immediately became friends. Since it was summer and I wasn't teaching, I found myself spending time with her.

"Adele had fallen for Tim in a big way. As I got to know her, I realized she was rather naive and vulnerable. She'd lost her parents when she was young and had been raised by relatives who never gave her a sense of belonging. Tim, who could charm anyone when he chose to, saw how pretty and smart she was and set out to win her over. Suddenly, he liked the idea of marrying and settling down. That's why he'd come back to Dickens Island. He was hoping William would give him a share of the farm.

"Now, William was no fool. He didn't quite trust his brother to be a responsible adult, but he wanted to do right by him. He told Tim he'd give him a portion of the farm once he proved he could do the work and stick to it. At first, Tim made a big show of getting up early and doing chores, but he quickly began to slack off. He found every excuse to get out of whatever job William told him to do."

"Did Adele see this?"

"She did, and it bothered her, because it was very clear to her that Tim wasn't fulfilling his part of the arrangement. By

August, Adele and I weren't getting together as much as we had been. My family went on vacation for two weeks. When I saw her a month later, she seemed different. Quiet. But strangely happy. She finally told me that she and William were in love."

"Oh." *Weren't you jealous of Adele?* I had more questions I wanted to ask Helena, but instead I pressed my lips together and let her tell the story.

Helena continued. "The relationship had its complications. A month after that, Adele told me she and William were going to marry, but that William was overcome with guilt for having poached his brother's fiancée. He decided he and Adele would leave Dickens Island, and he'd gift the farm to Tim as recompense. She agreed to leave the farm and stay at the only hotel on the island—it was small and more like a B and B than a hotel—and William would join her right after he spoke to Tim."

I grimaced. Something told me things weren't about to go as planned.

My grandmother exhaled a long sigh. "Adele called me the following day, crying hysterically. I went to see her at the hotel. She showed me the letter William had dropped off for her. In it, he said he was awfully sorry, but he couldn't get past thinking of her as his brother's fiancée, and therefore he couldn't bring himself to marry her. By the time she received this, he would be miles away. And lastly, she should reconsider marrying Tim."

"Oh no! Poor Adele!"

"Adele was beside herself, especially since she'd just discovered she was pregnant and hadn't told William yet. Abandoned and misused, Adele was at her wits' end. I invited her to stay with us until she figured out what to do, but she insisted she didn't want to be a burden."

My mouth fell open. "So what did she do?"

"Adele said she couldn't go home to her parents; they were too conservative to be able to deal with a grandchild born out of wedlock. But she was close to an aunt—her mother's younger sister—who lived in upstate New York." Helena's eyes got a faraway look. "She took off on the first ferry the following morning. I asked her to keep in touch, but I never heard from her again." Helena sighed again. "I suppose Dickens Island held too many bad memories for her to stay in contact with someone who lived here."

I grimaced. "So Tim does own the VanPatten Farm. It's just a matter of finding that letter."

"So it seems. He made a fine mess of running the farm the first three or four years. Then he married Velma." Helena laughed. "Velma comes from good farming stock. She knew how to set the farm right again and turned it into the successful enterprise it is today. Or was, until a few years ago."

Chapter Twenty-Four

What a sad story, I thought as I got ready for bed. Poor Adele, abandoned by the man she loved. I felt a flash of anger toward William VanPatten. First, he broke my grandmother's heart. Then, after making plans to marry Adele, he ghosted her because he suddenly felt guilty for stealing his brother's fiancée. I sighed. My last thought as I drifted off to sleep that night was that William was probably one of those men who should never marry anyone.

My dreams were strange that night, and why wouldn't they be, with the kind of day I'd had? In one, I'd gone to a local farm that didn't look at all like the VanPatten Farm to buy fruit and veggies. The sunny afternoon had just turned into a violent summer storm, and there was a tornado warning. I was desperate to get home. The farm owner invited me to join him in the farmhouse, which I'd never entered before, to wait out the storm. Both choices—going into the farmhouse and driving in the downpour—terrified me. I ran to my car, and though I knew it was dangerous, I started driving home.

Then I woke up, shivering with fear.

I knew I wouldn't fall back asleep anytime soon, so I got up and made myself a cup of tea. Riley padded over to me from wherever he'd been sleeping and rested his head on my lap. I gave him a few treats and sipped my tea, glad for his company. Then I returned to my bedroom, and Riley went into Connor's room.

My head was filled with the story that Helena had told me. Such a sad romantic tale. Hours later, I woke to the sound of the ringing telephone. It was my father, who sounded agitated.

"Delia, I need you to open the store at nine thirty and keep an eye on things until I get there. I'm taking the next ferry to bring Brad to the hospital for a CT scan. Someone hit him over the head as he was getting into his car to go to work."

"Oh no! Is he going to . . . ?" I couldn't bring myself to say the words.

"He'll be all right, honey. But I want to make sure he wasn't concussed."

"Did Uncle Brad see who hit him?"

"No."

I grimaced. "I bet it was Tim VanPatten."

"Who else? I called Gregg to let him know what happened. I'm coming over now to give you the keys to the store."

I disconnected the phone just as Connor padded into my bedroom, followed by Riley. "Who called?"

"Gramps. Someone hit Uncle Brad over the head. He's okay, but Gramps is taking him to the hospital on Long Island to be checked out."

"Was it the guy who owns the farm? He blames Uncle Brad for holding up the sale."

"How did you know?" I asked. "It only came out at the meeting last night."

"Gramps called me while you were reading in Grandma Helena's room. He likes me to be up on issues concerning the island."

A surge of anger rose inside me. I remembered how my father and Helena had done their best to instill in my brother and me the obligation to become guardians of the island when we were adults.

"You know, Connor, you don't have to live on Dickens Island after college. You can go wherever you like."

"I know, Mom, but I like knowing what's happening. After all, this is my home."

"It is," I agreed.

"I hope Gregg arrests that VanPatten guy. It's gotta be him. He has shifty eyes."

We both laughed. Tim *did* have shifty eyes. "At least he'll bring him in for questioning."

All humor was gone when he said, "I asked Gramps if there was any news about Madison's boyfriend. The guy's disappeared into thin air."

"They'll find him," I said, mostly to cheer up Connor.

"They'd better."

I hesitated, then ventured to ask, "Was it weird seeing Trevor in school yesterday?"

"Didn't see him. He was absent."

"Oh." I was at a loss for words.

Connor glanced down at Riley. "I'll get dressed and walk him."

I showered, got dressed, and went downstairs to make us breakfast. I was relieved to see Connor playing with Riley. Though my son's trust in friendship had taken a beating, he could still get joy from other aspects of his life. It was strange that the authorities hadn't yet found Guy Lovett. It wasn't like he was a master criminal with plenty of available money and places to drop out of sight.

Dad dropped off the keys to the general store on his way to the ferry. I arrived there at nine twenty and was pleased to find people waiting at the back door to be let in as soon as the store opened.

The influx of customers was partly because, I was sure, I'd included news about the new shipment of merchandise in *The Chronicle* and on our Facebook page. I greeted customers, reviewed a few things with Meg and Derrick, then started writing a paragraph about the Book Nook—why I had created it and a few thoughts about future meetings—for the new abbreviated flyer I planned to print regularly. My cell phone rang and I fished it out of my pocketbook.

"Hello, Delia. This is Mavis O'Hara from the high school."

"Hello, Mavis. Is Connor all right?"

"He's fine, except for his bruised knuckles. The nurse gave him an ice pack to take down the swelling. He's sitting in the office right now."

"Mavis, why is my son's hand swollen? Was Connor in a fight?"

"Yes, he was. He and Trevor Sykes got into it the start of second period. Your son gave Trevor a black eye. Dr. Rizzoli has spoken to both boys. They've been suspended for three days, starting today."

"Oh."

"Please come and pick up Connor at your earliest convenience."

Chapter Twenty-Five

Connor wasn't in the office when I arrived at the high school. Mavis told me she'd sent him to get his books from his locker and that his teachers would be emailing him his assignments.

"I'm sorry about this, Delia. Connor's never done anything like this before, while I can't count the number of times Trevor's gotten into trouble. He refused to tell Danielle why he hit Trevor, except to say that Trevor knew and deserved a black eye and worse."

"I'm afraid this is the result of something very serious," I said.

"The break-in the other night at your place?"

I shrugged, not wanting to discuss it. "I'll speak to Connor. Regardless, he shouldn't be starting fights in school."

"Danielle will be calling you later. She's busy now, trying to track down an adult in the Sykes family who can come pick up Trevor."

Connor entered the office, his backpack weighed down with textbooks. We walked to the exit.

"I'm sorry you had to come get me," he said as soon as we were outside the building.

"I'm sorry you got suspended. What were you thinking, fighting with Trevor in school?"

"I wasn't thinking," he admitted. "There he was, joking with a few kids, and I saw red. How could he be kidding around after what he did to us?"

"If it's any consolation, from what Gregg told me about his interview at the Sykes' house, Trevor gave him information I'm sure his sister would have liked to keep quiet. It implicates Madison's boyfriend, whenever they find him."

"That doesn't make any difference," Connor said. "Madison found out about the log because Trevor kept at me to tell him where I got the map. I told him not to tell anyone, but he couldn't keep his mouth shut. That whole family is a bunch of thieves."

I pressed my lips together so I wouldn't remind him of the times I'd questioned the wisdom of his being friends with Trevor, given Trevor's reputation. This was a life lesson, and we were both learning it.

I dropped Connor off at the house. "Please stay home until I get back from the store."

"Sure, Mom." Connor grabbed his heavy backpack from the back seat and, to my surprise, kissed my cheek.

I watched him unlock the door and saw Riley greet him before he even stepped into the hall. Once again, I was grateful that Riley had found us.

When I got to the store, I decided to postpone writing the introduction to the Book Nook and instead spent time walking around chatting with customers. My parents were always a presence in the store, ready to answer questions and help with purchase decisions. Engaging the attention of a Dickens was an added perk, I now realized, and something I needed to start doing if I planned to continue being involved in the future of the general store.

It also gave me a chance to observe customers as they checked out the merchandise. I decided to ask a few shoppers what they'd like us to carry and was surprised at some of their requests. They ranged from pup tents to washing machines, neither of which I planned to add to the inventory, but a few suggestions, like umbrellas and basic tools, made sense.

At noon, Dad called to tell me Uncle Brad had been seen by a doctor and they'd be taking the next ferry back to the island.

"What did the doctor say?" I asked.

"He checked him out, said he didn't need a CT scan, but to take it easy today and tomorrow."

"So why do you sound so worried?" I asked.

"Gregg called Brad. He asked him to come into the precinct as soon as he was up to talking."

"To talk about what?"

"Missy's murder. It seems he and Billy Watson went back to the Faraday house to have a second look around. They found something Gregg wants to ask Brad about."

My heart began to race. "Something of Uncle Brad's."

"I have no idea." My father's voice went cold. "I wish my brother had been more circumspect regarding Missy. Even if there was nothing between them, at times his behavior certainly made it appear they were more than friends."

I remembered what Jack had told me about Missy's behavior. "That was how Missy operated—acting helpless and needy around men. That last night of her life, I had the definite feeling that Uncle Brad was just being helpful and kind."

"Unfortunately, sometimes appearances count more than reality. This is especially true in murder cases and trials. As a lawyer, my brother knows this better than anyone. Or should know," Dad muttered.

When he arrived at the store an hour later, Dad said I was free to leave if I liked. I told him about Connor getting suspended for fighting.

He shook his head. "I warned Connor about becoming too friendly with Trevor. I reminded him that Trevor has been known to steal from local stores. I caught him in the act myself a few years ago."

"What did Connor say?" I asked.

"He said he knew what Trevor used to do, but he wasn't like that anymore."

"I'm stopping at the supermarket, then I'm heading home," I said.

"Delia, I hope you don't mind, but I told Brad he could call you when he's finished at the precinct and that you would drive him back to my house. I don't want him walking that far. The doctor said he needs to take it easy the next few days."

"Of course. I'll pick him up when he's done answering Gregg's questions."

I drove to the supermarket, wondering what Gregg could possibly have found in Missy's house that made him want to question my uncle again.

When I got home, I found the TV on in the family room and Connor fast asleep on the sofa with Riley on the floor beside him. Riley woke up when I came into the room and padded over to me. I decided to let Connor sleep. The fight with Trevor and then being reprimanded and suspended must have wiped him out. I went into the kitchen to put away the groceries I'd bought.

Connor woke up and came into the kitchen. He took a box of crackers and the jar of peanut butter from the pantry, got a knife from the drawer, and smeared cracker after cracker with gobs of peanut butter, and gulped them down.

"Connor, enough," I said.

"It's my lunch."

"Why don't you eat a banana? Or a few clementines? I just bought some."

"What are we having for dinner?" he asked as he heaped a few tablespoons of peanut butter on another cracker.

"Pork chops."

"Sounds good." He got up and went to the fridge, where he took out a bottle of soda. He opened the bottle and was about to drink from it when he caught me watching him. He sighed dramatically and reached into the cupboard above the dishwasher for a glass. I was torn between wanting to comfort him and feeling like I should be firm. Firmness won out.

"Connor, you're not on vacation now. You were suspended from school."

"I know, Mom. What do you want me to do—write 'I must not fight' one hundred times?"

"I expect you to do your homework and to think about why getting into a fight in school is a bad idea."

My cell phone rang then, putting our discussion on hold. *Thank God,* I thought. It was Uncle Brad.

"Hi, Delia. I hate to bother you, but I could use a ride from the police station to your dad's whenever you're free. I'd walk, but the doctor wants me to take it easy today."

"No problem, Uncle Brad. I'll come get you now."

The landline phone rang. Connor answered it. I watched him reach for the pen and pad I kept on the small desk in the corner. "Got it. Thanks." He listened as he wrote, then said, "Okay. Thank you," and hung up.

"Who was that?" I asked.

"Mrs. O'Hara. My English teacher gave her my assignments for the next few days. She'll text me the work from my other classes as soon as she gets it."

"I hope you'll get started on it so you won't fall behind."

Connor rolled his eyes.

I slipped my phone into my pocketbook. "I'll be back soon. I need to drive Uncle Brad over to Gramps's house."

"Why? Where is he?" Connor asked.

I hesitated. "At the police station. Gregg wanted to talk to him."

"About Missy's murder? But he questioned him last week."

"The police often go over a person's statement a few times—in case they missed something the first time around."

Connor looked frightened. "Gregg can't think Uncle Brad killed Missy. You saw how he put up with her the other night."

"I'm sure he doesn't consider Uncle Brad a suspect," I said more confidently than I felt. "But he knew her, and Missy might have told him something important that could help find her killer."

"Like the black car trying to run her down?" he asked.

"Exactly. Why don't you get started on your English homework while I'm gone?"

"I might as well. I have nothing else to do."

Talking about the murder case seemed to put my relationship with Connor on a better footing. But as I drove to the precinct, I wondered if it was wise to discuss Missy's murder with my fifteen-year-old son. Would it have a damaging effect on his psyche and cause him to have PTSD? Not that he seemed especially frightened. Connor was more concerned that his great-uncle not be considered a suspect. And since Connor had spent time with Missy the night she was murdered, it was only natural that he was curious about the case.

Five minutes later, I pulled up in front of the entrance to the police station. Uncle Brad came out to the car. Since he'd been attacked on his way to work, he was wearing a suit under his parka. He looked pale and totally worn out. For the first time I realized he was only a few years younger than my father.

"I'm glad that's over," he said as he slid into the passenger seat. "All I want to do now is crawl into bed and sleep for twenty-four hours."

"Are you hungry?"

"A little. Your dad and I stopped at a diner before the ferry ride home, but I couldn't eat much."

"Why don't you have something to eat at my house, then I'll drive you to Dad's?"

"Sounds like a plan." Uncle Brad leaned back in his seat and closed his eyes.

He was nodding off by the time I arrived home. I parked in the driveway and shook him awake. Uncle Brad stumbled out of the car. I took hold of his arm and didn't let go until we were inside the house.

Riley greeted us at the front door. Music drifted down from Connor's bedroom.

"Connor, I'm home," I shouted up to him, hoping he would hear me. "Uncle Brad's here with me."

The music stopped. Connor came downstairs.

"Uncle Brad's not feeling well," I told my son. "I brought him here to eat something, then I'll drive him to Gramps's house."

Connor followed us into the kitchen. Riley trailed after us.

Uncle Brad sank heavily into a chair at the table. He asked me to make him scrambled eggs and toast.

"Coffee?" I asked.

"Tea, I think."

"Okay," I said, though I was surprised. Uncle Brad never drank tea. "What instructions did the doctor give you?"

"Nothing really. Your father has the printout. A few days rest."

"Does Gregg know who attacked you?" Connor asked.

Uncle Brad shook his head, then grimaced as he immediately regretted the movement.

"Where did it happen?" Connor asked.

"Outside your grandfather's house. I was getting into my car. No witnesses. And I certainly didn't see him."

"I bet it was Tim VanPatten," Connor said. "Did Gregg question him?"

"He did. Tim denied it. Said he was fast asleep at seven thirty."

"So how can they ever prove he whacked you?" Connor asked.

"Unfortunately, many crimes are never solved."

"You mean they may never find out who murdered Missy?"

I didn't like the way this conversation was going. "Connor, Uncle Brad's not feeling well. He needs peace and quiet. Why don't you go back to your homework?"

Connor made a face. "All right. Come on, Riley. We're not wanted here."

I served Uncle Brad his food and watched him eat his eggs and sip his tea. When he was done, he smiled at me. "That hit the spot, Delia. Thanks."

"What did Gregg think was so important that you had to see him the same day you were assaulted?" I asked.

"Gregg and Billy Watson went back to the Faraday house to see if they could find any clues identifying Missy's murderer. They found Missy's diary, and Billy discovered letters written to me taped to the underside of a drawer in her bureau." Uncle Brad gave a bark of humorless laughter. "Who would have thought a sane person could make up such stories and pretend they were real."

My pulse quickened. "What did she write? What did it have to do with you?"

"The letters were addressed to me as if we were in a relationship. A sizzling, romantic relationship. A few times she wrote how happy she was that I was going to divorce Reenie and marry her." Uncle Brad regarded me, totally bewildered. "Where on earth did she get that idea? I was never anything but supportive and helpful."

Perhaps too helpful, I thought but didn't say. "And that's why Gregg had you come in for questioning?"

"Yes. Missy went on and on about our love for each other." By now his ears were bright red. "It was over the top. I imagine Gregg thought so too but felt obliged to question me about it."

"At least he no longer considers you a suspect."

"It looks that way, but . . ." Uncle Greg hesitated. "There was something else she wrote about, something she'd told me in confidence the day she was murdered."

I had a flash of insight. "Was that what you two were exchanging looks about that night at Dad's? Acting like you were sharing a big secret?"

He nodded. "Missy started speaking rather freely about her life, until I reminded her that she didn't want anyone besides me to know something momentous she suspected until she had further proof." He paused. "Missy was beginning to think she'd been adopted."

I thought back to that night. "She mentioned her parents were older. I thought she was implying that they weren't much fun when she was growing up."

"Just before Frank died, he said something to Missy that led her to believe that he and Essie had adopted her. But he never got around to telling her more. Gregg said that she wrote a few entries in her diary about it. In one, she wondered what secret her parents had kept from her, insisting adoption couldn't be it. In another, she wondered if she had any siblings."

I felt a stab of pity for Missy. How confusing and upsetting those last six months of her life must have been.

"In a third entry, she remembered Tim VanPatten telling her a few times over the years how much she looked like his sister, Gloria."

"Wow!" I exclaimed. "Do you think Missy was Tim's niece?" *More likely William's child than Gloria's,* I thought.

"I have no idea. But Gregg told me the last line in her diary said that she planned to talk to Tim and ask him if they might possibly be related."

Chapter Twenty-Six

I dropped Uncle Brad off at my father's house, then went home to do some research for my article. I found three books in the secret room that had information about the island's history and carried them, along with my laptop, into the family room to take notes. But after a few minutes, I realized there wasn't enough information about the women of Dickens Island for an article.

I had to come up with another topic, but what? I decided instead to read everything available about the island. Then I'd decide what the topic of my first article would be.

The reading part was easy enough. So easy, in fact, that I dozed off. The sound of my cell phone's jingle jarred me awake.

"Hello?" I managed to croak.

"Hi, Delia. It's Jack. Are you all right?"

"I'm fine. I was reading and must have fallen asleep."

"I called to see how everything was and to ask if the police had any luck tracking down your stolen pin."

"Not yet," I said.

"That's too bad. I hope everything else is okay."

"Not really." I told Jack about Uncle Brad being assaulted and Connor getting suspended because of his fight with Trevor.

"I'm sorry to hear that. I was wondering if you were free on Thursday. I'm off from work and thought we might drive out east on Long Island and have a leisurely lunch."

"Sounds lovely. I could use a day off the island. Connor will still be home from school, but he can look after himself."

"How about I pick you up at twenty to eleven in time to catch the eleven o'clock ferry?"

"Sounds like a plan."

"Great. See you then."

* * *

It was close to six o'clock when I started preparing dinner. Connor came downstairs, followed by Riley. He grabbed a few chips from the pantry, then took Riley out for a walk. The pork chops and veggies were roasting in the oven and I was dressing the salad when they got back. Connor fed Riley then, without my asking, washed his hands and set the table.

"What are you so happy about?" he said after downing a large glass of OJ.

"What do you mean?"

'You've been humming," he said. "You hum when you're happy."

I shrugged. *Am I happy?*

"Do you have a date or something?"

I didn't answer, but my face must have given me away.

"The vet! You have a date with the vet."

"He called," I said. "We're getting together on Thursday."

Connor thought that over. "He's all right."

"I'm glad I have your approval," I said, going for sarcasm. But the truth was, I wanted Connor to like anyone I dated. Not that Jack and I were dating. Or were we?

"Yeah. He's a good guy. At least he is now."

I grimaced. "You've been talking to Gramps."

Instead of answering, Connor said, "Are you ever going to tell me about my father?"

A rush of adrenaline coursed through me. "Did Gramps ever mention him?"

A shrug, and then, "He and Grandma said that was for you and me to discuss."

Of course my father kept far away from that topic. But he was right to. It was my job to tell Connor about Mitch and why he wasn't in his life. "And I will."

"When? When I'm thirty-five?"

I laughed. Thirty-five must have seemed ancient to Connor. "Whenever you like."

"How about now?"

"How about right after dinner?"

He nodded. "That works for me."

Connor and I ate dinner, not saying much. I felt a bit nervous as I cleared our dishes. I hadn't planned how I was going to tell my son about the most difficult time in my life. In both our lives, actually. I could only hope I'd find the right words to convey the facts with a minimal amount of pain.

"Would you like ice cream for dessert?" I asked him.

"With chocolate syrup and nuts," Connor said, making a beeline for the freezer while I reached for the dishes.

We both scooped generous helpings of pistachio and chocolate ice cream into our bowls and added the trimmings. I ate a heaping tablespoon that had a bit of everything on it and savored the taste. That done, I pushed my dish back a bit and cleared my throat as Connor stared at me.

"I met your dad in my junior year of college. Mitch was a senior. We were in a few business classes together and ran into each other in the library and started going out. You look a lot like your father, Connor. He's tall, a bit over six two, and slender. He wasn't on any college sports teams, though he played pickup baseball and basketball games occasionally."

"Did he have friends?" Connor asked.

"Good question. There were guys he did things with—played sports, went out for drinks—and he had a few guys he studied with. After we started to date, we had a group of friends, mostly couples, but Mitch didn't have any one particular friend he was close to."

"Was he smart?"

"I'd say so. He had a sharp mind. Got good grades. We fell in love and decided to get married. After he graduated, Mitch got a great job in Boston. I went there on weekends or he came down to the college. We got married two weeks after my graduation." I took another tablespoonful of my now melting ice cream.

"So far it sounds pretty good."

"It was, for a while. I liked living in Boston. I liked my new job. I wasn't crazy about the apartment we were living in that your dad had rented, but the lease was only for two years. After that, we were free to move wherever we liked." I drew a deep breath. "And then I got pregnant."

"With me?"

"Of course with you! I was deliriously happy. We'd planned to wait a few years before starting our family, but sometimes things don't go according to schedule."

"And I'm guessing Mitch wasn't thrilled," Connor said.

"No." It came out as a whisper.

Tears welled up in my son's eyes. Angrily, he rubbed them away. "So he never wanted me."

"Oh, honey, it wasn't you he didn't want." I reached out to touch Connor's arm, but he pulled away. "Mitch expected me to put him first. Always. He wasn't capable of sharing me with anyone. I didn't see it at first, and then when we were living in Boston, it was usually just the two of us. But when I found out I was pregnant—"

"My own father didn't want me." Connor said the words as though he was trying to understand the concept. "What kind of father doesn't want his own kid?"

"A man who expects his wife to cater to him and no one else." *A controlling man. A dangerous man,* I thought.

Connor stared at me. "And what about you? What about a mother who hands her son over to her parents and visits him on special occasions?"

"Connor, there were reasons why I made those arrangements. Let me explain."

But Connor was off and running to his room, with Riley close behind. His door slammed shut with a powerful bang. Some job I did explaining why his father wasn't in the picture, and I hadn't even gotten to the part that hurt him the most. Poor Connor believed neither of his parents wanted him, and I'd failed to make him understand that that wasn't true. *I* wanted him. He was the most important person in my life.

I waited a few minutes, then went upstairs and knocked on his door. "Connor, please let me tell you why I asked Gramps and Grandma to take care of you."

I waited. No response. Silence.

"You were better off with them here on Dickens Island."

Now wasn't the time to be angry, but I couldn't stop myself.

"You asked what kind of mother hands over her three-year-old to be raised by her parents. A mother who was terrorized, that's who. A mother who saved her child from his father's anger and refused to go through that again."

I sank down to the floor and started to cry. I heard the door open, but I didn't look up.

"And afterward?" Connor asked. He was close to me now, but I didn't look at him. "After you got divorced and we went to live in Manhattan?"

I reached in my pocket for a tissue and blew my nose. "I tried to manage on my own, I swear I did. But there was always something—you were sick, and I needed to find a babysitter. The daycare closed midyear, and I couldn't find another nearby that would take you."

I sniffed and looked at Connor. "My mother came and stayed a few days. Then she started bringing you to the island. You liked it here." I gave a little laugh. "You liked being wherever you were. It just seemed easier all around if you stayed with my parents. But don't think for one moment I didn't love you because I did. And I do."

We hugged for what seemed like a very long time. When we separated, I smiled at Connor. "Please don't ever doubt that I love you."

My son put his hands to his head. "This is a lot. I think I just need to chill for a bit."

"Got it," I said.

Connor went into his room. I went downstairs and collapsed in a kitchen chair. I felt drained but somewhat relieved. I'd managed to tell my son what I'd been wanting to tell him since I'd moved back to Dickens Island. The basics, anyway. I'm sure he had many more questions for me, and I had no way of knowing how he was going to react to me tomorrow.

Connor's feelings of being abandoned weren't going to disappear overnight because he'd finally allowed me to briefly talk about our lives after I divorced his father. But it was a start. A therapist could help him understand and eventually accept the facts of his life so that he wouldn't see himself as unwanted or as a victim. I gave a little laugh. That was, if Connor was willing to see a therapist. That would be up to him too.

Chapter Twenty-Seven

Thursday turned out to be seasonably warm and sunny. It was the perfect day to drive out to the North Fork of Long Island. Connor woke up a few minutes before Jack picked me up at ten forty. My son seemed to be all right and not traumatized by our discussion on Tuesday night. He'd spent Wednesday close to home except for walking Riley a few times. He didn't mention his father again, and I certainly didn't bring up the subject.

I told Connor I'd be happy to cancel my Thursday plans with Jack and stay home with him, but he insisted he'd be fine. All good news, but it was going to take time for him to wrap his head around everything I'd told him, and I prepared myself as best I could for future bursts of anger.

Now, driving east on Sound Avenue with hardly another car in sight, I was feeling calm and at peace. I must have been quiet for some time because Jack placed his hand over mine and asked, "Everything all right?"

"I'm fine. Actually, better than fine. I finally got to tell Connor about his father and the kind of person Mitch turned out to be."

"Connor didn't know?"

I shook my head. "My parents never told him about Mitch. They felt that was a conversation for me to have with Connor. A few times, I tried telling him why I'd left him with my parents when he was little, but he always shut me down. Then, Tuesday night he asked me to tell him about his father."

"That had to be difficult."

I squeezed Jack's hand. "Oh, it was. No kid wants to find out that a parent didn't want him, or even worse, that a parent tried to hurt him, though I didn't go into that."

"Mitch did that?"

I turned to meet Jack's gaze. "That's when I left. Grabbed Connor, my pocketbook, and flew out the door. I drove nonstop to the island."

"You and Connor both suffered a trauma."

I nodded. "Thank God Connor doesn't remember it." I bit my lip. "And now I'm back to feeling insecure about being a mother to a teenager, wondering if I'm handling issues that arise correctly. I worry—am I being too lax? Too rigid?"

"Maybe you should talk to someone—professionally, I mean."

"Maybe I will," I said. I laughed. "I want to send Connor to see a therapist, and now I realize that I could benefit from one as well."

Jack merely nodded. It was amazing how I'd opened up to him as easily as I used to all those years ago.

We sat quietly. A minute later, he was exclaiming, "Look, there's a horse!" He was pointing to the field at our right. Jack's way of lightening the mood.

"Two horses," I said when another one came into view.

"Imagine how busy this area will be once the weather turns warm, then even more so when people drive out to visit the farm stands and the wineries."

"The fall is the busiest season of all," I said. "With pumpkins sold at every stand."

We chatted as we slowly made our way east on Sound Avenue, talking about everything and nothing in particular. Nothing personal, at least not about our present lives. At twelve thirty, we stopped at a restaurant that was the picture of rustic elegance. We both had a glass of wine with our chicken potpies that the restaurant was famous for and shared a dish of hot apple cake covered with vanilla ice cream and chocolate syrup.

"No dinner for me tonight," I said as I climbed into the car and we headed for home.

We drove back to the ferry via Route 25 for a change of venue. I tried calling Connor's cell phone as well as the landline and got no answer. It was a sunny day, and I hadn't told him he had to stay in the house, so there was no reason why he'd be answering on the landline. But he never left the house without his cell phone, so I wondered why he wasn't answering.

Now I was eager to get home. It was only three thirty, but the charm of the day's outing had been replaced by concern for my various responsibilities, starting with my son. Jack noticed the change in me immediately.

"Something's worrying you."

"Connor isn't answering his phone."

"Could be he's in the woods or riding his bicycle and doesn't hear the phone."

"That's possible," I admitted. It wouldn't be the first time he hadn't picked up when I called.

We drove onto the ferry. Pete Osbourne, who sat on the town council with Uncle Brad, pulled up next to us in his Subaru. We exchanged waves. Pete made a call on his cell phone while Jack and I left the car to stand at the ferry's bow. A minute later, we were moving across Long Island Sound.

We stared out at the water in comfortable silence. Finally, I was the one to speak. "A ferry to Connecticut would be so nice to have."

"It sure would make traveling a lot easier."

"Oh? Where are you planning to go?"

"A summer week on Cape Cod would be awesome. And I've been thinking of taking a few days off to visit the Connecticut art museums in the fall."

"You could check out the fall foliage at the same time," I said.

Jack turned to me. "Would you like that, Delia?"

My heart was thumping when I met his gaze. "I haven't been to the Yale museums in ages."

"They're at the top of my list, along with the Wadsworth Atheneum in Hartford."

"Let's not forget the New Britain Museum," I added.

"Or the Aldrich in Ridgefield."

When I didn't answer, Jack said, "So that's settled. I'll block out a week's vacation. Shall we say mid-October?"

"Are you serious?" I asked.

"Dead serious."

I was saved from answering when the ferry attendant approached to tell us to return to our vehicle. We got into Jack's Grand Cherokee. He turned on the ignition and prepared to disembark.

Four cars were lined up outside the Dickens Island ferry terminal, ready to load on the ferry for the trip to Long Island. One of the cars was a dark-green, dented wreck. A skinny twenty-something dude with a wispy beard wearing a baseball cap turned backward was behind the wheel. Sitting next to him was Madison Sykes. When she caught me staring at her, she ducked down out of sight.

"Jack, look! Madison Sykes is in that beat-up jalopy! I bet the guy driving is her boyfriend."

Jack turned to see the other car as it drove onto the ferry.

"All I caught was the rear end of the car. Call Gregg Fanning. He can notify the Suffolk County Police, and hopefully they'll reach the ferry before it disembarks."

I called Gregg's cell number, but it went to voicemail. Frustrated, I left a message as Jack drove me home. As we approached the house, Riley ran up the outside stairs and barked at the front door.

"There's Riley!" A shiver ran up my spine. "Where's Connor?"

"Riley's come to get you," Jack said. "He thinks you're in the house."

He stopped the car, and I got out. Riley came bounding over to me, barking as he ran.

"He wants to take you to Connor," Jack said.

"I know, but . . ." I wasn't sure if I should chase after him on foot or get back into the car. Riley stood still and barked twice. Then he took off down the road that curved around the point. I climbed into Jack's car. "Follow him!"

As Jack drove, I clasped my hands together, praying that Connor was all right. Had he hurt himself digging for pirate gold after I told him not to? Or even worse—my heart was pounding now—had Guy Lovett found Connor digging and struck him so badly he couldn't make it home?

My fears grew as we passed Marley's Beach and approached the bird sanctuary. Five or six vehicles filled the road in all directions. Riley darted past a police car and a van as Jack drew to a stop. We raced out of the car.

"Mom! Mom! Hurry up. You gotta see this."

"Connor! Are you all right?"

I ran past a group of men standing around a hole in the ground to reach my son. I wrapped my arms around Connor so tight, he stumbled and nearly fell.

"Mo-om." His ears were blazing red.

I'd embarrassed him. "We just got back, and Riley led us here. I thought something bad had happened to you."

"I'm fine."

I drew back and realized several pairs of eyes were observing me. Gregg and Billy Watson were there, and so was Trevor Sykes and a few other islanders. I peered down into the hole and received the shock of my life. There lay the skeletal remains of someone who had clearly died many years ago.

"Who is that?" I asked.

"I have my suspicions," Gregg said, "but I won't venture a guess at the moment. We'll send the remains to the crime lab and find out for sure."

"Gregg, I just tried calling you. Madison Sykes and a man who I assume is her boyfriend are on the ferry to Long Island."

Gregg turned to his deputy. "Billy, contact the Suffolk Police in Riverhead. Tell them to pick up Guy Lovett at the ferry and to take him and Madison Sykes to the precinct for questioning."

I turned to my son. "What are you doing here?" I stared at Trevor. "The two of you."

Connor shrugged. "Trevor called this morning. We got to talking and ended up here."

"I hope you weren't digging for gold," I said.

"We found my sister and Guy digging." Trevor started to giggle. "You should have seen them when they hit bones instead of gold pieces."

"Trevor, those bones were once part of a living person," I said.

"Sorry," Trevor mumbled.

He began to tremble, and I found myself putting an arm around him, saying "It's a lot to take in."

A van filled with workers in uniforms arrived. I figured they'd come to remove the remains of whoever had been buried here years ago. Gregg spoke to the forensic technician in charge, then turned to us.

"You're going to have to leave the area while the remains are being removed."

"Connor, I'd like you to come home now," I said.

"Can Trevor come too?"

"Trevor, is anyone home at your house?" I asked.

He looked down as he shook his head.

"Then by all means, come home with us."

Riley followed the boys as they went to retrieve their bicycles. Jack and I got into his car.

I released a deep huff of air as we set off for my house. "A skeleton in the bird sanctuary is the last thing I expected to see today."

"It was a man, and I'd say someone buried him there thirty or forty years ago."

I shuddered. "A man whose partner murdered him while searching for pirate treasure?"

"Could be a man who lived on Dickens Island."

I glanced sharply at Jack. "What makes you think that? Besides Missy, I never heard of anyone being murdered here since I don't know when."

"Me neither. But there was talk." Jack pulled into the driveway and turned off the motor.

"What kind of talk?" I asked, suddenly alert as though every nerve in my body was on edge.

He shrugged. "I was about thirteen when I heard this, and for some reason, it stuck in my mind. My parents had friends over for drinks and dinner—Harlan Trott, the judge, and his wife, Ginny, who died a few years ago. They got to talking about island people—who bought this and who sold that. Who got married, who died. Harlan asked my dad if he'd ever heard from William VanPatten. My father said no, he hadn't. From what Tim told him, William wanted to move his new bride as far from Dickens Island as possible. The judge said that whole business of William leaving the farm like that to go live someplace he'd never been was odd.

"A week later, I overheard my dad telling my mother that when he ran into Tim, he made a point of asking about William and his wife. Tim said they were doing fine living in Cincinnati, Ohio, and had two kids. But Tim looked kind of squirrely when he said it, Dad added. Mom said Tim always looked kind of squirrely, and they both laughed."

"And that was the end of it?" I asked.

"As far as my parents were concerned. I always wondered if there was more to the story. But then again, I was reading lots of Robert Louis Stevenson at the time."

As we walked up the outside steps, Jack said, "I have a few evening appointments at the Riverhead office, but if you'd like me to stay, I'll cancel them."

"Thanks, but I'll be fine. Connor's okay. He's even back on good terms with Trevor."

"I feel sorry for Trevor. He's torn between loyalty to his thieving sister and to Connor."

"I noticed."

We stopped outside the front door. "I'll say goodbye," Jack said.

"Goodbye. Thank you—"

He kissed me unexpectedly, and I found myself kissing him back. I pulled away, realizing that Connor and Trevor would be coming along any second now.

"Are you free Saturday night?"

I nodded.

"Great. We'll do something. Let me know if you find out who was buried in the bird sanctuary." He started down the steps.

"I will," I called after him.

What am I getting myself into? I wondered as I unlocked the front door.

Chapter Twenty-Eight

The boys came in five minutes later. They went straight to the kitchen and finished off a package of cookies. I gave Riley a few treats.

"You guys sure had an exciting afternoon," I said. "What made you decide to go to the bird sanctuary?"

The boys looked at each other.

"Well?"

"My sister got a phone call when we were watching TV in the family room," Trevor said. "Madison turned all secretive and went into her bedroom to talk, so I knew she was talking to Guy."

I nodded. "And?"

Again they looked at each other.

"I called Connor," Trevor said.

"Yeah, we talked. About things," Connor said.

Trevor turned to me. "Ms. Dickens, I feel bad about Guy ripping you off and stealing the map. My parents always tell me that family should stick together no matter what, but Madison had no right butting into our business, Connor's and mine."

"Your digging for pirate gold business?" I said.

"Yeah."

I nodded, seeing Trevor in a new light. He'd apologized to Connor and me for what his sister and her boyfriend had done, even though his parents had taught him to stick by his family no matter what.

"How did you know what they were up to?" I asked.

"Guy came over, and they closed themselves in Madison's bedroom. I tried to listen to what they were saying. When I heard Guy say 'shovels' I figured out what they were planning, so I called Connor back. We arranged to follow them."

"They went digging for treasure," Connor said, a broad grin on his face.

Trevor giggled. "We knew what they were planning, but they must have read the map different from us, because they started shoveling about twenty feet from where we dug that day."

Now Connor was giggling too. "Mom, you should have seen their faces when Madison uncovered that first bone. I had to poke Trevor so he wouldn't make a sound."

"She jumped back. Guy thought she was acting weird until he shoveled away more dirt and saw more of the skeleton."

"Then what happened?" I asked.

"They grabbed their stuff and ran to Guy's car like they'd seen a ghost," Connor said.

"We saw them getting on the ferry," I said.

"And now Madison's gonna get arrested," Trevor said, no longer laughing.

"I suppose so, since she was in on the burglary," I said.

Trevor looked down. "If only she'd never gotten involved with Guy. He's bad news. Even my father said so."

I had my doubts about who had instigated the burglary. "Trevor, I think you should call your parents. Let them know what's been happening."

"Okay. I'll call my mother. Dad won't be home till tomorrow."

Trevor wandered off into the dining room to make the call on his cell phone. A minute later, he was back, holding out his phone to me.

"My mom wants to talk to you."

"Hello, Delia. I'm on my way to a police station in Suffolk County. They're holding my daughter on a trumped up charge because of her scuzzy boyfriend. My husband's on an overnight, and I have no idea when I'll be getting home. Would it be too much trouble if Trevor stayed with you tonight?"

"No trouble, Thelma, but he probably should stop by your house for a change of clothes and whatever he'll need for school tomorrow."

"Oh yeah. Trevor can go get them now."

"Sure. Connor can ride over with him and help carry what he needs to bring back to my house."

"Thanks a lot, Delia." Thelma exhaled loudly into my ear. "Kids. How many times have I told Maddie to stop seeing that Guy Lovett? But does she listen?"

"Does Madison have a job?" I asked.

"She was working at a car dealership in Riverhead, but the hours interfered with her classes. Why do you ask?" Thelma asked, sounding suspicious.

Because she's always home with too much time on her hands. "I was just wondering. I'm glad to hear she's going to college."

"She's taking two courses at Suffolk Community—online, actually. She'll enroll full-time when she decides what she wants to major in."

"Uh-huh."

"Thanks for looking after Trevor. Tell him I'll call him later."

"Sure. No problem," I said. "Trevor's welcome here."

I handed him the phone. "Your mom asked if you could stay here overnight. She's on her way to the police station where they're holding your sister."

"So the police caught them after all," Trevor said.

I nodded.

Trevor looked like he was about to cry. "Maddie's in jail. This time she went too far."

"She's done other things?" I asked.

Trevor shrugged. "Nothing serious. She likes to boost a few things when we go to the mall, mostly for the fun of it."

"Boost?" I asked.

"Shoplifting," Connor supplied.

Suddenly I wished I hadn't invited Trevor to stay over. "Let me tell you, boosting, as you call it, isn't fun if you're a store owner. It's an expense, and it's illegal!"

"Mom," Connor said.

"I'm sorry," Trevor whimpered. "I didn't want to tell Maddie why Connor and I cut school that day, but she wormed it out of me. Then she insisted on hearing about the map, and she just had to see the log. She started in on Connor too. When that didn't work, she told her goon to steal them."

"He got the copy of the map, along with my grandmother's pin," I said.

"I'm so sorry," Trevor said again. His voice dropped. "Do you think the police will come after me as an accessory?"

"I doubt it," I said. "Your sister coerced you into giving her the information. But then, you shouldn't have told her anything about the map and the log if you had even the slightest idea that she'd send her boyfriend to steal them."

"I was hoping she wouldn't." Trevor scraped away his tears with his fists. "Sometimes I wish Maddie wasn't my sister."

"He's told you he's sorry, Mom," Connor said. "Can we please drop it?"

"All right, as long as nothing like this ever happens again," I said.

"It won't. I swear it won't!" Trevor said.

Connor was right. Enough had been said about Trevor's unfortunate part in the burglary. "Connor, why don't you ride home with Trevor so he can pick up his books and notebooks for school, along with his pj's and his clothes for tomorrow?"

"Sure," Connor said, relieved that I hadn't changed my mind about having Trevor stay over after what he had admitted. "Let's go, Trev."

Trevor pressed his lips together. "You don't have to come with me, Connor."

Connor opened his mouth to say he wanted to go with him, then realized his friend needed some alone time after his emotional outburst. "Yeah. Sure. Don't forget to bring that game we played the other night."

"Sure thing. See you both soon." Trevor shot me a little smile, then left.

As soon as the door closed behind him, Connor turned to me. "You didn't have to come down on him like that. Trevor's having a hard time."

"Is that so? We were robbed because of Trevor. Or did you forget?"

"Mom, Trevor has an awful family. His parents do all sorts of illegal stuff, and Maddie sits around the house dreaming up all kinds of heists and crimes. It's like she's researching the subject instead of doing her classwork."

"Connor, I have no proof, but I've heard from other store owners that Trevor has stolen things from them. They watch him carefully whenever he enters their shops."

"I know, Mom. Trevor used to do some of that stuff, but he stopped."

I gave Connor a look of pure skepticism. "I'm sure he told you that because he doesn't want to lose you as a friend."

"Right, he doesn't want to lose me as a friend, and somehow he's realized that what his family's doing isn't the way he wants to live."

When I didn't answer, Connor went on. "It's a big deal when a kid can recognize something like that."

"I suppose."

"Trevor was furious with Maddie when he realized what she'd done. He knows she's going to blame him for her and Guy getting caught."

"But he didn't call the police. I did."

"That's why. She'll blame him for siding with us. So will his parents. He's really in for a rough time."

"Poor Trevor," I said, somewhat sarcastically. But I was touched by Connor's loyalty.

"You don't know the half of it. He wants to go to college and work with AI. His father wants him to drive trucks like him and do whatever other business they deal with on the side."

"I had no idea."

"He's not lucky like me. I have you and Gramps and Grandma. And Uncle Brad and Aunt Reenie."

I put my arm around him. "I'll tell you one way that Trevor is lucky. He's lucky to have you as a friend." *And I'm lucky to have such a great kid.*

Chapter Twenty-Nine

As soon as Trevor got back, the boys set off on their bikes, with Riley running after them. I felt a pang of concern regarding Riley's safety, then decided that after all that time of being on his own, he was pretty savvy when it came to avoiding cars. Except for the village, traffic was always light on the island this time of the year.

Connor and Trevor piled back into the house an hour later, chatting and laughing as they set up Trevor's game in the family room. Their oohs and ahs over points made and lost, along with good-natured squabbling, reached me in the kitchen where I was preparing dinner. I was glad that Trevor was enjoying himself after his emotional afternoon and realized it must have been cathartic for him to talk about his feelings. Though it was only a temporary respite, considering his family's values and what he was going to endure now that he was no longer in sync with them.

I'd made a salad to go with the meatballs and pasta and was surprised that I managed to eat heartily after the delicious lunch I'd had with Jack. As Connor and Trevor chattered away, our pleasant afternoon outing seemed to have taken place long ago.

The boys helped me clear the table, then took their bowls of ice cream upstairs to hang out in Connor's room. I was still dealing with pots and pans when the landline phone rang. It was Gregg, calling to give me an update on today's events.

"Maddie Sykes made bail. Her mother showed up to save her, but it looks like Guy Lovett will be a guest of Riverhead Township until next week, when they're both arraigned." Gregg laughed. "A little birdie overheard him pleading with Maddie to ask her mother to post bail for him, but Thelma didn't, of course."

"Trevor's spending the night here. Thelma asked if he could, and I said he was welcome. I don't think she's aware that Trevor wants nothing to do with his sister's shenanigans. He's angry that Madison wormed the information about the supposed pirate map out of him, then had her boyfriend break into my house to steal it and the log."

"I'm going to have to question Trevor in the presence of a parent," Gregg said.

"I know. But talking to you with one of his parents in the room will intimidate him," I said. "He's breaking the 'family first' rule."

"Do you think he'd be willing to speak to me in your presence?"

"Is that allowed?" I asked.

"I don't see the problem if that's what Trevor prefers. He's not being charged with a crime."

"Go easy on him, please, when you question him."

"Don't worry, I will. It sounds like your son has had a good influence on Trevor. For a while, it was starting to look like he was turning out like Maddie."

"Any word on the skeleton remains?"

"It's as I suspected as soon as I spotted the difference in the leg bones. We've uncovered the remains of William VanPatten."

"Oh!" A chill ran down my back. Though Jack had told me he thought the remains might prove to be William's, knowing that Helena had once cared for William, then years later he had plans to marry Adele, his brother's former fiancée, made me feel as though someone I knew had been murdered.

"We've managed to get William's medical history from the doctor who bought the local practice some years ago." Gregg chuckled. "Turns out Ron Caruso doesn't believe in throwing out any records in case they might ever be needed. Sure enough, there are X-rays among William's medical records that ID his withered left leg. The ME said that much is evident, though he plans to follow up with his dental records. Ha, I doubt we'll be so lucky to get those as well."

"How do you think William ended up buried in the bird sanctuary?" I asked.

"Someone killed him. Shot him three times. A bullet was found lodged in the body, though it will be damn near impossible to match it with any weapon after so much time."

My pulse quickened. "Did Tim murder his brother all those years ago?" I asked.

"Maybe. I sure would love to talk to him about it."

"What do you mean? Tim's gone?"

"Looks that way. He must have heard about the remains being found. By the time I got to the farm, he was off the island."

"Both he and Velma are gone?"

Gregg exhaled loudly. "Just Tim. He jumped into the water taxi as it was about to cross to Connecticut."

"Interesting," I mused. "It sure makes him look guilty."

"The good thing is, he can't get far. Sure, he can catch a taxi or an Uber, but we can track any vehicle that picks him up."

"What a day!" I said. "Two sets of criminals on the run. At least you stopped Madison and her boyfriend."

"Don't you worry. We'll get Tim VanPatten too. Now we know why Tim couldn't come up with the papers that show he owns the VanPatten Farm."

"I heard William was planning to leave Dickens Island with Adele, who was engaged to Tim when she and Tim came to stay at the farm, and handing over the farm to Tim as recompense." I drew a deep breath. "I also heard that William took off alone, feeling too guilt-ridden to marry his brother's ex-fiancée."

"Either way, no one ever felt the need to question William's leaving Dickens Island."

"Do you think their sister, Gloria, would know what really happened all those years ago?"

"My, my, Ms. Dickens. You certainly are well informed about a generation of islanders and things that happened before we were born."

I felt my ears grow warm. "I've been doing research for articles that Wayne wants me to write for *The Chronicle.* I've been gathering anecdotes and stories from some of the older residents." *And from one resident who's dead.*

"Speaking of older residents, I stopped by my parents' house to see if they had an address for Gloria VanPatten. My mom had an old address, so I managed to track her down to a nursing home. Unfortunately, Gloria has Alzheimer's and rarely speaks. The nursing home director told me her husband died a few years ago. So did their only child, a son who never married. Gloria's nephew—her brother-in-law's son—looks after her and takes care of her finances. As soon as I get a free moment, I'll give him a call."

"Thanks for filling me in on what's been happening," I said.

"Delia, before you hang up, there's one more thing . . ."

"Yes?" The change in Gregg's voice told me I wasn't going to like what he was about to tell me.

"Are you dating Jack Morrison again?"

"We've gone out a few times. Why? Is there something I should know?"

Gregg hesitated as if he couldn't decide how to answer me.

"Come on, Gregg," I said. "What is it you're not telling me?"

He exhaled loudly. "Okay. Jack's not a suspect, but he's a person of interest in the Faraday case."

For a moment, I was too shocked to speak. "Come on! You can't believe Jack had anything to do with Missy's murder."

"Billy and I went back to the Faraday house and found Missy's diary."

"I know. Uncle Brad told me about that."

"Missy wrote about Jack in her diary. According to her, they were dating."

"Oh, please!" I scoffed. "Jack told me she made a play for him after they sat next to each other at a meeting. Those entries of hers are wishful thinking, like the letters she wrote to Uncle Brad."

"Honestly, that's what I thought, except I've got a witness who saw them together in a bar a week before she was murdered."

"Could be they just both happened to be there at the same time," I said.

"That's possible. But until I talk to Jack, I won't know his side of the story."

So Jack's in for an interrogation. "What about Missy's ex-boyfriend?" I asked.

"Peter Maris claims he was home at the time she was murdered, but he has no one to support his alibi," Gregg said.

"Do you think he might have killed her?"

"It's possible. I plan to talk to him again real soon."

I thanked Gregg for bringing me up to date and went back to cleaning up the kitchen. His subtle warning about Jack bothered me. Surely he couldn't possibly think that Jack had murdered Missy. If anyone was a viable suspect, it was Missy's ex. He was aggressive and violent, and probably the type of person who would use a gun to kill someone. Aunt Reenie said that Missy had taken out an order of protection against him after their breakup.

I reflected on everything that had happened earlier that day—lunch out on the North Fork with Jack, seeing Madison and her boyfriend leaving the island, staring down at the remains of a man murdered and buried many years ago, hearing about Trevor's sad family situation. And now Tim VanPatten was on the run, making it obvious that he had murdered his own brother and had gotten away with it until now.

I wanted to tell my grandmother about the day's events. Helena had spoken to me at length about William and Tim. They were old friends of hers and had been very important to her at one point in her life. She had every right to know that William had been murdered, most likely by Tim. And while the news was upsetting and as bad as could be, she deserved to be informed.

Going on the assumption that the boys were busy and probably wouldn't need me for anything urgent in the immediate future, I entered the secret room and closed the door behind me. *Please, please appear,* I silently pleaded. And to my amazement, Helena did.

"I sense you have something to tell me," she said.

"I do. The remains of William VanPatten have been uncovered, and his brother, Tim, has fled the island. It's assumed that he murdered William over forty years ago."

My grandmother exhaled loudly. The stream of air chilled me. "How absolutely horrible, though somehow I'm not surprised."

"You suspected Tim murdered William?" I asked.

"No. I had no reason to believe William was dead. Adele showed me the note she'd received—supposedly from William. Like Adele, I assumed it was genuine."

Helena hovered a few feet above the ground as she wrung her hands—a sign of how much the news I'd brought had upset her. "I never thought much of Tim, to be honest. He was a precocious child, full of tricks and practical jokes, and he never grew up. He developed a sense of entitlement, and his tricks grew meaner and nastier. But to go so far as to murder William . . ." Helena was lost in thought.

"He must have been furious that Adele chose William over him," I said. "Maybe Tim did it to get the farm. For all we know, William never offered it to him. Or maybe William told Tim he would hand it over after a trial period—to see how serious he was about maintaining the farm that had been in their family for generations."

Helena mused, "Could very well be. Frankly, I was surprised that Tim ended up running it. He hated farm work when he was younger."

"Maybe Velma helped change his mind."

"Velma was always a hard worker." Helena thought a minute. "Did Velma leave with Tim?"

"No. Isn't that odd?"

"It is," Helena agreed. "But tell me, where did Tim bury William?"

"In the bird sanctuary. Madison Sykes and her boyfriend, who stole Connor's copy of the supposed treasure map, went digging for gold."

Helena cocked her head in puzzlement. "Treasure map? Digging for gold?"

"Sorry. I never had a chance to tell you about Connor finding what he thought was a map to pirate treasure." I proceeded to fill her in about everything, including the theft of the pin she'd given me.

"So instead of finding gold, Madison and her boyfriend unearthed William's remains," Helena said. "Has anyone tried to contact Gloria? She'll be terribly upset to learn that Tim murdered William."

"Gregg said Gloria has Alzheimer's and rarely speaks. She's living in a nursing home. Her husband and her son are both dead."

"Alzheimer's. How very sad. And I heard that her son never married, so no grandchildren."

"Didn't you stay in touch with her?"

"No, we drifted apart," Helena said, sounding sad. She began to fade away. "I have to leave now, Delia. We'll talk soon."

Her rather abrupt departure puzzled me, but I told myself that the news about her old friends must have come as a shock and might have weakened her ability to remain any longer. I exited the secret room.

The landline phone was ringing. I hurried into the family room to answer it.

"Hi, Delia." It was Jack. "Did you hear the news?"

"What news?" I asked.

"Tim VanPatten's been apprehended in Connecticut. The police have him in custody."

Chapter Thirty

Jack and I spent a good hour rehashing the events of the day. He wasn't at all surprised when I told him the victim had been IDd as William VanPatten. I also filled him in on what Trevor had shared with Connor and me.

"I feel for the kid," Jack said. "A year ago, he brought an injured bird to the animal hospital and asked if he could help out there. I had to tell him he was too young to work.

"His father's rumored to be moving all kinds of illegal cargo on his truck routes, and it looks like his sister is following the family tradition that laws weren't made for the Sykes."

"What about Thelma?" I asked. "She's a nurse and strikes me as hardworking."

"She may be, but she was fired from one hospital under suspicion of stealing drugs. I think she got the job she has now because they're so hard up for nurses. I bet they watch her like a hawk."

"They have this 'family first' rule that Trevor is beginning to find hard to follow," I said. "He kept apologizing to me for telling Madison about the map when he suspected she'd send her boyfriend to rob us. He wants no part of her criminal ways."

"His family will give him grief over this," Jack said.

"Trevor knows that."

I hesitated, then asked, "Has Gregg contacted you recently?"

"I got a text from him this afternoon asking me to stop by the precinct tomorrow. Why?"

"Gregg and Billy found Missy's diary. She wrote about you as though you and she were dating."

Jack burst out laughing. "That's absurd."

"I know. She did the same with Uncle Brad. In his case, she even wrote letters to him. They found them hidden away."

"I told you, she came on to me—calling when I'd made it very clear I wasn't interested."

I drew a deep breath, then asked, "Did you spend time with her at a local bar?"

"You mean, did she come over to me when I was out with friends and not leave until I very pointedly told her to go back to her own table?"

"It seems someone saw you there with her and mentioned it to Gregg."

"Well, I'll set Gregg straight when I see him."

I heard a ping on my cell phone and glanced at the message. "Uncle Brad has called an island-wide meeting for tomorrow night."

"No big surprise, with all that's been happening."

"You're right. That's exactly what he wrote. 'In view of the many events that have taken place on Dickens Island, both Ravena and I think it essential that we meet tomorrow at eight o'clock in the village hall to discuss urgent matters. Please attend.'"

"So I guess I'll be seeing you there tomorrow evening," Jack said.

"I suppose."

"Till then, Delia."

I was still smiling when I disconnected.

* * *

The boys got ready for bed around ten o'clock and turned out their lights half an hour later. I walked Riley, then read in bed for a while. When I peered into Connor's room at eleven, he and Trevor were sound asleep. Riley slipped past me and lay down on the floor between the two beds.

Having Trevor stay the night proved to be no additional work for me. He was a polite and considerate guest, and it was obvious that he and Connor were in sync with each other. My opinion of Trevor was definitely changing. Now I could fully appreciate how angry Connor had been when he felt Trevor had betrayed him and had been in on the burglary. I was glad they'd made up and felt bad that Trevor's family life was so awful.

The house seemed very quiet after the boys left for school. I finished writing up the Book Nook announcement, added information about upcoming sales, then ran off forty copies on my printer. After a quick lunch, I drove to the general store to drop off the flyers and to add last minute touches to the Book Nook. I was delighted to find four customers sitting in the Book Nook, looking through the books and chatting.

Harriet Lewis glanced up from a book she was leafing through. "Creating a Book Nook is such a cozy idea, Delia. Are you planning any book-related events?"

"I was thinking of having one next month. Here's the flyer I just made up," I said as I handed one to her, glad that I'd kept a few copies with me.

"Have you decided what the event will be?" Harriet asked.

I grinned. "I'll announce it once all the plans are set. I'll print up a flyer and leave copies in front of the store. I'll also post about it on our Facebook page and in our local newspaper." *It was the least Wayne could do for me now that he had me writing articles for him.*

Because suddenly I knew how I wanted the first meeting to be. After I explained why I'd created the Book Nook, whoever attended would talk about a book he or she had recently enjoyed. It was a good way to get things started. I'd also serve a few refreshments. Having something to nibble on always made things cozier.

I waved to my father, who was chatting with Harriet's husband, Hector, in the men's clothing section. A few customers stopped me to ask store-related questions. Sadie Alvarez, who was a member of the town council, called me over. I went to see how I could help her. Sadie was an accountant in her fifties, married with three grown kids. She was generally upbeat, but today she looked troubled.

"Hi, Delia. Are you coming to the meeting tonight?"

"I sure am. I wouldn't miss it, with all that's going on."

Sadie grimaced. "I don't know what's happening to our peaceful island. First, Missy is murdered, then your house is burgled, and now this terrible business of discovering William VanPatten was murdered all those years ago. With Tim scurrying off like that as soon as he heard the news, we can only assume he killed his own flesh and blood for the farm."

"It's all very upsetting," I agreed. "But why is there a meeting tonight? Any updates on the two cases?"

"Your uncle didn't say." Sadie pursed her lips. "Any chance you can talk some sense into Brad and Reenie?"

I was taken aback by her question and must have shown it, because Sadie was quick to apologize.

"I'm sorry, Delia. I'm very fond of them both, and I certainly don't have a prurient interest in their personal relationship, but their public squabbling is polarizing our community."

"What do you mean?"

Sadie released a long exhale. "People are taking sides—some with Reenie and some with Brad—and some are ready to fight. Ralph Caccini got into it with Don Withers this morning at the All Day Breakfast Café. Ralph was bad-mouthing Brad, saying he should resign and let someone with progressive ideas run the council, and Don said he wasn't in favor of any gambling resort like Reenie was pushing, and maybe it was time to choose a new town manager.

"Harlan Trott tried to explain that Reenie never said that's what would happen, but before you knew it, Ralph and Don were edging up to each other, their hands balled into fists. Harlan got between them and almost got knocked down. Good thing your brother happened to come into the café just then and put a stop to their posturing."

"Oh boy." I shook my head, picturing the scene. "I think we're all on edge because of recent events."

"No doubt. See you tonight," Sadie said. "Probably more fireworks."

* * *

The rest of the afternoon passed peacefully enough. The order of three huge cartons of pool floats and inflatables that I was expecting arrived. I asked Meg to help me open the boxes and stack the floats and blow-up toys on shelves in the back room since they wouldn't be needed until the end of May.

As we worked, Meg chatted on about the VanPattens. "I remember going to the farm when I was little—for corn and tomatoes. William always teased me, but in a nice way. He was so handsome. He limped from having polio, but after a while, you didn't notice because he was always moving, always doing something."

"I heard he was nice too," I said. "My grandmother told me she used to visit William and his siblings. They were distant cousins."

"Indeed they were!" Meg proceeded to tell me how Helena's family was related to the VanPattens.

The new merchandise taken care of, I found myself at loose ends and decided to leave after speaking to my father.

Dad came into the office and bent down to kiss my cheek. "Hi, Delia. Every time I'm on my way to the office to see you, a customer waylays me."

I grinned. "Not a problem. Meg and I unpacked the delivery and I'm off."

If you're planning to go to the town meeting, I'll pick you up."

"Thanks. Much appreciated."

"Tell me, was Connor upset by seeing those remains?"

I thought a minute. "I don't know. When we talked about it, he didn't seem upset."

"Delia, honey. Chasing after pirate treasure is one thing. Watching someone dig up and expose human bones is something else. It could be traumatizing."

Dad was right! I felt like the most irresponsible parent. How could I not have spoken to Connor about his reaction after seeing the remains of what once had been a living, breathing person? "I'll talk to him when he comes home from school," I said.

"Good idea, Delia." Dad patted my shoulder. "I'll see you later. Twenty to eight?"

I nodded and walked over to the bakery to buy Connor a blueberry muffin. When he got home, I was in the kitchen, ready to give him a snack and reassurance, should he need it.

"Hi, honey. How was your day?" I asked.

"Okay," he said just before biting into the muffin. "Hey, this is really good," he said as he chewed.

I stopped myself from telling him not to talk with his mouth full. Instead, I said, "Did it feel funny, going back after you'd been suspended?"

Connor shrugged and took another bite before chugging down half the milk in his glass.

"Are you behind in any of your subjects?"

"Nah. In fact, I'm ahead in math. I already did the problems we were assigned for homework." He bent down to give Riley a two-handed rub, then he jumped to his feet. "I'm going riding with Trevor. Oh, he said to tell you thanks again for letting him stay over."

"He's welcome anytime," I said. "Before you rush off, I'd like to talk to you about something."

Connor sat down. "I figured something was up. All those questions. You don't have to worry. School's okay."

"It's not about school."

Connor looked worried. "So what is it?"

"Yesterday you and Trevor were there when Madison and her boyfriend found the remains of someone who died many years ago."

"Yeah. And?"

I drew a deep breath. "Did seeing that upset you? Your grandfather's worried it might have."

"Oh." Connor cocked his head as he thought. "The truth is, our first reaction was to laugh. We had no idea some dead guy was buried there—we couldn't see what was buried from where we were hiding. But the way Maddie and her boyfriend reacted cracked us up. They literally jumped up with horrified expressions on their faces. They raced to Guy's car. It was only when they ripped out of there that we looked to see what had scared them so much."

Connor shuddered. "Seeing those bones *was* scary, Mom. I called Gregg. He asked us to stay until he and Billy got there.

Good thing they got there real quick because we wanted to get as far away as possible."

"I bet."

"Trevor and I talked about it while we waited, wondering who the guy was and why someone buried him there. Then finding out he was Tim VanPatten's brother who he killed all those years ago! How spooky is that? Tim's been living here on Dickens Island, and no one had any idea he was a murderer."

I reached out to put my arm around him. "Don't you worry. Tim VanPatten's in jail right now."

"I'm all right, Mom." To my surprise, Connor wrapped his arms around me. "Oh." He released me just as suddenly and ran toward the stairs. "I have to go or I'll be late. I told Trevor I'd meet him fifteen minutes after I got home."

When he reached the top of the stairs, he shouted, "By the way, Trevor says I'm lucky to have such a great mom."

Chapter Thirty-One

This time, the parking lot was full when we arrived at the village hall, and Dad had to park on the street. We entered through the front door and were greeted by a cacophony of raised voices. The sound had an aggressive edge that made me think my fellow islanders were disputing rather than discussing. I hated to think that part of the divisiveness was because my aunt and uncle's personal hostilities had spilled over onto the issues they supported.

I glanced up at the dais and waved to Aunt Reenie. Uncle Brad was there too, in deep conversation with the other council members.

"Quite a crowd tonight," Dad said.

"Almost every seat is taken."

I scanned the rows, looking for Jack, but he hadn't arrived yet. I pointed to three empty seats in the third row. "Let's take those seats."

"Save one for Jack. I'll catch up with you later," Dad said.

I watched him stride off to join a group of his friends, not sure if he left because he didn't want to intrude on my time with

Jack or because he disapproved of my resuming a relationship with the man who had broken my heart.

I heard fragments of conversations all around me. Most concerned the VanPattens.

"I figured William had come to a bad end," Ralph Caccini was telling Jeanie and Larry Boden, a couple in their fifties sitting behind me. "There was no way he was about to leave that farm he loved so much."

"Did you mention it to Chuck Kroll?" Larry asked. "He was the police chief at the time, wasn't he, Jeanie?"

"I believe he was," Jeanie agreed.

"Nah. I was nineteen at the time, and I had no proof. It was just a thought that flitted through my mind. Besides, Chuck should have known better than to take Tim VanPatten's word."

"I heard Tim showed Chuck a letter that William supposedly wrote," Larry said.

"I heard that too!" Ralph's booming laugh had me covering my ears. "'Supposedly' being the operative word in that sentence."

"Thank God the police have Tim in custody," Jeanie said.

"How long do you think he'll be there?" Ralph asked. "What kind of a case can they build against him? With what evidence? Mark my words, Tim VanPatten will be set free before the trees have leaves next month."

I shuddered because Ralph was right. What kind of a case could they build against Tim after all these years?

Minutes later, Uncle Brad stood at the front of the dais and asked for order. Conversations ended. I looked around as Jack entered the room through the back door. I waved to him, and he took the seat beside me.

"Good evening, fellow Dickens islanders," my uncle began. "Our small island has been going through a tragic and turbulent patch. Only a week ago, poor Missy Faraday was shot to death by an intruder in her home in the middle of the night. Since then, a home has been burgled and a valuable antique pin stolen. Yesterday, the alleged burglar and his accomplice thought they were digging for pirate treasure in the bird sanctuary according to the map they'd stolen. Instead, they ended up exhuming human remains."

There was a titter of laughter, which quickly subsided.

"The remains turned out to be those of William VanPatten who, it was believed, had left Dickens Island for parts unknown forty-five years ago. At least, that's what his brother, Tim, told the police, basing his information on a letter William had supposedly written to explain his departure."

Supposedly. I couldn't help grimacing when I heard that word again.

"What?" Jack whispered.

"Tell you later."

"As soon as the news got out that the remains of his brother had been dug up, Tim VanPatten fled the island and was eventually located and apprehended in Connecticut. Those of you who attended our last public meeting will remember that Tim, though eager to sell the VanPatten Farm to Dickens Island, was unable to provide us with the proper deed indicating that he is indeed the owner of the farm."

Uncle Brad waited for a sudden spate of comments to die out.

"It's not my duty, responsibility, or even within my jurisdiction to say with any certainty that Tim murdered his brother. That is for a court of law to decide. But as president of your town council, I need to speak to you about the property known as the VanPatten Farm as well as the house that Melissa Faraday owned."

So this meeting was about property. I wasn't the only one disappointed, judging by the frowns and whispered comments around the room. Uncle Brad paused, then continued.

"I'll start with the house that Melissa Faraday lived in her entire life. It was purchased by her parents, Frank and Essie Faraday, forty-three years ago. Frank died this past September and stated in his will that Missy was to inherit it, along with all his earthly possessions.

"Missy died intestate, meaning she did not have a will at the time of her demise. I urged her to write a will, and she said she would—eventually. I suppose she was in no rush since she was only forty-five and claimed she had no living relatives. Like Missy, both Frank and Essie Faraday were only children. Sadie and I have been searching records, and it seems that Missy was right. We couldn't find any record of her having relatives.

"What this means is the state decides where all her possessions, including her home, will go. From my experience with past intestate deaths on Dickens Island, the house will most likely become the property of Dickens Island.

"Our preference would be to sell it as a private home since it's located in a residential area. Another possibility would be to sell the house as a home-office or as a non-polluting home business that won't have a negative impact on neighboring homes. Since the Faraday home is a beautiful hundred-year-old Victorian house, I believe we'll have no trouble finding a buyer."

Uncle Brad cast his eye on his fellow council members and his wife, sitting on the other side of the dais. "Now on to another matter. "

Silence reigned as Uncle Brad drank from his water bottle. "What happens to the VanPatten Farm is a bit more complicated because, right now, we don't know who the rightful owner is. That being the case, no one has the authority to sell us the property.

"According to the medical examiner's report, William VanPatten, the farm's last owner of record, died after being shot three times. He was a homicide victim. After much searching, we have been unable to locate any will that William might have made.

"Tim VanPatten claims the farm is his, but since he is unable to provide the deed to the farm and since he is a suspect in his brother's murder—having possibly murdered William to gain possession of said farm—he cannot be considered the farm's rightful owner.

"Before I go into further complications related to the question of who owns the VanPatten Farm and who has the right to sell it, I want to reassure you that we are doing everything we can to resolve this matter as quickly as possible."

Sighs and groans rose from the audience.

"Like all of you, I'm hoping for a quick resolution of this matter. As it stands, the VanPatten Farm is zoned as farmland and can only be used as such. Not many people are taking up farming these days."

A few people chuckled. There had been two other farms on Dickens Island. Both had been repurposed years ago—one as a B and B and the other was now the Dickens Island junior-senior high school.

Uncle Brad continued. "We—the council and the town manager—are the only authority with the power to change property zoning. That said, Reenie and I have very different ideas regarding the future use of the property. While I envision it as a farm with a showcase house and barns for visitors, possibly raising a few crops and keeping livestock, along with a gift shop, making this a place where visitors can come and see how a farm was run in the early twentieth century, my wife, our esteemed town manager, would like to see this property put to a more practical use—building housing to enlarge our population.

"I know you must have many questions concerning the future use of both these properties. I'll try to answer them as best I can."

Hands shot into the air. The first to speak was Ralph Caccini. "If Tim doesn't own the farm, then who does?"

"Possibly Tim and William's sister, Gloria. Gloria moved to Indiana many years ago to live near her husband's family. She is suffering from Alzheimer's and heart disease and isn't expected to live much longer. Gloria's husband and son are both deceased, and there are no grandchildren. There is, however, a nephew, her husband's brother's son, who has been looking after Gloria while she's been living in a nursing home. The nephew, Perry Addison, is her rightful heir, and upon her death will inherit everything that Gloria owns."

More conversation rose, and once again hands shot into the air.

My uncle acknowledged the owner of the All Day Breakfast Café. "Yes, Bennie?"

"Will this Perry Addison be willing to sell the farm to the island as we previously thought would be the case, or does he want to try his hand at farming?"

Laughter broke out.

"Mr. Addison has power of attorney for Gloria's business affairs and has been informed of our interest in obtaining the property. We'll have to wait and see what he plans to do with the property, though I doubt that he'll want to move to our island since his family and his business are in Indianapolis. I did mention that property taxes were due next month, which might give him some incentive to make up his mind sooner rather than later. I also told him what we had been prepared to pay Tim for the farm."

"He'd have to put in about $300K to get that farm working full-time again," someone called out.

Other comments followed. Uncle Brad brought the room to order, but before he could speak, Aunt Reenie stood and asked to address the meeting.

"As Brad said, both properties were previously owned by persons now deceased and, coincidentally, were unfortunately murdered. Both died intestate, which usually means complications. That said, I'm hoping our governing board will soon have access to the Faraday house. I'm afraid that acquiring the Van-Patten Farm will take considerably longer than our esteemed council president has led you to believe."

Mouths fell open. Aunt Reenie swept on, ignoring several raised hands. "Eventually, we will be in possession of both properties. Now isn't the time to discuss how they will be used."

We all stared at Uncle Brad. He started to dispute her words, but Aunt Reenie never paused.

"Right now, our priority is to come together as a community and decide: Do we want to move ahead and grow and welcome visitors—yes, tourists—which means building more housing, providing more accommodations, and sprucing up our shops? Or do we want to remain a quaint little island reminiscent of the early twentieth century, when Dickens Island was a place for summer residences and the few year-round residents? Once we agree on which twenty-first century version we want, we'll easily find many wonderful uses for the properties under discussion."

Several people stood and clapped as Aunt Reenie sat down.

Uncle Brad's face was red when he addressed his wife. "Thank you, Madam Town Manager, but I'm afraid you strayed too far afield of tonight's agenda, which was merely to share what information we have regarding the two properties we hope to acquire in the near future. What you have suggested is a topic for another meeting. For several meetings, I'd venture to say."

Behind me, Ralph Caccini jumped to his feet. "Now hold on a minute, Brad. Reenie's right. Most of us see the need for more housing, for a ferry to Connecticut, and for setting up a real village instead of just a few stores and a bar on the side facing Connecticut. But every time someone proposes we tackle these issues, you and the council shoot down the idea. You claim a ferry to Connecticut and more housing would change life here on Dickens Island. Maybe it's time we made some changes."

Fists raised in the air with shouts of "Yeah! Yeah!" The commotion finally ended when Uncle Brad pulled out a whistle and blew it three times.

"I promise you, we will address the modernization of Dickens Island in the near future. But first, there are two murders that need to be solved."

"One has already been solved," someone shouted.

"Possibly," Uncle Brad conceded, "though it's far from official. It will take months, maybe years, before there's a trial and a verdict regarding William's murder."

A woman in the back row raised her hand. "Brad, isn't the burglar who broke into your niece's house now sitting in jail?"

"He is," Uncle Brad said.

"So we're down to one homicide that needs solving," Ralph said. "Can you assure us there will be an open forum to discuss modernizing the island once Missy's murderer is apprehended?"

"Well, I suppose we could start to talk about it," Uncle Brad said begrudgingly.

Hector Lewis raised his hand. "I kinda like the idea of keeping the farm a farm. This way, tourists get to see the real Dickens Island—or how it used to be."

"The real Dickens Island?!" one of Ralph's cronies shouted. "That's a laugh, since we were never a farming community."

"Did you say the farm's in disrepair?" someone else asked. "Haven't been there in years."

"Tim and Velma have been living in the farmhouse, though it's not in great shape, and it's been years since the farm's functioned at full capacity. In fact, if we decide to go with the farm museum project, the buildings will require serious renovations. But this is all a moot point until we speak to Mr. Addison and find out his intentions."

"You have it wrong, Brad. My intentions are the only ones that matter when it comes to the VanPatten Farm."

We all turned to stare at Velma VanPatten standing at the rear of the room.

"I'm sorry, Velma," Uncle Brad said, "but you and Tim have never provided us with the official deed to the farm. And now that William's remains have been found and the—er—complexity of the situation exposed, you have no claim to the property."

Velma laughed. "You mean if Tim is found guilty of offing his brother?"

"Well, yes."

"I certainly had nothing to do with William's murder. I didn't even know Tim at the time William disappeared."

"Regardless, you cannot benefit from a murder, and if Tim is found guilty, you would be benefiting from your husband's crime."

Velma dismissed his words with a wave of her hand. "Of course not. Perish the thought. But according to my lawyer, I've lived and worked on the farm for forty years. What I have are squatters' rights."

Stunned, Uncle Brad was at a loss for words.

"The VanPatten Farm is now mine. But there's no need to worry. I'm all for going ahead with selling it to Dickens Island."

Chapter Thirty-Two

Uncle Brad brought the meeting to an end. He had started to explain to Velma that her lawyer was wrong, but he stopped when she slipped out of the room and left us staring after her.

"Is that true?" I asked Jack. "Can she really claim squatters' rights?"

"You wouldn't think so, but laws involving squatters' rights are complicated."

"I've read about people taking over houses that aren't occupied and owners having a problem getting them back," I said.

"Then there's the law that a person can't benefit as the result of a crime. If Tim killed William, as I imagine he did, then he never owned the farm and Velma has no claim."

"It is complicated," I said. "Uncle Brad can have his para research it. Then he can address the matter accordingly."

We stood and joined the line of people exiting the room.

"Do you know what you'd like to do tomorrow night?" Jack asked.

"Dinner? A movie, if there's something really good playing nearby."

"I'll check both out and get back to you."

I watched Jack stride off to the parking lot as I waited for my father to finish talking to his friends.

"What did you think of Velma's performance?" Dad asked as we headed to his car.

"Very dramatic, if what she says is true."

"I don't buy it for one minute. Brad will get to the bottom of this. I hope it doesn't turn into one of those long, drawn-out cases," Dad said, sounding worried. "They could take years before they're settled. Meanwhile, the farmland will sit there unused."

"It may take time, but I think Gloria's nephew will end up selling the farm as originally planned." We climbed into my father's SUV, and I turned to him. "Dad, I'm curious. What would you like to see the property used for?"

For a minute or two, he drove on without answering. "That's a good question, Delia. I find myself somewhere in the middle between Brad's desire to keep things as they are and Reenie's push to move us into becoming a larger community. When it comes to the store, you know how difficult it is for me to make too many changes all at once. But the island needs some new projects. More housing. Maybe a small village on the shore facing Connecticut." He chuckled. "And even a ferry to Connecticut."

"Wow! I wasn't expecting that."

Dad sent me a sharp look. "Your desire to make changes in the general store has made me realize we've been standing still these past ten years. Standing still is stagnating."

I patted his arm. "I'm glad you see it that way."

* * *

By Saturday morning, it was obvious that the events of our island had caught the attention of the media in the tri-state area. We'd made the front page of *The Times*. "Murder and Mayhem

Wreak Havoc on Tranquil Dickens Island" screamed the headline of a Long Island newspaper, followed by an article about the capture and arrest of Tim VanPatten soon after his brother's remains were discovered. The next page had photos of Madison Sykes and Guy Lovett looking grim and thuggish under the headline "Local Thieves Apprehended." Wayne was going to have to feature both stories in *The Chronicle.*

Sure enough, while Connor was out walking Riley and I was finishing my second cup of coffee, my brother called. "Hi, Delia. I need a favor pronto."

"And hello to you too."

"Sorry about that. With so much happening on the island, I'm going to press a day earlier, and I need articles on the two latest criminal cases affecting our little island—your house being broken into and William VanPatten's remains getting dug up instead of pirate's treasure. And since you're involved in both of them, I'm asking if you'll please, please write two short articles—an update on what's been happening. So if you can swing this, I'll be eternally grateful."

"And?"

"And what?" Wayne asked in surprise.

"I'll reward my clever, enterprising sister, if she agrees to do this, by . . ."

"By treating her to dinner at the restaurant of her choice."

I thought a minute. "When do you need these stories?"

"ASAP."

"The latest?"

"Tomorrow morning."

"Okay, if it's dinner for two that you're offering."

"Sure, if you want Connor to come along with us."

With us? I don't think so. I laughed. "I was thinking of a dinner guest other than Connor," I said, and disconnected.

I had no idea why I wanted to include Jack when I had dinner with my brother. The idea had flashed by, and I went with it. I could always change my mind, but if I didn't, I'd ask Wayne to arrange a time when Lauren could join us.

I cleared the breakfast dishes and got to work on the two stories Wayne wanted me to write. Surprisingly, they didn't take long at all. I was simply recording what I'd seen and what I already knew. Perhaps preparing to work on the historical article had flexed my writing muscles. I read the two stories over, made a few edits, then emailed them to my brother.

Jack called midday to say a foreign film he thought we'd both enjoy was playing in a theater on Long Island.

"Sure. Sounds good," I said when he finished reading the blurb describing the film.

"I'll pick you up at six. This way, we can grab an early dinner."

Feeling virtuous for having accomplished my assignment so quickly, I drove to the supermarket to do a little food shopping. Then I stopped by the bakery to buy cookies as well as half a dozen rolls.

I was handing Jodie my credit card when I heard a grating voice. "Imagine running into you twice in one week."

"Hello, Peggy."

"I see they've caught the thieves who broke into your house. You must be relieved."

"I am."

"I spoke to Amanda this morning. I told her we had a nice chat and you're dating Jack Morrison again. She sends her love."

Jodie handed back my card and receipt. I stuck them in my pocketbook and flew out of the bakery. How had Peggy ever produced a daughter like Amanda?

* * *

At five o'clock, Connor went over to my father's for dinner. An hour later, Jack and I were heading for the ferry. We had burgers at a popular Long Island restaurant, then drove to the movie house. The foreign film was a poignant love story with funny parts that made us both laugh. Jack held my hand in the theater and on the drive home. We talked about the lovers in the film and about the goings-on on Dickens Island.

"I went to the precinct this morning to talk to Gregg," he told me as we drove onto the ferry heading back home. "I gave him the name of the people I'd been sitting with at the bar the night Missy decided to come over to my table. He said he'll be checking my story."

I laughed because Jack was obviously put out by the experience. "It can't be easy for Gregg to have to question people he's known all his life. My aunt and uncle had the same reaction as you."

"He doesn't have any viable suspects, and they never found the gun that was used to kill Missy," Jack said.

"What about Missy's ex?" I asked. "I thought he had no alibi for the night Missy was murdered."

"True, but there's no evidence linking him to the crime," Jack said. "And there's no record of his ever having owned a gun."

He walked me to my front door and kissed me tenderly. While he held me in his arms, I debated about asking him in. Before I could come to a decision, he stepped back. "I had a good time tonight."

"Me too," I said.

"Talk soon." Jack turned and walked down the steps to his Jeep.

Connor heard me come in and barreled down the stairs with Riley to tell me about his evening with my father. I told him about the French film I'd seen. It felt good coming home to my son and having a normal conversation. But getting ready for bed, my thoughts turned to Jack and our evening together. I was puzzled by the abrupt way he'd left.

Was Jack shying away from getting involved with me again? Was I? What did I want? The truth was, I didn't know.

* * *

The next morning, to help me sort out my conflicted emotions, I decided to finally give my old friend Amanda a call. She was thrilled to hear from me, just as Peggy said she would be. I was in luck. She was out on her five-mile walk, which she managed to do a few mornings each week. Amanda was as warm and caring as ever, eager to hear about my life and to tell me about hers. At first, we talked about our kids. I told her how often I wondered if I was making the right decisions regarding Connor.

Amanda laughed. "I think every parent who takes parenting seriously feels that way at times. But from what you've told me, Connor is thriving."

"He seems to be. Lately, we've even been having conversations."

She laughed again. "That's more than many parents can say about their relationships with their teenagers."

Amanda knew all about Missy's murder and the fact that our house had been robbed.

"You know my mother. She's up on everything that goes on on Dickens Island. Besides, that information's on the internet, the papers, and Facebook."

"I suppose."

There was a pause, then Amanda said, "Mom told me you're seeing Jack again."

"I am. Something else I'm not sure about."

"How does it feel to be spending time with him again?"

"Good. Wonderful. Then I think about the way he ended it with me, and I worry he'll hurt me again."

"What's your sense of him now?"

"He's got his head on straight," I said. "He told me he broke things off with me because he realized he was falling in love with me and that frightened him."

"So he admitted that," Amanda mused. "I think that says a lot. And things are going well?"

"They were, but now I'm not sure. Last night he kissed me good night and left suddenly. I'm thinking maybe he's having second thoughts about us."

"Or could be he's picking up signals from you, that you're being cautious."

"Maybe," I agreed. "But how will I know?"

"Ask him," Amanda said.

"Just—ask him?"

"Uh-huh. Just a sec."

Amanda had to take another call. She was back a minute later. "Sorry, Delia. That was my daughter. She wants me to pick her up at her friend's house ASAP. They had a fight. I need to call my friend and find out what happened."

"Okay."

"We'll talk again soon. Better yet, let's get together. I'll call you in the next few days and we'll make a date."

I smiled as I disconnected the call, glad that I'd reached out to Amanda. Talking to her had left me feeling better about things in general. Connecting with my old friend who knew me so well helped remind me that I was capable of deciding what I wanted from my relationship with Jack. Maybe I simply needed more time.

Jack called after dinner to say hello and to ask me out for the following Saturday night. We chatted for a while. *Maybe he needs to take things slow too,* I thought when I said good night. And that was all right too.

Chapter Thirty-Three

On Monday morning, Gregg called me with the good news that the police in Riverhead had been able to locate my stolen pin. I went to the police station to retrieve it. He handed it over with a smile. "We'll be keeping the copy of the map as evidence, if you don't mind."

I shuddered. "Be my guest. I wish Connor had never discovered that log supposedly written by Captain Kidd."

Gregg slipped on a pair of gloves and showed me the map, now stained with dirt. "How ironic that Maddie and her boyfriend dug up bones instead of a treasure."

"That map is far from precise. Connor and Trevor went digging in a completely different area."

Gregg laughed. "I think the map is phony."

"I do too. Maybe the log is fake too."

"Someone probably just stuck that poor excuse for a map in the log ages ago. But the log, from the way you described it, might be authentic. You should have it appraised. "

"Oh, I intend to," I said, making a mental note to work on that very soon.

After Gregg had me sign the necessary form saying he'd released the pin to me, I asked for an update on Maddie and her boyfriend.

"They both will be charged—differently, of course, since Maddie didn't break into your house. Most likely, her charges will end up being dismissed."

I grimaced. "She planned the break-in and deserves whatever her boyfriend gets."

Gregg turned up his palms. "I'm with you, but that's not always how it turns out."

"And Tim?" I asked.

"He's being held in the Sheriff's Office in Riverhead. The DA felt that his taking over the farm without a deed or letter to show ownership, coupled with running as soon as he heard William's remains had been discovered, were enough circumstantial evidence to keep him. But I'm afraid, without visible evidence or a confession, they'll have to let him go soon."

More disappointing news, I thought. "You can't expect evidence of a murder from over forty years ago to suddenly turn up."

"That's true, Delia. But this case is full of surprises. Maybe we'll be lucky and get a few more."

"Is Jack off the hook?" I asked.

"Looks that way. I spoke to the people he was with the night someone saw him with Missy at the bar. They backed up Jack's story." Gregg grinned. "And we have a new lead. We managed to reach all the homeowners in the vicinity of the Faraday house to find out if any have a security camera. Sure enough, one does."

"And it shows someone entering Missy's house that night?"

"It shows someone approaching the house after midnight."

"That's great news. Is it Peter Maris?"

"I'm not at liberty to say until everything's checked out," Gregg said. "But I've got a feeling we're finally getting closer to solving Missy's murder."

Back home, I put away Helena's antique pin, then took Riley for a long walk.

Connor called me from school to ask if Trevor could have dinner at our house.

"Sure," I said. "Any special reason why?"

"Maddie found out we were watching them dig. She's angry at Trevor and blames him for getting caught."

"But Trevor didn't call the police. I did."

"I know that. I think Maddie's mad at Trevor because she can't boss him around anymore and tell him what to do."

"Tell Trevor he's welcome at our house anytime."

"Thanks, Mom. See ya soon."

I gave Riley a few treats, then went into the secret room hoping that Helena would show up so I could bring her up to date on the happenings on our little island. Riley followed me into the small room. I sat in the chair, and he hunkered down beside me.

I patted his flank, noting that his coat was starting to grow in. "You like coming here when I meet Helena," I said. "Are you a descendent of Duncan, Helena's Beardie?"

Riley wagged his tail and licked my hand.

"Of course you aren't. That would be too much of a coincidence."

I called to my grandmother, and eventually she appeared.

"Hello, Delia. Vibrations of stress and discord are emanating from Dickens Island, strong enough to churn up the waters of the Sound."

"I'm afraid we're in a state of upheaval," I admitted. "Tim's in jail facing homicide charges, though he'll probably be out soon for lack of proof. Now Velma's claiming the farm is hers based on squatters' rights."

Helena chuckled. "That Velma is a piece of work. Did she tell the police Tim confessed to her that he murdered William?"

"I don't know, but from her stand on the matter at the meeting Friday night, it sure looks that way."

"I always suspected Velma would do anything for money, including turning on her husband—not that Tim doesn't deserve it."

"Not if he killed his own brother," I agreed. "Uncle Brad is looking into her claim. I'm hoping she can't benefit from Tim's actions. There's a good possibility the farm now legally belongs to William and Tim's sister, Gloria."

"Last time we spoke, you said that Gloria has Alzheimer's."

"Yes, and she's failing. Her nephew has power of attorney, and he's also her heir. Before Velma made her proclamation at the meeting, Uncle Brad assumed we'd be dealing with him."

Helena sighed. "How I wish I could see Gloria one last time."

"Were you and Gloria close?" I asked.

"At one time, we were very close."

"Oh." I finally got it. Helena wasn't in love with William when they were young. She and Gloria were—together. I stared at my grandmother.

"Am I shocking you?" Helena had an amused smile on her face.

"I'm—surprised, that's all. I . . ." I didn't know what else to say.

Helena laughed. "I know how difficult it must be, learning about your grandmother's unexpected love life."

"But you married Grandpa," I said. "You had children."

"I did." Helena nodded. "I put all my energies into living the typical life of a middle-class woman of my time. It wasn't easy. I loved your grandfather for being the good person that he was, and I mourned him when he died so young, but the truth is, I don't know if our marriage would have survived."

"It must have been so difficult for you," I said, "being married to Grandpa and loving someone else." *A woman.*

"We'll talk about this another time," she said. "Now let's focus on what's happening here on the island."

I smiled. "One good thing. The police were able to get back the antique pin you gave me."

Helena waved her hand. "That pin is more trouble than it's worth. Your grandfather gave it to me when I gave birth to your father. It's so ornate, I only wore it once or twice." She grinned. "I bet you've never worn it."

"Maybe not, but I love it because you gave it to me."

"I appreciate the sentiment," Helena said. "Any new leads on Missy's murder?"

"Gregg told me a security camera filmed someone in the area around the time of the murder. He wouldn't say who, but I think it was Missy's ex. Gregg didn't mention if a black car was parked near her house at the same time."

"Have the police looked into who owns a black car?"

"Gregg said they did. And they still haven't found the gun used to kill Missy. "

Helena pressed her lips together. "There has to be a reason why Missy was targeted. The killer had it in for her and wanted her out of the way."

"It sure looks that way. But the question is, why."

"How is Connor doing?" Helena asked.

"Great. He and Trevor made up. In fact, they're closer than ever since Trevor told us how angry he is at his sister. He's been spending more time here with us. He feels alienated from his family."

"The Slippery Sykes is what some people call them. Others call them worse. I'm glad Trevor has the good sense to want to break away from them."

"I don't know about breaking away from them," I said.

"He'll have to, Delia, if he doesn't want to end up stealing and cheating like his parents and his sister. I hope he'll have a haven with you and Connor. He needs a base with good, honest folk."

"As I told Trevor, he's welcome here anytime."

Helena was smiling as she faded from sight. "Goodbye, Delia. We'll talk again soon."

* * *

My thoughts spun in my head as I prepared dinner for Connor, Trevor, and myself. To think my grandmother had been in love with a woman! Did my father or uncle have any idea about their mother's inner life? Did Helena have other lovers? I'd never heard that she did. This was one huge secret she had kept, one she wouldn't have to keep today. Or so I'd like to think.

My curiosity shifted to Helena's comment about Missy. Why *did* someone want Missy dead? Who besides her ex-boyfriend even had strong feelings about her? I shuddered as Aunt Reenie came to mind, but I couldn't conceive of my aunt killing Missy, or anyone, for that matter.

Had Missy offended someone? Did she have something the murderer wanted? I doubted that since the house hadn't been ransacked the night she'd been murdered—sure signs of a search. And there were no reports of anyone breaking into Missy's house afterward.

Maybe the murderer was after the house itself. It was a lovely Victorian, somewhat smaller than the house Helena had left me and where I now lived. In fact, both houses had been designed and built by the same architect and builder. But unlike the Van-Patten Farm, no one was claiming the Faraday house. Since Missy hadn't made a will, the house would go to the state and eventually to the island.

Unable to come up with a reason why someone might want to murder Missy, I allowed myself to mull over what Helena had said about Trevor. Given her insight and the many years she'd spent teaching elementary school, I wasn't surprised by her keen assessment of what he'd need in order to have a chance at a good future. She knew enough about the Sykes family to foresee the problem Trevor would have if he no longer went along with their "family first" rule. As I'd told her, Trevor was welcome to spend time with Connor and me whenever he wanted. I chuckled, finding it ironic that while I worried about being a good enough mother for Connor, Helena considered me a safe haven for Trevor Sykes.

* * *

At dinner, Connor and Trevor kept up a running conversation about sports, other kids in school, and TV shows they watched. They teased each other in a good-natured way, occasionally including me in their banter. They complimented me on the food, and both ate enough to prove that they were enjoying their meal. I was glad to see them both so happy.

Afterward, the boys took Riley for a walk while I loaded the dishwasher. I asked Trevor if he'd like me to drive him home. He hesitated, then accepted my offer. Connor went upstairs to do his homework.

"Thanks again for dinner, Mrs. D," Trevor said as I pulled into the Sykes' driveway.

"You're welcome, Trevor. Come again soon."

He shot me a grin. "You bet I will. Your house is so much fun!"

My house is so much fun? I waited till Trevor crossed the cracked walkway and let himself in. The kid was beginning to grow on me.

I made a U-turn and started for home but found myself driving past my house and continuing in the direction of town. I made a left on Clydesdale Road and drove the half block to number 17, where Missy Faraday had lived all her life. I stopped in front of the Victorian house. The drapes were drawn, the blinds closed, but there was a glimmer of light showing through a break in the curtains in an upstairs room.

I felt a thrill of excitement. Someone was in Missy's house! Was it the murderer, searching for whatever he or she was after? I looked around to see what cars were in the vicinity. No car was parked in the driveway. I drove farther down the block and burst out laughing when I spotted my uncle's Lexus. Parked in front of it was Aunt Reenie's red Rav4.

What on earth were they looking for in Missy's house? I turned around and pulled into Missy's driveway and rang the bell. When no one came to the door, I rapped the knocker several times. The drape in a downstairs window moved aside a few inches. A minute later, the front door opened.

"Delia, what are you doing here?" my uncle hissed.

"What are you and Aunt Reenie doing here?"

"How did you—? Never mind. Come inside! Gregg gave us the okay, and we're looking for evidence. Now that you're here, we can use your help."

"Sure. I'm happy to." I entered the house just as my aunt traipsed down the stairs.

"There's nothing upstairs that I could see. Hi, Delia," she greeted me when she saw me there. "What brings you here tonight?"

"I don't know exactly. I've been thinking about Missy and trying to imagine why anyone would want to murder her. But why are you and Uncle Brad here?"

"Let's sit down in the family room and chat," Uncle Brad said. "I could use a break."

The layout of the house was similar to mine, but on a smaller scale. I followed my aunt and uncle into the family room. Two fabric recliners, with a sofa between them, faced a large TV screen. My aunt and uncle chose to sit side by side on the sofa, so I perched on one of the recliners and turned to face them.

"Gregg and Billy have thoroughly searched the house, looking for important papers like the deed to the house and property tax records. They came up with zilch," Aunt Reenie said.

Uncle Brad was shaking his head. "I don't know how many times I advised Missy to make a will after her father died, but she kept putting it off."

I looked around. "Missy must have had a laptop."

"Oh, she did," Aunt Reenie said. "It's upstairs. She kept a pile of credit card statements, and I found her bank statements and income tax records for the past ten years."

"What an odd coincidence that the deeds to both the farm and this house are missing," I mused.

"And both are linked to murder victims," Aunt Reenie said.

"True, though there's no connection between the two murders," Uncle Brad said.

"None that we know of." Aunt Reenie got to her feet. "I'm going back upstairs to finish going through the file cabinet in the room Missy and her father used as an office. Though from what I've seen, it's all copies of tax returns of the few clients Frank kept these past seven years. I don't expect to find anything personal or related to the house, but you never know."

"I was about to tackle the desk in the kitchen," Uncle Brad said as he stood. "Delia, we found a few items stashed in one of the drum table drawers in the living room. There's another drum table and an antique desk under the window in the living room. See if there are any papers in them."

"Examine the table and the desk for a possible secret panel or false bottom," Aunt Reenie said. "They're antiques. Who knows what they're hiding."

"Will do," I said. "I suppose you've already checked with local banks to find out if Missy had a safety deposit box."

"We did, and she didn't," Uncle Brad said. "All right. Let's get to work and not make this an all-night affair."

Aunt Reenie got a glint in her eye I knew well. She opened her mouth to come back with a caustic comment but thought better of it.

I waited until she'd reached the second floor, then went into the kitchen where Uncle Brad was dumping the contents of the desk drawer onto the table. "Did you and Aunt Reenie make up?"

"No, but I think we're getting there."

Not if you keep micromanaging, you won't. "Whose idea was it to go through the house in search of the deed?"

"Mine." He grinned. "But she went along with the idea."

"At least you can agree on some things," I said. "But to really get back into her good graces, you'll have to start meeting her halfway when it comes to island issues."

"I thought you were here to help, not play marriage counselor."

It was worth a try. "I'll go in search of hidden drawers and important papers."

There wasn't much in either of the drum table drawers. The antique desk—made of beautiful rosewood with curved cabriole legs and five drawers—held more promise. I found a few old charge card receipts in the long center drawer, and odds and ends in the four smaller drawers. Something inspired me to pull out each of the drawers. A very small envelope was affixed to the bottom of the left-hand drawer. I removed it and opened it up. Inside was a key.

"Look what I found," I said as I showed the key to Uncle Brad.

"Now that's interesting. He followed me back into the living room. We looked around to see what the key might open. There were wall-mounted cabinets filled with figurines on both sides of the bookcase that took up most of the long wall of the living room. I felt a surge of excitement when I noticed they had key holes. But they were too large for the key I held in my hand.

"What about the credenza in the dining room?" Uncle Brad suggested.

We tried the credenza filled with two sets of dishes, but the key didn't fit, and the doors opened readily.

"What are you doing?" Aunt Reenie asked.

"Trying to figure out what this key opens," I said, holding up the key.

"Find anything more upstairs?" Uncle Brad asked Aunt Reenie.

She shook her head. "What about you?"

"Nothing," Uncle Brad said.

"Too bad. I was hoping we'd find some important papers in the house."

As they chatted, I returned to the living room and started removing books from the middle shelf of the bookcase.

"What on earth are you doing?" Aunt Reenie exclaimed.

I had no intention of mentioning the secret room in my house. Of course there was a good chance Uncle Brad knew about it since he'd grown up there, but then again, maybe he didn't since he didn't bring it up. I ran my palm along the back of the bookcase, hoping to come upon a protruding button similar to the one that opened the hidden door in my house, but felt nothing.

"I've read that sometimes architects and builders include a built-in niche to store jewelry or important papers," I said. "I'm checking to see if there's one in this house."

Though I was disappointed, I started removing the books from the higher shelf. I gave a shout of glee when I felt a square knob protruding, similar to the one in the bookcase in my house. I tugged on it, and though it moved a bit, there was no opening the compartment until all the books on the shelf, on the shelf above, and the shelves themselves were moved out of the way.

Finally, the door opened, revealing a space the size of a large medicine cabinet only considerably deeper. Inside was a metal box like the large safety deposit boxes you could rent at a bank.

"Look what's here!" I exclaimed.

"Good for you, Delia!" Uncle Brad hugged me.

Eagerly, I reached for the small key that had been taped under the desk drawer. It slid easily into the keyhole. "Voilà!" I opened the box, exposing a large manila envelope. Beneath it were two smaller envelopes.

"I think we're about to find everything we're looking for and more," Aunt Reenie said.

Chapter Thirty-Four

I carried the box into the dining room and set it down on the long wooden table. Aunt Reenie reached for the manila envelope and spilled out its contents for us to see.

"Just what we need," she said. "The deed to the house and property tax returns for the past five years."

"And here's a copy of Frank's will, leaving everything he owned to his daughter, Melissa Faraday," Uncle Brad said. "Now, if only Missy had agreed to have me draw up a will, the paperwork would in order."

Aunt Reenie reached behind me to rub her husband's shoulder. "Still, this is very helpful and will facilitate our getting possession of the house quickly."

"You're right, Reenie. Thanks to our clever niece."

They each kissed a side of my face, the way they used to when I was a little girl.

"Okay," I said, embarrassed, "there are two more envelopes. Let's see what's in this one."

I opened the number ten envelope. It held a three-page form yellowed with age that was folded in thirds. I unfolded it carefully.

"Oh my God!" Aunt Reenie exclaimed. "These are adoption papers. Brad, did you know that Missy was adopted?"

"No, but Missy had started to think she was. According to this, her mother was Adele Parsons."

"And it says her father is William VanPatten!" I said.

"Let's see what the smaller envelope has to offer," Uncle Brad said.

I picked up the smaller envelope and drew out a folded piece of paper. The page was filled with cursive writing in a neat, masculine handwriting.

"What is it, Delia?" Uncle Brad asked.

"A letter Frank wrote to Missy. It's dated August of last year."

"He wrote it shortly before he died," Uncle Brad said.

"Frank must have planned to give her the letter or leave it for her when he died," Aunt Reenie said, "but was suddenly too weak to retrieve it from its hiding place."

"Yes," Uncle Brad and I both said.

"Dear Missy," I read aloud.

> "When you read this, I will be gone. I hope you won't be too sad at my passing. I have lived a long life, and you have been a wonderful daughter. You gave your mother and me a great deal of joy.
>
> There is something important I need to tell you, something your mother and I wished we'd shared with you many years ago. Each time we considered doing it, something momentous was happening in your life, and we were reluctant to add to the turmoil. And so we delayed and delayed, until we've come to this point in time.
>
> Your mother and I discovered we were unable to have children. While on vacation in upstate New York, we met a very pregnant, very unhappy young woman.

Her name was Adele Parsons, and she's your birth mother. Adele told us she'd been abandoned by your father. She was staying with her aunt until she gave birth because her parents had disowned her. Adele insisted there was no way she could take care of you on her own. Essie and I knew immediately that we wanted to adopt you, and Adele accepted our offer. We made the necessary arrangements, and you became our Melissa as soon as you left the hospital. Sadly, your birth mother developed an infection that led to a high fever. She died when you were only seven days old.

Missy, my sweetheart, though this must come as a shock, I hope you come to realize that this fact about your birth makes no change in your life. Essie and I adored you from the moment you were born and couldn't possibly have loved you any more if you were of our own flesh and blood. You are the child of our hearts, and everything I possess now belongs to you.

Your mother and I tried to find out more about Adele's family. We wrote to her parents, but they never responded. Your father's family is another story. You were almost two years old when we moved to Dickens Island. We ended up buying produce at the VanPatten Farm and learned that, years earlier, the farm was owned and run by Tim VanPatten's older brother, William. When I asked Tim about William, he gave me the strangest look and said William took off for parts unknown, and he and his wife now owned the farm.

I'm not proud to say I let the fact that Tim and his wife are rather gruff, unfriendly people kept me from telling him you were probably his niece. I let the matter slide. I shouldn't have. Your mother and I found it eerie that you were always drawn to the farm and even worked there one summer when you were in high school. It was only in later years that I began to wonder if the farm might actually belong to you. But again, I delayed taking action. I'm ashamed to admit that I never looked into this matter, though of course it could very well be that Tim and Velma are the rightful owners."

Though there was another paragraph, I stopped reading.

"That's quite a story," Uncle Brad said.

"So, maybe the two murders are connected after all," Aunt Reenie mused.

Uncle Brad was nodding as he thought. "If Missy was William's child, and Tim has no bill of sale, then she probably *was* the rightful heir to the farm."

"So Tim killed them both," I surmised.

"Let's not jump to conclusions," Uncle Brad said.

"As soon as he heard his brother's remains were found, he couldn't get off the island fast enough," I reminded him.

"That's still not proof that he killed William."

"Velma claims the farm is hers, implying that Tim killed his brother. He must have admitted it to her," I said.

"Except she never said that, did she?" Uncle Brad said. "And even if she had, it's still only circumstantial. In order to convict Tim of murder, they need evidence or a confession, and I don't see either happening. Gregg and Billy searched the farm for the gun that killed William and couldn't find it,"

"Both father and daughter were shot to death," Aunt Reenie pointed out.

"Certainly not with the same gun," I said.

Aunt Reenie made a scoffing sound. "Tim's not an idiot. He wouldn't keep a murder weapon around for over forty years."

"But no one ever considered him a killer," I said.

"A bullet was found among William's remains," Uncle Brad said.

"You're thinking . . . ?" Aunt Reenie said.

"It's possible," my uncle agreed.

"Brad, you're so clever!"

Behind me, my aunt and uncle were locked in a fierce embrace. Who would think that solving a murder or two would bring them together?

Only it didn't, of course. They released each other just as quickly, stepped back a foot or two, and returned to island-business mode.

"That's quite a discovery we made tonight," Aunt Reenie said, "thanks to Delia."

"It sure is," Uncle Brad agreed.

I slipped the papers back into their respective envelopes, placed them beside the metal box, and locked it.

"We should hand all of this over to Gregg ASAP," Aunt Reenie said.

"I will, after I make a copy of everything," my uncle agreed.

"And the key?" I asked.

My aunt and uncle exchanged glances. "Why don't you lock the wall cabinet and give the key to your uncle?" Aunt Reenie said. "He can give it to Gregg when he hands over the papers we've discovered."

We returned to the living room. I locked the cabinet and handed the key to Uncle Brad. Then the three of us put the bookcase shelves and books back in place. I walked out with Aunt Reenie and Uncle Brad, kissed them both good night, and got into my car. I watched them hug briefly, then go to their own cars. I was disappointed not to see . . . What? A passionate kiss? A romantic embrace? They had come here tonight in search of some answers regarding an island issue. They had both remained civil. Uncle Brad hadn't been argumentative. Aunt Reenie hadn't made any snide remarks. Still, I saw no sign of their getting back together again as a married couple.

For all I knew, it wouldn't happen at all.

* * *

"Jack called," Connor said when I came into the house. He was in the kitchen eating. Riley was at his side. "On your cell phone. You didn't bring it with you. What took you so long? You drove Trevor home ages ago. I was beginning to worry that something happened to you."

Teenagers worry about their parents? "Sorry. I saw lights on in Missy Faraday's house and found Uncle Brad and Aunt Reenie giving it the once-over, so I decided to join them."

"Find any clues?"

"Some papers that might prove useful. Uncle Brad has them. He'll hand them over to the police."

Connor didn't ask about them, and I was happy not to explain.

I went into the family room and called Jack.

"How would you like to have dinner at an Indian restaurant Saturday night?"

"Sure. I love Indian food," I told him. He said he'd get back to me regarding the time after he called to make a reservation.

"Something exciting's happened, hasn't it?" he said.

"You can tell?"

"Of course."

"Something has, but I don't want to go into it now."

"I can't wait to hear about it Saturday night."

"Till then," I said.

We both laughed. I loved the sound of Jack's laughter. It was so cheerful and masculine.

"I'm looking forward to seeing you," he said.

I hesitated, then said, "Me too."

Connor appeared in the doorway. "I'm going upstairs."

"Okay. I'll take Riley out now."

"See you in the morning." He came over and planted a kiss on my cheek.

"Don't stay up too late."

He rolled his eyes.

The evening's discoveries had revved up my excitement. I was bursting with energy, my thoughts shooting off in all directions. Instead of taking the path that ran along the shore, I found myself walking along the street that led back to the Faraday house. Essie and Frank had adopted Missy. They'd found out early on that she was William VanPatten's daughter but never told Missy. I wondered if they'd ever told anyone who lived on Dickens Island. If they had, perhaps Tim found out somehow and murdered Frank and later Missy.

No, I remembered that Frank had been ill and died in the hospital. If Tim had no idea that Missy was his niece, then he had no reason to kill her. It struck me that we might be on the wrong track completely. There was still Missy's ex to consider. All I knew was that now, more than ever, I wanted to help catch the person who had murdered Missy.

I was deep in thought when Riley began to growl. The sound startled me.

I turned around and saw a car behind me. It was driving on the wrong side of the road. I jumped to my left, into the narrow space between two bushes. The speeding car created a breeze as it passed inches from me, its wheels squealing as it disappeared into the night.

I'd been unable to make out the license plate or see who was inside the vehicle, but I thought it was black—the same as the car Missy claimed had tried to run her down.

Chapter Thirty-Five

I called Gregg when I got home and left a message on his cell phone. He called me back ten minutes later.

"Hi, Delia. It's been a long day." He exhaled loudly. "I'm finally on my way home after finishing the paperwork for Tim VanPatten's release."

"You released Tim VanPatten? When? Why?"

"Two hours ago. He hired a top lawyer who insisted that we let him go." Another deep exhale. "Since we only have circumstantial evidence, I can't hold him any longer."

"Soon as he heard his brother's body was exhumed, off he ran," I said.

"That doesn't prove that he killed William. We need more than that to arraign him and bring him to trial."

I made a scoffing sound. "Velma all but said the farm was hers since Tim was guilty of killing his brother."

"Except she never said that exactly. Even if she had, it's still only circumstantial," Gregg said, repeating what Uncle Brad had told me earlier. He released another deep sigh. "Believe me,

I'll be questioning Tim VanPatten again, with or without his expensive lawyer."

"Gregg, someone tried to run me down a few minutes ago. Or maybe they were just trying to scare me. I was walking my dog near the Davenport house. I think the car was black like the one Missy said almost hit her. Maybe it was Tim VanPatten. You said you released him two hours ago."

"Are you all right?"

"I'm okay."

"That's a relief. I appreciate your telling me about the incident, and I'm glad you weren't injured. I'm pretty sure Tim drives a truck."

"He might also have a car that's black."

"Delia, lots of people have black cars."

"I'm sure you checked to see if any of the people connected to Missy's murder drive a black car."

"Of course I did, and there are a few: her ex-boyfriend; Jodie Reinking, who owns the bakery where Missy worked; and your uncle Brad."

"It wasn't Uncle Brad's car. I would have recognized it."

"In the dark?"

I let out a sound of exasperation. "I was with Uncle Brad earlier this evening. We were with Aunt Reenie going through Missy's house. Did you know Frank and Essie had adopted Missy?"

"I had no idea. How did you find out?"

"There's a secret niche hidden behind the bookcase. We found the adoption papers and a letter that Frank had written to Missy but never got to give to her."

"Where are these papers? Why weren't they brought to the station?"

Oops. Me and my big mouth. "Uncle Brad will bring them to you tomorrow. I called to tell you about the car that almost knocked me down."

"I'm glad you escaped unharmed, and I'll certainly look into it tomorrow. Sleep well, Delia. And please leave the investigating to me and my men."

Well, that was no help, I thought. Tim VanPatten was out and about and Gregg had the nerve to suggest that Uncle Brad might have tried to run me down. But the fact that he hadn't known Missy was adopted was interesting. I wondered if Helena knew. I went into the secret room and sat down in the chair, hoping she'd show up. Thankfully, she appeared five minutes later.

"Twice in one day," Helena said. "I'm honored."

"A lot happened this evening." I told her about going to the Faraday house and what we found there. "Did you know that Frank and Essie adopted Missy?"

"No, I didn't. The three Faradays moved to the island when Missy was very young. But it was strange . . ."

"Yes?" I prompted.

"I didn't notice it when Missy was my student, but when she was a teenager, I was startled by how much she resembled Gloria."

"That's interesting," I said.

"I wasn't the only one," Helena said. "One or two people mentioned it to me in passing. I kept the photo album from my high school days. You can see for yourself how much she looked like Gloria."

Helena pointed to the other end of the bookcase where I'd found her journals, and I picked up the album. The black pages held old-fashioned photos with zigzag edges. Some were black and white, others were in color. All were photos of the same two boys and two girls, though the number of people in each photo varied. All had been taken at the VanPatten Farm.

I paused to study a picture of two teenaged girls standing in front of a barn, their arms around each other's waists. I recognized Helena, her fair hair in disarray, a grin showing how happy she was. Gloria was tall and slender, and very pretty.

"Missy looked just like her!" I exclaimed.

"Yes, she did.

"Frank wrote that Missy was drawn to the farm. I wonder if Tim ever noticed how much she looked like his sister," I mused.

"If he even noticed," Helena said. "And why would he be suspicious that Missy was his niece? He never knew Adele was pregnant. William didn't even know. Nobody knew but me, and I had no idea there was a connection."

"What was Missy like as a student?" I said.

Helena pressed her lips together. "She had learning disabilities, and a few personality issues that grew more apparent every year. I think these days she would have been diagnosed as bipolar. The few times I suggested that Missy be tested, Essie got angry that I dared to insinuate something was wrong with her daughter. She and Frank hired a tutor to help Missy with her schoolwork. That worked for a while, until Missy resented having additional work.

"At that time, the kids went to junior and senior high school on Long Island. Missy got in with the wrong crowd and started cutting classes." Helena exhaled. "She was a handful. By the time she was sixteen, she was running wild. She had an older boyfriend and started staying out all night. Essie and Frank were frantic. Then Essie got sick and Missy changed. It was the most amazing thing. She became a devoted daughter, spending her afternoons in Essie's sick room.

"She was devastated when her mother died. She managed to finish high school by the skin of her teeth and settled down." Helena gave a little laugh. "Well, settled down for Missy. She couldn't keep a job for more than three months and kept getting involved with the poorest excuses for men. But she was always pleasant and cheerful and completely devoted to her father. She was too flirtatious for her own good, but I think that was part of her bipolar disorder."

"I'm glad you told me all this," I said. "It gives me a better understanding of Missy. I suppose Uncle Brad knew she had problems, which was why he was so kind to her."

Helena nodded slowly. "That boy always had a soft spot for vulnerable people and animals."

I skimmed through the photos and came upon a loose one at the end.

"Who is this?" I held up the photo of a young woman. She was sitting in a garden and had a sad expression.

"That's Adele. I took it when she was staying at that small hotel," Helena said.

"Frank mentioned Adele in the letter he wrote to Missy but never gave her. In it, he claimed he and Essie never found the right time to tell her she was adopted."

"Never found the right time in all those years?" Helena scoffed. "Hard to believe. I think they simply shied away from a subject they found difficult to broach."

"I'd like to show this photo of Adele to Tim VanPatten and see his reaction when I tell him I know Adele was Missy's mother and his brother was her father. He figured out that Missy was his niece, and that's why he murdered her!"

"Cordelia Dickens, don't you go putting yourself in danger! Let the police link the two murders and find the evidence they need."

"Yes, Helena," I said meekly.

"I mean it," Helena said sternly. "Gregg Fanning is intelligent, and he worked in homicide before coming back to Dickens Island. The adoption papers alone testify that Missy was William's daughter. Once you've told him everything I told you about William, Tim, and Adele's story, Gregg will understand how angry Tim must have been when Adele broke their engagement and fell for his older brother. He'll investigate further to prove that the two murders are connected."

"I can't very well tell Gregg you told me all this—er, in this form."

Helena burst out laughing. "Of course not! Tell him I told you about my friendship with the three VanPatten siblings and Adele a long time ago, and be sure to include that I knew Adele was pregnant. Reading Frank's letter stirred your memory. You went looking for information in my journals and came upon this photo of Adele. That should be enough to convince Gregg there's a connection between the two homicide victims."

"I sure hope so." But I was speaking to myself. Helena had vanished.

Chapter Thirty-Six

On Wednesday morning, I took the ferry and drove to the Long Island Railroad station in Riverhead. The Captain Kidd journal and the "treasure" map were in my tote bag. Ten minutes later, I hopped on the train to Penn Station. I had a noon appointment with Gerald Edelson, an archivist who specialized in antique naval logs, to have them analyzed.

It was a lovely sunny day, perfect for a train ride into Manhattan. Since it was past the morning rush hour, I had few companions in the car I occupied. The relative quiet gave me the opportunity to let my thoughts swarm freely in my mind.

The mysteries surrounding the two murders were being revealed, one by one. The adoption papers were solid proof that the two victims were related. And once the bullets used to murder them both were tested, we'd know if they'd been shot by the same gun. Not much of a chance, of course, since more than forty years separated the two homicides.

I shook my head. Getting valuable information from a ghost was difficult enough. Getting the police to follow up on it was another.

I exited Penn Station and hailed a taxi. Mr. Edelson's office was in a gallery on the East Side in the mid Seventies. As I rode north on Madison Avenue, I gazed out the cab's window as eagerly as any tourist. Working in the city all those years had rarely given me the opportunity for a midday drive.

A very slender, very shapely young woman in a black midi dress and stiletto knee-high boots greeted me as I entered the gallery. When I told her why I was there, she directed me straight back to the office on the right. I passed giant, colorful oil paintings and free-form sculptures on stands as I made my way to the elderly gentleman who stood waiting for me.

Mr. Edelson and I exchanged greetings. His eyes lit up when I handed over the log and the map. After studying the log's cover for a long minute, he told me to return in three hours for his report.

It was a short walk over to my old apartment where I was having lunch with my mother. I opened the door to the aroma of a freshly baked quiche, one of my mother's specialties. Mom greeted me with a warm hug and a kiss on each cheek, enveloping me in a circle of warmth and belonging.

"Lunch will be ready in five minutes," she said as I followed her into the kitchen. "A glass of Chardonnay?"

"Most definitely. I don't lunch like this very often."

"Neither do I." She reached into the fridge for the bottle of wine that was already uncorked and poured a generous amount into both glasses. We sat in the padded kitchen chairs and faced each other.

"So, how is everyone back home?" Mom asked. She looked lovely as always in her sky-blue silk tunic and jeans, her hair subtly highlighted and shaped perfectly to fall inches below her shoulders. The total Manhattanite.

"Fine. Dad misses you."

"He said so?"

"Not in so many words, but I can tell."

Mom raised her eyebrows and sipped her wine.

"When are you coming home?"

"Soon."

How soon? I longed to say but knew better than to ask.

"How's Connor?"

"He's fine. We're getting used to living together. With our new dog."

"Dog?"

I told Mom about Riley. "And Trevor Sykes is over quite a bit. I'm growing fond of him."

"I'm not surprised. He'll be fine as soon as he's free of that family of his. Anything new on Missy's case?"

I told my mother what my aunt and uncle and I had discovered the night before.

"Interesting," she mused in such a way that I wondered if she was referring to Frank's letter or to Aunt Reenie and Uncle Brad being there together. "And you've turned everything over to Gregg?"

"Of course. At least Uncle Brad will as soon as he's made copies." To change the subject, I asked, "What have you been up to?"

"Would you believe I've started writing a novel."

"Oh. Another writer in the family."

"Your brother suggested I take a short-story writing class at the New School with a friend of his. The novel grew out of the story I wrote as a class assignment." Mom beamed with excitement. "A few of us formed a critique group. We meet once a week."

"That sounds . . . exciting," I said.

"You don't seem very excited," Mom said.

"It's just that you sound like you're settling into life here in the city."

"Oh? Do you want your apartment back?" Mom asked in a teasing tone.

The oven timer sounded.

"Our quiche is ready. Want to get the salad from the fridge? And there's iced tea or seltzer, if you prefer."

Minutes later, we were too busy eating to speak. The broccoli and mushroom quiche was outstanding, as was the beet salad. When we were finished, Mom pushed back her plate.

"I know you'd like me to give you a date when I'm moving back to the island, but I can't do that, Delia. Not yet, anyway."

"Why? We all miss you."

"Believe me, I miss you too, but if I go back now, nothing will have changed. I'll be in the same rut. I can't live like that."

"Like what exactly?" I asked, though I had a pretty good idea what she was talking about.

"Living behind the times. Seeing the general store turn into a seedy old store instead of a place that sells trendy clothes and fun items tourists would buy." She sighed. "Your father says he wants to update the store, but every time I wanted to bring in something new and different, he stopped me."

I chuckled. "Yeah. He tried to do the same thing to me."

"Tried?"

"I told him I'd quit if I couldn't make changes." I nodded. "And we're making them, believe me."

For the next fifteen minutes, Mom listened agog as I told her about the new merchandise I'd ordered and my plans for the Book Nook.

"I take my hat off to you, Delia. Your father's a stick-in-the-mud when it comes to that store."

"When it comes to the island," I said. "Uncle Brad's the same way, wanting to keep Dickens Island 'unspoiled.' Which, translated, means the way it was fifty years ago. That's part of the reason Aunt Reenie threw him out of the house."

"Don't I know it. She calls me every other day, sometimes to ask if she's being too hard on Brad. I keep telling her not to cave."

We both laughed.

"How did Helena's two sons get to be that way?" Mom mused as she stood to clear our dishes. "She always gave a thought to the island's future."

"Maybe it's because their father died so young," I said. "Something inside them wants to keep things how they were when he was alive."

"That's very insightful, Delia, and not something I ever considered." Mom served us warm apple cake with vanilla ice cream and coffee.

"Why don't you invite Dad to spend a weekend here with you?" I said.

"Maybe I will," Mom said. "Have you seen Jack again?" she asked, quickly changing the subject.

"I have." Something in my voice must have informed her that I didn't want to talk about Jack, because all she did was smile and nod.

I stood to leave and hugged my mother. "Thanks so much for a wonderful lunch."

"Feel free to drop in anytime," she quipped. "Give your father and Connor a hug for me."

"And tell them you miss them?"

"Of course."

I found myself humming as I walked back over to the gallery. It was time I had a talk with my father, and this one wasn't going to be about his brother and sister-in-law.

* * *

"The log is real enough, and I can verify it belonged to William Kidd," Mr. Edelson told me when I was comfortably ensconced on one of the two love seats in his office. "May I ask how you obtained it?"

I held out my hands and shrugged. "I found it in my grandmother's bookcase. She left me her house and everything in it. My son first came across it a month or so ago. The truth is, I have no idea if she bought it or if someone else did or when."

"Well, it's worth at least fifteen thousand dollars. I'll be happy to verify the provenance." He proceeded to tell me the many reasons why this was the genuine article. "And I'll be happy to buy it from you."

"I couldn't do that without discussing it with my son," I said.

Mr. Edelson handed me the map, which he'd placed in a plastic sleeve. "Alas, this map has nothing to do with the log or anything written in the log."

"I kind of figured that," I said, "though my son thought it would lead to treasure that Captain Kidd had buried."

Mr. Edelson laughed. Then he said, "I did read about two young people digging on your island and uncovering a corpse buried over forty ago. Don't tell me . . ."

I forced a laugh. "That had nothing to do with this map."

Mr. Edelson gave me a piercing look. "Just a coincidence, then."

I shrugged. I had no intention of telling him the truth.

I paid him his fee, and we chatted as he walked me to the door. Mr. Edelson told me what I'd kind of expected to hear—the log was real, the map was fake—but it was worth knowing for sure.

Chapter Thirty-Seven

Connor was thrilled to learn that the log had actually been written by Captain Kidd. "I'll include the log in my social studies report. I'll make a map of where his ship traveled when he wrote it."

"That will give your report a sense of authenticity. Will your teacher care that your subject was a pirate who was hanged?"

"William Kidd didn't start out as a pirate, something I plan to go into with great detail."

"Connor, as far as I'm concerned, the log belongs to you. You found it, and you can decide what to do with it—save it, donate it, or sell it. Mr. Edelson is willing to pay fifteen thousand dollars for it."

Connor's face glowed with joy. "Thanks, Mom. I'll keep it, of course."

"Unfortunately, the map has no connection to the journal. Mr. Edelson couldn't tell me what it refers to, if anything."

Connor frowned. "I figured that already. Trevor and I followed it exactly and came up with zilch. Maddie and her boyfriend did it their way and ended up finding a corpse."

I shook my head. "How they happened to choose that spot is beyond me."

Connor grinned. "Yeah, but it's a good thing they dug the guy up. Now maybe the police will find out who killed him."

"I sure hope so," I said.

Connor jumped up from the family room sofa where we'd been talking. "I gotta text Trevor to tell him the news about the log. Can I invite him to dinner?"

"Of course." I headed for the kitchen to see what I had on hand that the boys would like. I found a large lasagna that I'd recently bought in the back of the freezer, figuring it would last Connor and me two dinners, along with a package of frozen French fries.

Jack called while I was cutting up a salad.

"I made reservations for seven thirty at the Indian restaurant for Saturday night. If we catch the six forty-five ferry, we'll get there in plenty of time."

"Sounds good."

"What are you doing now?" Jack asked.

"Making dinner for Connor, Trevor, and me."

"Lucky Trevor. Sounds like he's a frequent guest."

"He likes coming here. His parents work crazy hours, and his sister isn't the most reliable when it comes to preparing meals."

Jack laughed. "First Riley, now Trevor."

"Well, I enjoy both their company." I thought a moment. "Why don't you come and join us? If you're free," I added, suddenly realizing he might have other plans. "And if you'd like to, of course. It's nothing fancy."

"I love nothing fancy. Shall I bring wine—for us, that is?"

"Always welcome."

"I should have told you, I'm in the Riverhead office. I'll take the six fifteen ferry, then stop at home to walk Baron. I hope seven fifteen isn't too late." Jack asked.

"Seven fifteen's fine. And bring Baron. Riley can use some doggie company."

"Thanks. Baron could use some too."

* * *

Baron turned out to be the guest of honor. The boys couldn't get enough of him. Finally, they let him race through the house with Riley while we had our dinner. We ended up having more than enough to eat. Trevor contributed a package of frozen appetizers that I quickly heated up, and besides a nice merlot, Jack brought soda for the boys and chocolate ice cream for dessert.

Connor, still on a high from the good news about the log, was more outgoing than he usually was with someone he didn't know well. Of course he'd met Jack a few times now, and they'd hit it off. I couldn't help but be glad that they obviously liked each other. And Jack sure knew how to relate to two fifteen-year-olds. Conversation ranged from Captain Kidd to sports to dogs.

As soon as the boys finished their ice cream, they deposited their dishes in the sink.

"Thanks, Ms. Dickens," Trevor said. "Another great dinner."

"You're most welcome, Trevor. Anytime."

"Mom, we're going upstairs to play some games," Connor said. He bounded out of the room with Trevor and the two dogs close behind.

Jack sat back and stretched out his legs while I finished loading the dishwasher.

"That was a delicious meal, Delia. And fun too."

"The boys are good company." I laughed. "And you fit right in."

"They're great kids," Jack said. "Connor's a good influence on Trevor."

"I'm so glad they got past the break-in and are closer than ever. Trevor felt awful that his sister manipulated him for information, then sent her boyfriend to rob us."

"And Connor has his genuine Captain Kidd log."

"As he's told us at least five times," I said.

We both laughed.

"So, I'm curious," Jack said. "What did you find out last night that might help solve Missy's murder?"

Just then, Baron came downstairs looking for his owner. Jack got on the floor, and they roughhoused a bit.

"Why don't we take the dogs for a walk, and I'll tell you about it?"

Jack grinned. "I thought you'd never ask."

* * *

I called up to Connor and told him to send Riley downstairs because Jack and I were taking the dogs out.

"Okay, Mom."

I slipped into my parka and clipped Riley's leash to his collar. Jack did the same with Baron. I grabbed a few plastic bags from the box I kept on the hall table and handed one to Jack. Outside, the wind was blowing, chilling my face. I pulled up my hood.

"Whew! Blustery, isn't it?" Jack exclaimed as he raised the collar of his jacket.

We started to walk in the direction of town.

"Last night, my aunt, uncle, and I spent time inside Missy's house. We discovered some important papers." I told Jack that Missy had been adopted. "Frank and Essie kept putting off telling her."

"And so Missy never found out," Jack mused.

"In the letter he wrote but never gave her, Frank mentions her birth mother's name was Adele Parsons. Coincidentally, I found a photo of Adele among my grandmother's journals."

Jack shot me a look of astonishment. "That is a weird coincidence."

I felt my cheeks grow warm. I didn't like lying to him, but I wasn't about to explain that my source was my grandmother's ghost. Not yet, anyway.

"Recently I've been reading Helena's journals. My grandmother was a distant cousin of the VanPattens and used to spend a lot of time on the farm with William, Gloria, and Tim."

"I've been to the farm a few times, but the only VanPattens I know are Tim and Velma."

"After college, Gloria and Tim moved away, and William inherited the farm. When the brothers were in their forties, Tim returned with Adele, his fiancée. Tim had bounced from place to place, job to job, and I suppose he expected his brother would give him a share of the farm. Tim and Adele settled on the farm, but Tim didn't do much work. Adele broke off the engagement when she saw him for what he was—a user and a con man.

"She and William fell in love and made plans to leave the island. Adele went to stay at a hotel on the island while William settled things with Tim, supposedly giving him the farm, as Tim told everyone. Then, instead of coming for Adele as they'd planned, *supposedly* William sent her a letter saying he was going far away. Without her."

"And actually never left the island, but ended up in a makeshift grave in the bird sanctuary," Jack finished for me.

"He never knew that Adele was pregnant with their child. Ironically, both William and Missy were shot to death."

"More than forty years apart." Jack stopped walking and turned to me. "You think Tim murdered them both?"

"Who else, unless Missy's ex murdered her? Peter Maris might have killed her because he was angry that she broke off their relationship. And he does have a black car."

"But why would Tim kill William, if William was giving him the farm?" Jack asked.

I pressed my lips together. I hadn't thought this through. "Either William wasn't planning to give him the farm—we only have Tim's word for that—or Tim was so angry that Adele chose his brother over him, he shot him and wrote a letter to Adele, supposedly from William, saying he was going away without her. Only Tim knows what happened all those years ago.

"Tim doesn't have the deed to the farm. He needs it in order to sell it to the island. If he figured out that Missy was his brother's daughter, he'd realize the farm belonged to her. That goes to motive, why Tim murdered Missy and why he ran off as soon as his brother's body was IDed."

"Lots of circumstantial evidence and possibilities, but no proof," Jack said.

"Both murders center around the VanPatten family and the farm," I said. "A coincidence?"

"From what you've just said, it's possible the two murders are connected. But considering the time span between them, I have to wonder if it makes any sense that the same person killed both victims. The fact that Missy's ex has no alibi leads me to think he might be guilty."

A car sped by. A black car.

"Did you catch the license plate number on that car?" I asked.

"No, why would I?" Jack said.

"I think it's the same car that nearly ran me down last night."

"You're saying a car intentionally tried to hit you?"

"Yes, or it meant to frighten me because I've been investigating the murders."

"Is it possible the driver didn't see you?"

"I had to jump out of the road." I exhaled a huff of irritation. "Why do you question everything I say?"

"Because it's the only way I can process what you've told me." His voice softened. "And it's my way of refusing to accept that someone is targeting you."

When I didn't answer, Jack said, "All I can say is, I'm glad the car didn't hit you last night, and I'm sorry I don't see the two murders necessarily linked the way you do."

Somewhat mollified, I said, "I can't expect you to view everything the way I do."

We waited in silence while the two dogs did their business, then we started walking back toward my house.

"What did Gregg make of the information you, Brad, and Reenie discovered?" Jack asked.

"Uncle Brad was supposed to hand everything over to him today. I haven't shown him the photo of Adele Parsons yet."

"Did your grandmother write Adele's name on the back of the photo?"

"She did." *Did she? I can't remember.*

"That's good. Otherwise, there's no proof that the woman in the photo is Adele."

"Of course." *We can't rely on a ghost's word.*

We walked back in silence. As we approached my house, Jack asked, "Are we good?"

I shrugged. "I guess so."

"You're not sure?" Jack said.

"I find it disconcerting that you question everything I tell you."

"Instead of agreeing with your suppositions automatically? This is a case of two murders where very little has been proven."

I stopped when we got to my walkway. "Shall we agree to disagree?"

"That suits me," Jack said. "As you said before, we can't expect to see everything the same way."

"Hmm."

"Are we still on for tomorrow night?" Jack asked.

"Of course." *I can always call and break the date.*

Neither of us made a move to kiss good night.

* * *

It's time to decide what to do about Jack, I told myself as I got ready for bed. He'd rarely left my thoughts in the preceding hours, and not in a good way. A few times, I actually reached for my cell phone to call and cancel our Saturday night plans.

His second-guessing everything I'd concluded regarding the two homicides really annoyed me, and that included the driver's intention the other evening. Jack thought it must have been bad judgment on the driver's part, while I was certain the driver—who else but Tim?—meant to hit me or frighten me to stop me from investigating further.

Pushing past the pain that our former breakup still evoked was like picking at a healed scab as I tried to recall how Jack had treated me all those years ago. It wasn't easy, because at sixteen I had been too smitten to think about the way he regarded me as a person—my thoughts, my dreams. At the time, I focused on what *he* did and said; how *he* looked. It had thrilled me to my core to know that he cared for me—until he no longer did.

I forced myself to continue. At nineteen, Jack was already the empathetic person that made him a wonderful vet today. He listened when I told him about my day and my observations, and he had comforted me more than once when I'd had a fight with my parents. Though I was three years younger, Jack had never put me down, even in a joking manner. But neither did he agree with me if he thought I was wrong.

We once had words about an argument I'd had with my father over something that had happened in the store. Jack had kindly but firmly told me he thought I was wrong and that I should apologize to my dad. I didn't speak to him for two days, during which time I saw the situation from Jack's perspective—and my father's.

I was forced to acknowledge that tonight Jack had reacted exactly as he always had—showing concern for me and respect for my conclusions, but not necessarily agreeing with them. I had spent hours investigating both homicides, and I was quite certain it was likely that Tim had murdered both William and Missy. I was really pissed that Jack didn't see it that way, or agree that if Tim hadn't murdered Missy, then Peter Maris was her killer. I took his not agreeing to mean that he had little regard for my judgment.

I'd been on the verge of canceling our date and refusing to see him again. Was Jack's questioning whether Tim had killed both William and Missy a reason to turn against him?

No, hurting me the way he had twenty years ago was a reason not to see him again.

"Wow!" I exclaimed aloud as the truth bomb hit. I was still angry at Jack for ghosting me twenty years ago, and it was coming out in different ways.

Riley, who had just poked his head in my room, cocked his head and gave me a quizzical smile.

I petted his flank. "I just had a big breakthrough. Nothing to be concerned about."

I got into bed and turned out the light. As though he sensed I'd appreciate his company, Riley settled himself on the floor beside me, and we both fell asleep.

Chapter Thirty-Eight

At the Indian restaurant, the smiling maitre d' led us to a curved banquette for two that, though we were situated in the middle of the room, offered us the sense of being in our own private space. I set down my large menu and gazed at the wall decorations, carved wooden screens, and the large god figures around me. The fragrance of jasmine scented the air while soft Indian music added to the atmosphere.

"You like?" Jack asked.

"Very much."

A portly, mustached waiter approached to ask if we'd care to order something to drink. We decided on a bottle of wine. As soon as he left, I said, "Jack, I need to tell you something you're not going to like."

"That sounds ominous. Planning to make this our last date?"

"No-o, but since the other night, I considered canceling."

"I'm glad you didn't."

He wasn't making it easy. I fingered the raised applique on one of the pillows next to me as I searched for the right words. "I got angry because you didn't agree with my assumptions about the two homicides or that the driver in the black car meant to hit me—or at least frighten me so I'd stop snooping around."

"Delia, it happens all the time. Two people often see things differently. You got annoyed because you uncovered information about Missy and her natural parents and from that made assumptions about the two murders. But I know something about court cases, and there's not enough evidence to convict Tim VanPatten of two homicides forty-five years apart or Missy's ex of killing her."

"You're missing the point. My getting annoyed is fine, but I was *angry,* and I needed to know why."

Our waiter arrived with our wine. After he uncorked the bottle and had Jack sample it, which I thought was sexist but then Jack *had* ordered it, he poured some in both our glasses and placed the bottle in the cooler beside our table.

We held up our wine glasses. "To a wonderful evening," Jack said.

We clinked and sipped.

"Nice," Jack said.

"Yes, it is nice." I cleared my throat. "Going back to what we were just discussing, when I went home last night, I thought long and hard about what I was really angry about. I finally figured out I'm still angry at you for how you ended things between us. That you ended them, period."

Jack sipped again. He put down his glass and returned my gaze. "I get it. You're mad at me for something I did twenty years ago. Something I'm not proud of and came to regret, and for which I apologized."

"Yes to all the above, but it doesn't wipe out the anger. The hurt."

"Are those the only feelings you have for me?"

"You know they aren't, or I wouldn't be sitting here, would I? I still care for you."

"And I care for you. I think I've made that pretty clear."

I was suddenly feeling vulnerable for having revealed I'd held on to negative emotions because of something that happened over twenty years ago. What did that say about me?

Our waiter returned, and we told him we weren't ready to order. As soon as he left, Jack said, "Why don't we decide what we want to eat, then get back to our discussion?"

"Good idea." After a few minutes of studying the menu, I said, "I'd like chicken tikka masala, onion or potato paratha, and saag and basmati rice as side dishes."

"And I'll have lamb saag. Shall we also get some samosas for an appetizer?" Jack asked.

"If you're getting saag, we shouldn't get it as a side dish."

"No, let's order it. You want it. Anything that's left over we'll bring home."

Our waiter reappeared and took our order. When he left, Jack smiled.

"Do you think we'd be out tonight if we hadn't broken up—if I hadn't ended our relationship all those years ago?"

"Good question. I had two more years of high school, then college ahead of me."

"We would have been apart more than we would have been together," Jack said. "Long distance relationships take their toll."

"Maybe we wouldn't have lasted."

"Maybe you would have been happier if you'd been the one to end things between us."

"Maybe," I admitted. I thought for a bit. "Then I wouldn't have thought my world had ended and that you stopped seeing me because there was something wrong with me."

Jack covered my hand with his. "I never thought there was anything wrong with you. I was the one who got scared, remember? Maybe because you were sixteen."

"See, there was something wrong with me," I said.

That struck us both as funny, and we laughed. But then I turned serious again. "Looking at it now, teenage relationships break up all the time. Relationships of all ages break up. It's painful at first, but then you move on. But sometimes it affects your ego. How you think of yourself."

"Is that why you ended up with your husband?"

I nodded. "He was very supportive at first but changed after the first few months. He had flashes of anger. He was more controlling. I saw the danger signs, but I refused to end things." I gave a fake little laugh. "Because then what was I? Someone who couldn't keep a relationship. Someone who was too picky. I thought maybe I was exaggerating the problems."

Our samosa dish and tawa chole (spicy chickpea stir-fry) arrived, and for a few minutes, we were too busy eating to talk. But when our dishes were cleared, I discovered I wanted to continue our conversation because I was learning as I talked.

"Getting divorced was traumatic, and a big part of that was leaving Connor with my parents. The only things I had going for me were a good job and a nice apartment. My personal life was nonexistent. I worked long hours and kept it limited."

"There must have been a few heartthrobs along the way," Jack said.

I smiled as I remembered. "Actually, there were one or two who I could have fallen for in a serious way. I could have settled down and married, only I never let it get to that point."

"You were afraid you couldn't sustain the relationship?"

I met Jack's gaze. "I didn't trust my judgment. I figured you'd ended things between us because there was something wrong with me, and I should have admitted to myself that Mitch was toxic and should never have married him."

"But then you wouldn't have Connor."

Our main dishes arrived, putting our conversation on pause. Everything was delicious, and I ate as much as I could, though quite a lot of food remained in the serving dishes.

"We'll be taking the leftovers home," Jack told our waiter. When the table was cleared, he said, "I can't tell you how sorry I am—not only for hurting you, but also for being the reason you lost faith in your BS radar regarding men."

I gave a little laugh. "Put that way, it sounds really pathetic."

"No, actions cause reactions."

I thought a moment. "They do, but I held on to your rejection too long. And the truth is, I saw signs of Mitch's dark side and chose to ignore them. I told myself that everyone had negative traits. I'd put up with them if I couldn't change them."

"But you were determined to stick it out to show that you could."

"I was."

Our waiter returned with our food in one package. Jack and I exchanged glances. We should have told him to make up two packages, but neither of us wanted to say anything now.

He beamed at us. "Did you save room for dessert?"

I shook my head.

"Just the check," Jack said.

I tucked my hand under his arm as we exited the restaurant. "I'm happy to see I can still talk to you about anything."

Jack pressed my hand against his side. "Always. Does that mean you're finally over being mad at me?"

I looked up at him. "I'm afraid it's not that simple. The anger's bound to flare up again, but now that I've gotten to understand it better, I think it will go away in time."

Outside in the brisk night air, he took me in his arms and kissed me. The old magic we'd had between us sprang up, and I kissed him back.

"Wow!" Jack said. "It's still there."

"It is. But I want to take things slow. I won't get hurt again."

"I hear you, and I'm happy to do it your way."

We held hands on the way back to the ferry and said little on the ferry ride home. As we drove off the boat, Jack said, "I'd invite you over to my place, but that wouldn't be taking things slow."

I grinned. "That's for sure. It's still early. You can come back to my house."

"Or we can have a drink at the Shamrock," Jack said. "It's a fun place to be on a Saturday night."

"Ah, the old Shamrock." I thought of the bar situated amid the small group of shops we called Little Village on the opposite side of the island. "I haven't been there in years. It was pretty rundown last time I was there."

"It's still the favorite of the old-timers, but Ronnie McMurtry's son Brian recently took it over, and it's gaining fans. The food's good, and the drinks are reasonable. There's even entertainment on the weekend."

"Sounds okay to me."

Only we didn't get to the Shamrock for at least another forty-five minutes. As soon as Jack drove past Little Village, past the road leading to the VanPatten Farm and the acres of land still as undeveloped as they were twenty years ago, I knew where he was heading. I had my misgivings, but I didn't stop him, just let out a little gasp when he turned onto the narrow spur of land that jutted out into the water. This, the most northeastern tip of Dickens Island, was where we used to come to make out.

For a minute, we both stared out at the Long Island Sound and the lights twinkling from Connecticut homes. Without speaking, we reached for each other. After an intense kiss, we came up for air.

"It's like coming home," Jack whispered in my ear.

"It is," I whispered back. And it was. Being in his arms was both thrilling and familiar. Exciting yet safe.

We made ourselves more comfortable in the roomy back seat of the Jeep and let things follow their natural course.

Afterward, Jack said, "So much for taking things slow."

I laughed. "So much for that."

"Still interested in stopping for a drink?" Jack asked when we were back in the front seat of the car.

"Of course. Did you think you were going to get off that easy?"

Jack reached for my hand and kissed it. "Your wish is my command."

I grinned as he put the car into gear and drove to the Shamrock. *Am I crazy to let down my guard? What if he hurts me again?* As quickly as the qualms rose, I brushed them aside.

Little Village consisted of six stand-alone stores and businesses that formed a semicircle around a statue of my great-great-grandfather, James Nathaniel Dickens, the leader of the group that had settled Dickens Island in the late 1800s. Like the main village, the parking area was in the rear, though there were spots along the semicircle. Those were all taken, as were the spaces closest to the Shamrock's back entrance.

"Busy night," Jack said as he parked at the rear of the lot.

The Shamrock's back door opened, and a wave of mixed beer aromas and the sound of Adele's "Rolling in the Deep" spilled outside to greet us. The volume was at the level I liked in a bar—audible yet allowing for conversation.

The interior must have been completely redone because nothing looked familiar. Now a five-foot-high divider separated the long bar and a scattering of tables from the wider seating area that had booths and tables, most of them occupied.

Jack led me to an available booth against the wall. I sat on the bench and he slid in beside me.

"Now for a nice, quiet drink to end a wonderful evening with my girl," he whispered in my ear.

"So I'm your girl, am I?"

"What do you think?"

I found myself grinning. If this was a dream, I didn't want to wake up anytime soon.

Chapter Thirty-Nine

Our server, a good-looking twenty-something guy who said his name was Drew, plopped down a dish of pretzels and a couple of menus. I ordered a chocolate martini. Jack asked for a single malt Scotch by name.

"I rarely drink hard liquor," he said when Drew left.

"I can't remember the last time I had a martini."

Jack kissed my temple. "Could be we're celebrating."

Celebrating? My anxiety returned with a vengeance. *How could I have let things escalate? Do I want to be Jack's girl? Do I want to be in a relationship?* I was practically vibrating with anxiety when I turned to Jack.

"I still want to take things slow," I said. "For my personal reasons and for Connor's sake. I've only been back in his life a few months, and he's just beginning to let me in."

"I understand. I want to spend time with Connor. Get to know him better."

"That would be great," I said, though I still felt nervous and vulnerable. I wanted to present Jack with a set of rules regarding our relationship, but nothing came to mind.

Jack must have sensed my anxiety because he pulled me close and held me tight. "Delia, relax. Being together again is new to both of us. We'll take all the time we need to get to know each other again. And this time, I promise not to leave."

I smiled. "We were so in sync twenty years ago, but we're not the same people we were then."

"A bit wiser, I hope."

Drew appeared with our drinks. Jack proposed a toast to us, and I gulped down too much of my chocolate martini. The liquor slid down the wrong way, and I began to cough. Jack thumped my back until I stopped.

Two figures walked past us and stopped at the booth behind us. The woman's voice was raspy. "Thanks, Brian. I'll take it from here."

"No problem. He's been quiet all evening. As long as he doesn't start one of his shouting binges, he's welcome to stay till closing."

"Yeah, well, I'm not waiting around till then." The voice sounded familiar. "I'll take him home and settle up with you tomorrow."

"Suit yourself, Velma," Brian said and left.

Curious, I peered over the high back that separated our booth from the one that Tim VanPatten occupied. He was stretched out on the bench opposite us. His head rested on his propped up hand and his eyes were half-closed.

"Hello, my lovely. Who invited you?" His voice dripped with sarcasm as he addressed his wife. The guy was seriously drunk.

"So this is where you've been all evening, wasting our money on booze." Velma shrieked—loud enough to make heads turn. Was she drunk too? Or stoned?

"Our money," Tim crooned. "The thing you care about most in the world."

"Lower your voice," Velma shrieked. "If we had enough money, it wouldn't be a problem, would it? Get up so we can leave."

Tim waved her away. "Go home. I'll come when I'm ready."

Velma reached out to grab his arm but knocked over two beer bottles instead. The sound of laughter sent her spinning around to see who was mocking her. She let out a curse when she noticed they had an audience. Some patrons from the bar side had come over to find out what the commotion was about.

Velma's eyes glittered with fury. She tugged at Tim's arm. "Let's go! People are staring at us."

"Staring at us, are they?" Tim sat up. "Let's give them something to really stare at."

He slid to the end of the bench and stumbled to his feet. He looked Velma up and down. "On second thought, why would I go home with someone who betrayed me and is planning to take what's mine?"

"Call Gregg," I whispered to Jack. "I'm recording them on my phone."

Jack stepped away and made the call.

Velma lowered her voice a decibel. "Don't be silly. I'm your wife."

"Ha! You want the farm, only you can't have it. It's mine, not yours." Tim's head bobbled. "You'll get *nothing* from the sale, no sirree!" He dropped down on the bench hard enough to make his teeth shake.

"You'll never see the proceeds from any sale, old man. It's not yours to sell," Velma shouted.

"Of course it's my farm. Whose else would it be?"

Velma grinned. "Well, let's see. Maybe it belongs to Gloria, the sister you haven't seen in decades. Or maybe it belongs to William's daughter, Missy. Oh, right. She's no longer with us since you did away with her."

Tim cocked his head one way, then the other. "Missy Faraday? What does she have to do with this?"

Velma chortled. "Come on. You know she's William's daughter. William and Adele Parsons. Your former fi-an-cée."

Tim's eyes swam in confusion. "The girl sure looked like my sister, but so what? They're not related."

"You knew they were related," Velma said. "That's why you killed William and Missy, shot them with the same gun."

"Ha! I haven't seen that gun in years."

Jack returned. "Are you taping all this?" he whispered.

I nodded. A flash went off. Velma spun around to see who had taken a photo. "Scram, all of you! This is a private conversation."

Laughter rose up again. "This is better than anything on Netflix," a thirty-something guy said to his tablemates as he filmed a short video with his cell phone.

Once again, Velma grabbed Tim's arm, and again he shook free of her hold. "Did you kill Missy?" he asked his wife, his tone conversational.

Velma's laugh was forced. "Don't be stupid. Why would I kill her?"

"I don't know. Because you thought she had the right to the farm?" He shook his head. "*Did* she have the right to the farm? But how could she?"

Velma was shaken. Her eyes darted from side to side as she tried to decide what to do. What to say. I didn't know what urged me to do what I did, but I reached inside my pocketbook and fished out the photo of Adele I'd put there earlier in the evening.

"Do you remember Adele?" I asked, holding up the photo so Tim could see it. "Your former fiancée? She was Missy Faraday's mother."

Gasps came from all sides of the room.

"My beautiful Adele." Tim reached across the table for the photo, but I put it away. "She left me for William." He giggled. "Then William left her and went far, far away."

Far, far way, indeed! I wanted to slap him. "Are the ballistic tests going to prove Missy and William were killed with the same gun, Tim?"

He shook his head. "I didn't kill Missy. Why would I?"

Velma turned and bolted for the front door. "How did you—?" she shouted as Gregg and Billy stepped in the bar and stopped her in her tracks.

"Release me at once!" she shouted as Billy handcuffed her while Gregg read her her rights.

"The gun," Tim muttered. "Velma found the gun."

"I never hurt that girl!" Velma was screaming as Gregg came to collect Tim.

"I taped it all," I told Gregg while Tim muttered that he didn't kill Missy. "Velma killed Missy. Tim had no idea."

I gestured to the other patrons. "A few of them must have taped part of their conversation as they snapped photos."

"As soon as I have these two safely locked up, we'll start searching through Velma's possessions," Gregg said. "Maybe we'll get lucky and find the gun."

Chapter Forty

The police found the gun that had been used in both murders in the trunk of Velma's car—a black sedan just like the car Missy claimed had been used in an attempt to run her over; the same car that Velma confessed she'd used to frighten me.

"I admit it, we never thought to look at Velma VanPatten as a viable suspect in Missy Faraday's murder." Gregg shook his head at the oversight.

Ten days had passed since Tim and Velma's dramatic scene at The Shamrock. A group of us—Dad, Aunt Reenie, Uncle Brad, Gregg, and I—were sitting around Aunt Reenie's office, rehashing the aftermath of the two murders.

"Sounds to me like a case of gender discrimination," Aunt Reenie said.

Gregg laughed. "Velma's one tough old bird. The way she saw it, she'd put all those years and efforts into the farm, so it was hers to sell."

"With or without Tim," Uncle Brad added.

Gregg nodded. "She knew he'd killed William, which was part of the reason why she had no compunction about throwing him under the bus."

Uncle Brad pretended to shiver. "Cold. Very cold. Velma was determined to get the money from the sale of the farm, come hell or high water."

"To think she murdered Missy and never told Tim," I mused. "He had no idea that she'd found the gun and used it to kill Missy."

"And all because she saw Missy questioning Tim. He must have been drinking that day, because he didn't think anything of it or even remember it afterward. Velma suddenly realized how much Missy looked like Gloria and, fearing she'd claim the farm, took matters into her own hands."

Gregg went on. "Once I told Tim that Velma told me he'd murdered William all those years ago, he admitted he killed his brother, which simplifies matters. A confession goes a long way to closing the book on a homicide." He gestured at Brad. "And he fessed up to walloping you. Said he was angry at you for being such a stick-in-the-mud about the deed."

Uncle Brad frowned. "The issue of who is the legal owner of the VanPatten Farm is more complicated."

Aunt Reenie dismissed his concerns with a wave of her hand. "What's so complicated? As I see it, Gloria is the one living descendent not guilty of killing William and Missy. Her nephew has power of attorney. He's happy to sell the farm to us."

"And insisting on a pretty penny for it," my father said with a sigh.

"Graham, don't be so negative, and have some faith in your sister-in-law's negotiating skills," Aunt Reenie said. "I've yet to remind Mr. Perry Addison that, as it stands now, the land can only be used for farming. We're the only ones who can change its zoning classification. And property taxes are due soon."

We all laughed.

Aunt Reenie looked at each of us in turn. "The VanPatten farm is a valuable piece of property that can be used for many wonderful projects."

"To be discussed at our next council meeting two nights from now," Uncle Brad said.

"I hope you and Graham can finally agree it's time we modernized the island," Aunt Reenie said.

"We're working on it." Uncle Brad slipped his arm around her waist. I was relieved when she didn't push him away.

Gregg stood. "Well, I better get going. See you guys Thursday night."

Uncle Brad and Aunt Reenie had called for another council meeting to discuss the latest happenings on Dickens Island.

We said our goodbyes, and I drove Dad home. He was in a state of nerves because Mom had called him the other evening to say she was coming to the island on Friday afternoon for a weekend visit.

"Delia, you're sure you and Connor don't want to come over for dinner Friday night?" he asked as soon as I pulled into his driveway.

"Dad, we've gone through this. You and Mom need some time to yourselves. Have dinner. Talk. Connor and I will stop by Saturday or Sunday."

"I suppose you're seeing Jack Saturday night," he said.

"I am."

There was an edge to his tone, which I ignored. I wasn't sure if he was annoyed because I wouldn't come for dinner Friday night to act as a buffer or because he still resented Jack for hurting me all those years ago.

"Do you think seeing him so often is a good idea?"

I met his gaze straight on. "I do. Shall I come get you Thursday night for the council meeting?"

"Sure. Thanks, honey." Dad shook his head. "Sorry to be such a grump. With your mother coming home and so many things happening, I'm feeling anxious."

I leaned over to kiss his cheek. "They're all good things, Dad. Remember what Aunt Reenie said. It's time you and Uncle Brad let go of the way things used to be and start planning with a thought to the future."

Dad exited the car as an incoming text pinged. I glanced at my screen.

Miss you, Jack wrote.

See you at the meeting Thurs nite, I wrote back.

That's a long time from now.

I hummed as I drove home in the light rain. Though I still got anxious when I wondered what lay ahead for Jack and me as a couple, I was getting used to having him in my life. Connor liked him, and I had the definite sense that things were falling into place.

I climbed the outside steps and entered the house. Riley met me at the door. I ruffled his growing-in coat. "Where's Connor?" His response was to lead me to the kitchen pantry, and I obediently got him some doggie biscuits. I noticed the note on the kitchen table.

"Mom, I walked Riley around four. I'm at Trevor's. His mom invited me to stay for dinner. If no one offers to drive me home, I'll call you."

Perfect, I thought. *I have plenty of time to chat with Helena—if she shows up.*

Riley followed me into the hidden room. I sat down in the chair and found myself musing about the Book Nook. Tomorrow I'd post a notice on the bulletin board and in *The Chronicle* that our first meeting at the Book Nook would take place on the third Tuesday evening in April.

I began to mentally compose: *Come prepared to talk about a book you've recently read and liked and why you would recommend it to others. Share your thoughts about the characters, the plot, and the author's writing style.*

With that in mind, I started rummaging through the novels on the shelves.

"Hello, Delia. Looking for something to read?"

I smiled at Helena as Riley skittered away from her transparent figure. "I am, as a matter of fact. To read and to talk about at the first meeting of the Book Nook."

"So things have calmed down enough for you to concentrate on island events now?"

"Looks that way. Both Tim and Velma VanPatten have been arraigned for the murders they committed."

Helena tsk-tsked as she shook her head. "What miserable creeps they both turned out to be. I suppose Velma knew all along that Tim had murdered William."

"She did. Velma is one smart cookie. She'd always known that Missy looked like Gloria and, knowing the Faradays were quite old when they had Missy, their only child, she wondered if they'd adopted her. What really set her off was after Frank Faraday died, Velma saw Missy talking to Tim a few times. She figured that Missy either knew or suspected she was related to the VanPattens. Either way, Velma decided it was time to get rid of her."

"And Tim had no idea," Helena said.

"How ironic that Velma found the pistol he'd used to kill his brother and used it to murder Missy."

"Or was it intentional?" Helena mused. "You told me she was quick to claim the farm as soon as it became obvious to everyone that Tim had murdered William."

"Which she knew all along."

We took a minute to wonder about Velma's ulterior motives.

"The only mystery left is the so-called treasure map that Connor found in Captain Kidd's log. It's not real, of course, but I wonder how it got there."

Helena burst out laughing. "I put it there. One rainy afternoon, Gloria and I were going through my father's collection of ephemera. As we leafed through the log, we decided it would be fun to create a map that led to buried treasure."

Her eyes lit up when she said, "It was Gloria's idea to fold it and leave it in the log, though I am sorry it caused so much trouble—Connor digging for gold; the reason you were burgled."

"Because of the map, William's remains were discovered, and it indirectly helped solve both murders."

"I suppose you're right," Helena agreed, then asked, "How are Brad and Reenie getting along? Has he moved back home?"

"Yes, today, and it's a good thing too. Mom's coming home for the weekend."

"Is she?" Helena's face beamed with happiness. "How did that come about?"

"I told Dad to call Mom and say he'd like to spend a weekend with her in Manhattan. He took my advice, and she said she'd rather spend a weekend on the island instead. He's a nervous wreck over this."

"I don't know what's with those sons of mine," Helena said. "Why can't they get along with their wives?"

"Dad and Uncle Brad are happy keeping things status quo, while Mom and Aunt Reenie are for change and development—Mom in the general store and Aunt Reenie on the island in general."

"Sounds about right, but why?" Helena asked.

"As I told Mom, I think maybe it's to keep things the way they were when their father was alive."

"Could be you're right, but Ellery was all for change and growth," Helena said. She studied my face. "Delia, honey, I'm relying on you to find a way to convince those boys to move on with the times."

"No need. I think they both got the message."

"Good." Helena grinned. "And how are things with Jack?"

I nodded. "I'm getting used to having him back in my life. So is Connor. Yesterday he asked when Jack was coming to dinner again because he and Trevor wanted to ask him something."

"That boy is over practically every evening," Helena said.

"He's welcome here," I said. "Connor's over there now."

"That's not a nice family. Better the boys spend time at your house," she said ominously.

"Do you know something—?" But Helena had disappeared.

I shook my head. Dealing with a ghost was tricky business. They showed up and vanished at will.

"That's it!" I exclaimed. "I have my theme for the second Book Nook meeting. Everyone will read a book that has a ghost as a character! I grinned as I thought of books they could read: the Topper books, *The Ghost and Mrs. Muir,* the Haunted Library series. I'd make a list and put it in the store's next newsletter and post it on the bulletin board.

I grinned as my next brilliant idea flashed in my brain. My first article for *The Chronicle* was going to be about my grandmother, Helena Catherine Whitcomb Dickens, who did so much for Dickens Island. I'd start with her early years, when she and her family spent summers on the island, then move on to the time she lived here year-round. There was so much to say about her adult life when, as a single mother, she taught elementary school on the island, ran the Dickens General Store, and, as the first female town manager, looked after the island's growth and upkeep.

I had her journals to work from as well as Helena herself to provide me with anecdotes and personal touches. My excitement grew as I realized this could comprise an entire series of articles. I'd divide it by decades and cover all aspects of the island as well as Helena's life. For the first time since Wayne had proposed I write a lengthy article, I felt a rush of excitement and was eager to get underway. I supposed this was what a novelist felt like at the start of a new book.

"Let's go, Riley," I said. "I want to make a rough outline of what I plan to cover in the articles about Helena."

Riley followed me into the family room where I'd left my laptop. He settled down on the floor where I was sitting and rested his face in my lap. As I stroked his coat, I thought of everything that had happened since Riley had come into our lives. I had helped solve the murders of Missy Faraday and her long-dead biological father. Connor and I were getting along, and Jack was back in my life. I now understood how I'd allowed our break-up all those years ago to form a negative self-image instead of accepting that most teenage romances ended at some point, and dealing with heartbreak was all part of growing up.

My parents and my aunt and uncle were getting along, and once again, Helena was a presence in my life. I grinned as I remembered her telling a teenaged Delia that though I might live somewhere else for a while, I'd come back to Dickens Island. She was right. Moving back had been the right thing to do. I was grateful for all the good things that were happening in my life and couldn't help wondering what was in store for me next.

the first female park manager, looked over the island's growth and upkeep.

I had her journals to work from, as well as Helena herself to provide me with anecdotes and personal insights. My excitement grew as I realized this could comprise an entire series of articles. I'd divide it by decades and cover all aspects of the island as well as Helena's life. For the first time since Wayne had proposed I write a big city article, I felt a rush of excitement and was eager to get [illegible]. Anyway, I supposed this was what a novelist felt like at the start of a new book.

"It's a possibility," I said. "I want to make a rough outline of what I plan to cover in the article about Helena."

[illegible] followed me into the [illegible] room where I'd left my laptop. He [illegible] down on the floor where I was sitting and [illegible] his face in my lap. I [illegible] his ear and thought of everything that had happened since Riley had come into our lives. [illegible] helped solve the murders of Misty [illegible] long-dead biological father. Connor and I were getting along, and Jack was back in my life. [illegible] how I'd allowed our friendship all those years ago to turn into negativity [illegible] instead of accepting that most teenage romances end at some point, and dealing with that [illegible] was all part of growing up.

My parents and my [illegible] were [illegible] along, and once again, Helena was a [illegible] in my life. I [illegible] remembered [illegible] Helena [illegible] might live [illegible] there [illegible] while I [illegible] she was right. Moving back [illegible] the right thing to do. I was grateful for all the good things that were happening in my life and [illegible] help wondering what was next. [illegible]

Author's Note

Welcome to Dickens Island, the setting of my new series. Dickens Island, which I've set in the middle of the Long Island Sound between Long Island and Connecticut, is a creation of my imagination and cannot be found on any map. The island is part of New York State, and there is a ferry line between Dickens Island and Long Island. The history and geography of Dickens Island are as fictitious as the characters who live there.

Captain William Kidd was a real person—first a privateer and then a pirate. He was born in Scotland in 1645 and died by hanging in 1701 in England. Captain Kidd lived in New York City for many years. Stories about Kidd abound, many of which are not true. Most have to do with treasure because he was believed to have buried treasure in various places around the globe. He actually buried treasure on Gardiner's Island, and that was dug up. While Captain Kidd undoubtedly kept many logs, the log that Connor discovers in the secret room is not one of them.

Acknowledgments

Starting a new mystery series is a great undertaking. It involves creating a new cast of characters in a new setting where they create mayhem and murder. I loved writing about my characters' adventures in DEATH ON DICKENS ISLAND. Putting it all together in a book for readers to enjoy required the work of many others, for which I am very grateful.

As always, my many thanks to my wonderful editor, Faith Black Ross, who pointed out what was needed to make this a stronger, better book.

As always, I appreciate my fellow Plothatchers—Janet Bolin, Peg Cochran, Krista Davis, Kaye George, Daryl Gerber, and Janet Koch—for their assistance and support with plot suggestions and comments whenever I got stuck.

I absolutely love my cover. Thank you, Mary Woodin.

Many thanks to the copy editing team at Crooked Lane Books. Besides your comma knowledge, you caught a few name changes that somehow always creep into my manuscripts.

Thai, Dulce, Rebecca, and Mikaela—Thank you for all you do to get my books out to readers, and for always answering my questions so quickly.

And lastly, my many thanks to my granddaughter, Olivia Brooke Levinson, for supplying the necessary "teen slang."